AMERICAN VIKINGS

JACK R. WILLIAMS

PUBLISHED BY FIDELI PUBLISHING, INC.

Printed in the United States of America.

ISBN: 978-1-60414-992-0

Table of Contents

AMERICAN VIKINGS

JACK R. WILLIAMS

Introduction

Archeology for me started in 1956. That is when I read C.W. Ceram's book, '*Gods, Graves and Scholars*'. It was published in 1951. The book was a revelation for me, where unsuspecting civilizations and kingdoms could be discovered by kicking up the earth beneath our feet. Of course, this required some effort to find where to kick.

An early attempt at finding the place to kick was a part of the Italian Renaissance, particularly with respect to the Vesuvius volcano that erupted in the first century, CE. The destruction included Pompeii and Herculaneum in the year 62 and the great volcano in 79. For most people, the stretch of history after Roman times until the renaissance in the 17th century was a period of darkness. The European Renaissance period from the 14th to the 17th century, is regarded as the cultural bridge between the Middle Ages and modern history. During this renaissance, serious artwork was celebrated such as the Mona Lisa, David, The Last Supper, Pietà, and far more. The artists defining the renaissance were Michelangelo, Raphael, Botticelli, Donatello, Titian and many others.

But, history was a place for works in progress. Generally, our knowledge of those times is about Charlemagne who was a central figure. He wrote big as Charles I, King of the Franks from 768 CE, King of the Lombards from 774 and Emperor of the Romans from 800 until his death in his capitol of Aachen in northern Germany in the year 814. He united much of Europe during the early middle Ages. He was crowned Emperor of the Romans by Pope Leo III. This preceded the recognition of both the Eastern and Western Roman Empires. This book is to shed some light on that period.

After about the year 200, the real power shifted to the Eastern Roman Empire, or to Byzantium, whose capitol was Constantinople on the shores of the Golden Horn and the Bosphorus. Byzantium held that position of power until 1453. The Ottomans then took Constantinople. This was a period of about 1200 years. Later, Europe became a battleground over who was to be one of many kings. There were numerous kingships announced in the fighting over who was to rule whom. In the 7th century, an unlikely grouping occurred in this stewpot. This was to be the period of the Vikings. The Viking age began with the attack on Lindisfarne Monestary. This quote was according to the Anglo-Saxon Chronicle.

> In 793, a Viking raid on Lindisfarne Castle caused much consternation. Throughout the Christian west, this is now often taken as the beginning of the Viking Age.
>
> The raid was fierce. Foreboding omens came over the land of the Northumbrians (another name for Vikings), and the wretched people shook.
>
> There were excessive whirlwinds, lightning, and fiery dragons were seen flying in the sky.

The tidal island of Lindisfarne is located along the northeast coast of England, about a mile from the mainland and close to the border with Scotland. It is accessible, most times, at low tide by crossing sand beaches and mudflats, which are covered with water at high tide. Incoming tides can trap one as water may flow faster than can be outrun by waders.

The Vikings were organized sufficiently for a raid on Lindisfarne castle in 793. Evidence here and there indicates scattered activity in the 6th century. This castle was well known for its library, vestments and other valuables that attracted the vandals.

The Viking Age began with the attack on Lindisfarne Monastery led by Viking King Harald Hardråde and it ended with the Battle of Stamford Bridge in 1066, East Riding of Yorkshire, on 25 September 1066 when an English army under King Harold Godwinson and his brother successfully repelled Viking invaders. Lindisfarne signaled the Viking age was over.

The Vikings were a sea power. This led to the development of new areas along the Norwegian coast. The Norwegian Vikings also discovered Vinland and present-day America long before Columbus.

In the Viking period, the present day nations of Norway, Sweden and Denmark did not exist but the people were largely homogeneous and similar in culture and language, although somewhat distinct geographically.

We use here the calendar times of BCE and CE, denoting "Before the Common Era" and "Common Era" reference. Similarly, we favor the use of directional modifiers in lower case like western Atlantic instead of capitalized Proper Nouns like Western Atlantic.

The Vikings initiated their dominance period by building trade routes. These routes included much of central Europe, Ireland, the UK and Eastern Europe all the way from the Baltic to the Volga in the southeast. The Volga emptied into the Caspian Sea. Although not well known, trading beat a path down the Volga and Dnieper Rivers. The Baltic Sea in the north and the Black Sea in the south were connected by the Dneiper River. The Volga River connected the Baltic Sea to the Caspian Sea past convenient portages. Black Sea and Caspian waters completed the passages.

There were tribal divisions, called Rus, all down the Volga Valley and eastwards. These Rus were much later combined to form the Russia of Peter the Great.

Nevertheless; there were centuries intervening between the Vikings and Peter. Atilla the Hun filled part of this duration. Other Huns did the same from the 3rd to the 8th centuries or so. Vikings dominated the next period from the 8th to the 11th centuries. The later period was filled by a trade grouping called the Hanseatic League. The League's trade routes seem to have terminated in Bergen, Norway. This little town on the coast of Norway is beautiful. It hosted the Hanseatic League's terminus for centuries.

I have traveled to Bergen a number of times in this modern era. It is entered by ship, motor vehicle, aircraft or railroad. The port is a horseshoe U-shaped landing of about two football fields on either side of the horseshoe. The waterway inside the U stretches about one football field length. Houses and offices wrap around this horseshoe. They are rather plain two to three story wooden houses and offices but they are painted very colorfully. The roofs are also a bright color, contrasting with the houses.

The mountains fall right into the village of Bergen so it can only be visualized as a home for Heidi. The movie, Heidi, made in 1937, was a coup-de-grace for Shirley Temple. The movie was the spitting image of what we, the public, thought Switzerland was like. Although the movie was made in Lake Arrowhead, California, just outside Los Angeles, this drama in the idealized setting was a huge success. There were plenty of snow and blizzards, a crippled child, a fuzzy grandfather and a witch of an aunt. What more could one want? The film, Shirly Temple's best, is about an orphan named Heidi who is taken from her grandfather to live as a companion to Klara, a spoiled, crippled girl. Heidi is an eight-year-old Swiss orphan who is given by her aunt to her mountain-dwelling, goat-keeping grandfather. She is then stolen back by her aunt from her grandfather to live in the wealthy Sesemann household in Frankfurt as a companion to Klara, a sheltered, disabled girl in a wheelchair. Heidi is unhappy but makes the best of the situation. When Klara's body and spirits mend under Heidi's cheerful companionship, the housekeeper tries to get rid of Heidi by selling her to the gypsies but she is stopped by the police. Heidi is rescued and reunited with her grandfather. Everyone cried. Switzerland was memorialized.

The beautiful little Bergen houses swept to the seaport horseshoe. Then, a few houses rest here and there as the mountain ascends. There is even a funicular up the mountainside. This cogged funicular provides the most terrific view of all. The few minutes ride transcends time until you are looking at the Viking and Bergen of yesteryear. We see backward for a millennium.

A friend and I had caught a passenger train in Oslo, the capitol, heading to Bergen. On the train, one group of passengers consisted of four Norwegians. They had been partying, and we soon formed a single party. As it happened, they were on their way to the same conference in Bergen as we were. We watched that beautiful scenery as the train rose to nearly the mountaintops.

The early Goth, or Norsemen, aggression was first noted in about 378 CE. The Goth army led the Goth migration from southern Sweden, by way of Eastern Europe and Rus territory, down to the Black Sea. They secured a great victory in 378, killing Emperor Valens at Adrianople. Within 175 years, the army had conquered Italy, southern France and most of Spain.

The Goths did not leave their calling cards but they had made themselves well known in memories lasting seven centuries. These invasions were by land, not the sea. However, sea operations promised navies sometime in the future. Just as England is a sea-faring nation, geography predicts Norway with the Vikings and Scandinavians might go in the same direction. Europe saw this occur toward the end of the 7th century.

But, why did the Norsemen or Vikings abandon their way of life, going from simple traders and farmers to raiders of the sea? This answer seems to be that they underwent a revolution in shipbuilding. Many archaeologists write papers describing this. They have discovered many ancient Viking boats preserved in the bottom mud. Many of these have been raised and restored. They are beautiful. The design of boats was for trade early on. These needed room to store trade products and the longships needed to be light so they could go up the rivers and branches for trade. Later, the Vikings gave up trading for raiding.

As to the sizes of these Viking raiders, some used a single boat with a small crew while others reached more than a thousand ships and a combined crew of upwards of 65,000 men in their raid up the Thames on London, for instance. This was in the late 700's. Typically, the Viking longboats had an average of about 33 people aboard. These served as both warriors once they landed, and as crewmen when they were at sea or wrestling their boats over river portages.

Another scaling was a raid on Paris by the Vikings in 850. This put 350 longboats at the mouth of the Seine. Fortunately for Paris, the Viking army raided the vicinity but Paris was spared for the time being.

We wonder what happened to the Vikings. A simplistic definition calls the Vikings, "those people who lived in Scandinavia and the north Atlantic." The Viking age is defined as the years between 793 and 1066. It was during this time that these Northern people had the largest impact on other Europeans, through trade and through their Viking raids. Of course, some raids occurred before this time and many continued afterwards.

Raiding was the main aspect of the Viking culture that was recorded in the sagas and other documents. In these histories, the raiders are called Northmen or Norsemen, or the people who arrived from the northern lands. Unfortunately, very few historical artifacts were left to posterity. The artifacts consisted of rune stones and written sagas. Rune stones were basically rocks with etchings or pieces of wood with etchings.

After the Viking age, the Northmen continued living their lives in the Scandinavian countries, and in the settlements created during the Viking age, such as Iceland and Greenland. The end of the Vikings occurred when the Northmen stopped raiding.

Why did the Vikings stop raiding? The simple answer is that changes took place in European societies that made raiding less profitable and less desirable. Changes occurred not only in the Norse societies, but also throughout Europe where the raids took place. At the beginning of the Viking age, many European lands had no central authority figures, no kings. Instead, petty kings and local chieftains were the rule in most lands. At the beginning of the Viking age, the Norse societies avoided central authority. A story from the Frankish annals illustrates this aspect of the Viking culture. When a band of Danish raiders arrived in Frankish lands, they were met by a Frankish emissary, who asked to be taken to the leader of the Viking band. He was told, "We are all leaders here."

By the end of the Viking age, most European lands had strong central authorities, including trained, standing armies capable of mounting effective defenses against Viking attacks. Generally, the Vikings were not trained, nor had organized troops. Although skilled at arms, the Viking shock tactics were ineffective against trained, professional soldiers supported by their strong king.

The Christian church arrived in the Viking lands during this age. By its end, the Christians had taken over the Viking age. The Viking raids were not in keeping with some of the tenets of the Christian church, so it is not a surprise that the arrival of the church and the decline of raiding are closely tied. The raids slowed and stopped because the times changed. It was no longer profitable or desirable to raid. The Vikings weren't conquered. Yet, there were fewer and fewer raids to the rest of Europe. They stopped being Vikings but began to think of themselves as nationalists, as Danes and Swedes and Norwegians and Icelanders and Greenlanders.

The Christians had the same effect on the Middle Ages as those in the Roman Empire had on the Romans. Edward Gibbon described that in his book, *The Decline and Fall of the Roman Empire.* He took the position there that the Christians themselves contributed to the fall in a major way. In the cultural upheaval, the Roman institutions were undermined. The empire could not fend off all the attacks without and within. Gibbon was severely criticized for this opinion. It was, nevertheless obviously true. The Christian conquest was profound and ineluctable. Like the Roman empire described by Gibbon, the Vikings were destined to a similar outcome.

The Vikings designed unique boats that caused a revolution in boat design. In the early contacts with the Romans, the motive was trade. The Vikings had strange ships that had not been seen before. The boats had long sweeping midsections, terminating in tall prows often with dragon heads carved in the bow post. The boats had both paddles for maneuverability and oars for long distance. The oars fitted into oarlocks that were fitted permanently on the gunwales. The North Sea drove the design for boats that tended to founder in the brutal North Sea or to capsize. They discovered that boats with deep keels held the boats steady in heavy seas. Of course, the North Sea is known for its rough water and high waves. These are enlarged when they meet the Arctic Circle. Without keels, the boats were unstable and slow. The crew hugged the shore that slowed them even more.

The keel was a new invention for the Vikings. That keel stabilized the ship, making it seaworthy in rough waters. They could use a massive square sail that could accommodate the higher speed. Some reported that they had seen Vikings criss-crossing the Atlantic with cargos of timber, animals, and food covering distance of four thousand miles. This was in a time that few Europeans ventured to sea.

The Vikings also evolved a sideboard steering oar that was most efficient with heavy loads and rough seas. The sailors were very protective of this steering board. They developed a number of ship types such as cargo vessels, ferries and fishing boats. Their greatest achievements were the fighting ships, or longboats or longships. These were a combination of strength, flexibility and speed.

They also anticipated problems at sea and had designed their boats to recover if they foundered or capsized. Thus, when they capsized, they could right their boats and continue on their way. In shallow water, the light construction of boats purposely built without keels allowed portages around obstacles. This increased their range in the shallow waters of rivers and streams facilitating the transfer from one river system to another. They could attack along rivers and this opened the countryside for quick invasions and return to sea, often before the quarry even knew they were under attack.

The most frightening thing about the longboats was that they could carry up to a 100 men that served as warriors and crew. They could cover the 900 miles from Norway to the Seine River and Paris in about three weeks or 40 miles per day.

Their speed when propelled by oars was nearly as fast as being under sail in favorable winds. That made them nearly immune from most sailing limitations. The army they faced could only average 12-15 miles per day and that speed was attainable only if good Roman roads were available. Their speed was even worse with most roads. Enemy cavalry with horses could only manage 20 miles per day. The Vikings usually had a speed advantage of 5 times or more over their enemies where they could manage 40 miles per day.

The planking for the boats was made of oak. They had about one inch thick hulls or siding. Ragnar Lothbrok proved in 845 that the longships could achieve 40 miles per day or more. In 1893 a replica of a sunken Viking ship was made and crewed by only 12 men. It sailed from the Hanseatic town of Bergen, Norway, to Newfoundland in 28 days. This distance was 2,340 statute miles. This average speed was 83 miles per day. But, the boats had a minimum crew and no cargo or peripheral weight.

A longboat under oar could achieve the 150 miles up the Seine to Paris in 3 days. Then they attacked with dozens of boats and thousands of warriors. The boats were best suited for early-on trading and later for marauding and raiding.

Ragnar Lothbrok was a legendary Viking hero and ruler, known from Viking age, Old Norse poetry and sagas. According to this traditional literature, Ragnar distinguished himself by many raids against Francia and Anglo-Saxon England during the 9th century. According to one antiquarian writing in 1980, "certain scholars in recent years have come to accept at least part of Ragnar's story as based on historical fact".

On the other hand, another historian wrote in 2003: "although his sons are historical figures, there is no evidence that Ragnar himself ever lived, and he seems to be an amalgam of several different historical figures and pure literary invention."

Vikings were Norse seafarers, mainly speaking the Old Norse language, who raided and traded from their Northern European homelands across wide areas of northern, central and eastern Europe, during the late 8th to late 11th centuries. The term is also commonly extended in modern English and other vernaculars to the inhabitants of Viking home communities during what has become known as the Viking Age. This period of Nordic military, mercantile and demographic expansion constitutes an important element in the early medieval history of Scandinavia, the British Isles, France, and Kievan Rus.

Facilitated by advanced sailing and navigational skills, and characterized by the longship, Viking activities at times also extended into the Mediterranean littoral, the Maghreb of North Africa near the coast of the Mediterranean, the Middle East and Central Asia or what is now, Iraq. There was extended phases of exploration, expansion and settlement. Viking communities and polities were established in diverse areas of northwestern Europe, European Russia, Tangiers and Morocco. They augmented these by arctic North Atlantic islands and as far as the northeastern coast of North America. This period of expansion witnessed the wider dissemination of Norse culture, while simultaneously introducing strong foreign cultural influences into Scandinavia itself. The expansion into North America was highly significant since it occurred centuries before Columbus.

The recorded history of the Vikings is sparse, depending on a very limited number of runes and sagas. We don't know why but it was clearly not to convey historical continuity. All our exposure leaves huge holes. Try as we may, there is necessarily a lot of room for conjecture. We try to maintain a logical sequence. Unfortunately, much of it is trying to provide a logical time-line where the end result is sometime a hodge-podge. We do the best we can.

Popular modern conceptions of the Vikings—the term frequently applied casually to their modern descendants and the inhabitants of modern Scandinavia—often strongly differ from the complex picture that emerges from archaeology and historical sources. A romanticized picture of Vikings as noble savages began to emerge in the 18th century; this developed and became widely propagated during the 19th century Viking revival. Perceived views of the Vikings as alternatively violent, piratical heathens or as intrepid adventurers owe much to conflicting varieties of the modern Viking myth that had taken shape by the early 20th century. Current popular representations of the Vikings are typically based on cultural clichés and stereotypes.

The siege and sack of Paris in 845 was the culmination of a Viking invasion of the kingdom of the West Franks. Ragnar's fleet of 120 Viking ships, carrying thousands of men, entered the Seine in March and proceeded to sail up the river, but as the Vikings defeated one division, the remaining forces retreated. The Vikings reached Paris at the end of the month, during Easter. After plundering and occupying the city, the Vikings withdrew when they had been paid a ransom of over 5,000 pounds of silver and gold.

The Frankish Empire, the French neighbors of the Vikings in central Europe, was first attacked by Viking raiders. That led Charlemagne to create a defense system along the northern coast in 810. The defense system successfully repulsed a Viking attack at the mouth of the Seine in 820 (after Charlemagne's death), but failed to hold against renewed attacks.

The activity alternated between the two sides of the English Channel. Viking raids were often part of struggles among Scandinavian nobility for power and status, and like other nations adjacent to the Franks, the Danes were well-informed about the political situation in Francia; in the 830s and early 840s they took advantage of the Frankish civil wars.

The Vikings expanded into the islands of the north Atlantic including Iceland. After the settlement of Greenland, they defined their activity in terms of Labrador, Baffin Islands and Newfoundland. Thus, they could and did see themselves as settlers in North America. Most historians accept the fact that the Vikings in their migration south set up temporary dwellings in north and south Newfoundland. Many of them also accept as fact that the Vikings moved further south than this although the hard evidence of archaeological digs has not proved it yet. We have no doubt that this will be discovered in due time.

These settlements prompt the title here of American Vikings. Just as those settlers encompassed west, central and east Europe as their territory for trading and then for raiding, the Vikings also had a territory in America. This title recognizes the initial Americanization of the Vikings. We have faith that the stretch of north Atlantic islands and the North American settlements entitle the Vikings to a claim.

This story depends on freedom in time and space. The basic story is about ancient ages, shifting across 3,000 years from Homer's Troy until our modern observation age. We must feel free to refocus our lenses frequently and by large amounts. Our space horizons stretch from North America to the Middle East, similarly requiring wide azimuths. Agility in time and space surely enriches the story. That is, we shift around in time and space a lot.

CHAPTER 1

PRESENT TIME

Julia Hopkins and Shaun Rhodes

I was partial to fancy names as my mother always said. In fact, my name is Shaun Rhodes, which follows this theory of hers. She talked to me often about this. She was convinced that one's name held the key to career advancement just as male heights cause the same imperative. There is nothing better than a good name, she assured me. I often told her that I was in classes at school that did not respond to fancy names.

Somewhere she read this and held onto it. My avocation was to dig in the earth. My fate is to dig for debris, find shards that can be correlated or find patterns that give a clue as to what lies beneath them. I hunt for history, for the way men lived thousands of years ago and the cultures that define man's upward climb. I am destined to have dirty fingernails and carry the scent of a wet earth. Or, is it the scent of sweat after a hard day's work in a hole in the ground? The clothes become wet and have a stink that defies the dry-cleaners. Soon, they become salty with mildew and stiffening agents. Sweat colors my life in the summer and I am defined by freezing shivers in the winter. Life can be hard. But it is my choice.

My mother was horrified with my choice. She only saw the hard work, long hours and contentious surroundings in a desert somewhere or other. I had chosen such undesirable places to earn a living.

I was adamant that I get an archaeological degree and work in that area. I know that means digging or tending a museum, but that does not seem so bad. I go to the museum in Los Angeles and I can't get over it. Then, I can't wait to go to the next museum.

Their huge animals are breathtaking. As a matter of fact, the La Brea Tar Pits are right there, sharing grounds with the *Los Angeles County Museum of Natural Arts* (LACMA on Wilshire Boulevard). The 'Natural History Museum' of Los Angeles exhibits the Dinasour Hall with large animals dug from their environment that has lasted millions of years. That is not to say there are not numerous other museums in New York and elsewhere. I am proud when I am in their exhibits and know there is no other place for my aspirations. I know my passion for diggings will last through a whole career.

"Haarumph…." Cries a monster in his time. "Haarumph." I can hear the animal and see it. For me it is real. Just as the tar pits now show huge static animals jousting with one another in the chained-off pits, I look at them and they begin to move, to make sounds and jostle one another.

"Yeeeow…." Cries a pre-historic bird or fowl. Of course, this is millions of years ago. History moves on. It becomes the age of Troy, the ancient Egyptians, Pompeii and The Roman Empire, as the calendar puts us back 2,000 years or more. Following the calendar, one sees the Vikings in about the 7th century, 1,300 years ago. It concludes in our modern times.

"I mentioned the exhibits for large animals being exposed in some marsh somewhere. Yet, man, more often than not, digs to find man's treasures. His knowledge is found and anchored in these digs. The diggers find great treasure in many cases. And even when they don't find jewelry, gold and silver, they often find even greater treasures in man's quest for his past, and in his defining our cultural heritage."

I have found it difficult to finance the necessary education. Money was always tight. After graduation from high school, I got enough support to go ahead to university in fits and starts. In the end, I was successful in college through about my sophomore year. However, it was still hit or miss.

I carried only a partial study load in college. I worked during those years. It was a struggle to pursue my education while carrying a study load and a work schedule. But, it had to be done and I was sure to do it.

Julia Hopkins was a beautiful girl. She was a student in her junior year. She walked into the classroom and I could not take my eyes off her. The sky opened up and I saw nothing but gold and crimsons radiating from the sky above. I knew I could not exist without her. However, it was not a reciprocal relationship. She brushed me off. I pursued her as best I could. I was not a polished suitor.

School was a hell in those days. The students were pairing up or making their choices of who would be lifelong friends and who would be rejected. This was a dynamic process since who was wonderful today may be looked at as a pariah tomorrow. Further, cliques were being formed whereby the 'leader' of a clan decided who belonged and who didn't. It was an extremely painful process because acceptance is only probation while rejection is forever.

What was I thinking about? "Anyway, I had no chance of marriage. She was foot-loose, a free soul. I had no future with her but I could not help it. What is love anyway? Somehow the chemicals in our bodies re-arrange the molecules. Our antibodies shut down. The future is limitless and life is a blessing for all time. She affected me that way."

But, it was not to be. Life was a struggle. The stars did not align themselves according to my wishes. I grouped all events in just a certain way. My buddies, mostly George Grady, in the class tolerated me but that was not much fun. When one suggested we go for a hamburger or some other treat, I most always declined. There was not enough time. There was not enough money.

At any rate, my life moved on. I studied really hard in all my archaeological classes. I loved that so much.

"Hey!" George would shout loud enough for Julia Hopkins to hear. "Let's have a burger".

"Oh, I don't know," I would respond. "I don't think I have the time."

"You never have the time. That makes a dull boy, you know."

"How about it?" Julia was nearby so George asked her, "You want to?"

Her response was characteristic. "Get away from me, you bug."

No one said that love was easy.

I was put on notice to stay away from her. She had bigger fish to fry.

I could only grit my teeth and bear it. Love is not for the faint of heart. The embarrassment could be tolerated. Yet, down deep inside, the torch still burned ever so lightly.

How did I become so passionate about Scandinavia? Well, that is not so hard to decode.

"I'm half Scandinavian," I professed to George, my friend and classmate. "You know that Scandinavia consists of several central countries. These have changed since ancient times but they consist primarily of Denmark, Sweden, and Norway. These include the Faroes, Iceland, and Greenland, generally under Danish control.

There is evidence evolving that the Norwegian Norsemen had built as way points or for permanent settlement in the Baffin Islands, in Labrador and even as far south as Newfoundland. These outposts were to become part of Canada. I was in Argentia, Newfoundland in 1949 when the Newfoundlanders voted to become part of Canada. There was heavy politicking to determine the outcome. The strongest argument was that Newfoundlanders would be able to order from the Sears Roebuck catalog. This also promised a cheaper price if the plebiscite carried. This was curious.

"We talk about the Vikings and their golden age. This age consisted of approximately the years 700 until 1000, or about 300 years. Although this stretches the time that most scholars would endorse, these being 250 years or so.

At first, the Norsemen were traders. They later became Vikings and raiders. Their traders and raiders visited mostly the UK with its islands of Shetland, Faroe, Orkneys, Scapa and others as well as Ireland. The Vikings became mostly raiders in about the 8th through the 10th century. The Vikings found it harder and harder to support themselves by trade alone. Once the limits of trading became clear to them, they found it easier to raid, plunder and rob their way to wealth rather than through trade or farming. They sometimes used hundreds of longboats to cross over the hazardous North Sea and run upriver in Britain. There were often upward toward a hundred-man crew on each of these. They then overwhelmed the upper stretches of the rivers and streams they attacked. They usually launched attacks against the civilians, grabbed or plundered their victims and often left them headless or taken for ransom. Over the years, no one in Europe was safe. The plunderers often stayed through the winter, took slaves back to the north and married into the families of Britain, France, Ireland and Eastern Europe.

But a lot was going on in the world toward the Arctic Circle. For one, Charlemagne politicked his way to be the Christian King of the north, primarily Germany, and he had the Pope crown him in the Vatican. His domain was further east and south than most of the Vikings.

Charlemagne was the defender of the faith and the Pope's chosen instrument to spread Christianity and defeat Paganism. The relationship between one and the other Viking was often determined by this since part of the Vikings were Christian and the other, Pagans. This also appeared on the battlefield since Charlemagne was point man for the Christians and a significant portion of the Vikings was Pagan. Charlemagne even supported the Crusaders.

They continually plundered, mostly by the Danes. Central Europe provided ripe pickings, mostly by marauders sailing down through Britain, France and sometimes Italy. There were also paths down through Eastern Europe. These were only limited by the Volga river basin and Lake Ladoga near Saint Petersburg. This was Peter the Great's territory several centuries later. Eastern Norsemen flowed downward from the Baltic through Rus territory that defined Russia as she eventually became. This route was defined by the land of the Dnieper River, emptying into the Black Sea, and the Volga River, emptying into the Caspian Sea and then to the Black Sea. It eventually emptied into the Mediterranean Sea. The Volga in those days required only easy portage from the Baltic Sea to the Volga River and Constantinople, as often reported.

Constantinople was the fabled city on the Golden Horn that divided Europe and Asia and was the seat of power, first as the Eastern Roman Empire from about 300 and later as the Ottoman Empire from 1453 until this century. The Baltic-to-Black Seas passageway served as a Rus super-highway through the centuries and essentially defined the Russian Empire of modern times. This trafficking of Vikings lubricated trade and often provided soldiers, mercenaries and other interests of the Ottomans. It tied the Baltics to the Eastern Roman Empire for about 1,100 years.

These exotic places were easy for me to characterize and discuss. My Norseman background had prepared me and I had many long conversations on this subject. My grandfather talked about this often. However, he had stayed in the old country after my parents and our family immigrated to the US. He managed to visit the US for a long time when I was about 10 years old and again when I was about 15. He stayed for a considerable time on these trips.

My conflicts with Julia continued the whole time after college entrance. Nevertheless, my sun still rose and set with her. Her aloofness probably increased my infatuation with her. She said terrible things to me and embarrassed me for all this time. I asked her to parties…she refused. I gave her modest gifts …she trashed them. I wanted to ask her about this but she was totally unapproachable for me and avoided me like the plague. She still had classes with me since she was also taking archeology classes. I thought this might weaken her but it was a false hope.

"Why don't you leave me alone?" she asked.

"I just want to be friends," I lamely responded.

"Don't you know by this time that I don't like you? I just want you to go away. Leave me alone.

And yet, I imagined there was a spark there for me. Maybe it was wishful thinking but I just knew I had a chance. She did not think so.

The next subject we were to study in our classes was the volcanic eruptions of Mount Vesuvius with the destruction of Pompeii and Herculaneum. We were both Grade A students so we had a tendency to be near each other. Then, I made a serious blunder. I was helping out in a fast food restaurant and earned a few bucks. As I passed a jewelry store, I experienced a moment of weakness. I saw an Egyptian Scarab. It was one of the most well-known and sacred of all amulets in Ancient Egypt. It goes back as early as the year 2500. The amulet represented new creation, eternal life and gave immense protection against evil to the bearer. The Egyptian scarab became a representation of Khepri, the God of the Rising Sun and eternal life.

Considering the line of our education, I bought it as a present for Julia. I boxed it and wrapped it appropriately. I practically had to tackle her and force her to take the unexpected present. Finally and reluctantly, she accepted the little box and pushed it into her backpack. I was afraid it would never see the light of day. However, a few days later, her girlfriend made reference to the dung beetle so I knew the present had been opened. Unfortunately, the reporting by her friend was derisive and it was looked at with unexpected disdain. After all, it represents a dung beetle to her friend and that was all. In itself, to her, that was nauseating but their jeering made it worse. It was clear I had made a serious faux pas. I had only confirmed that I was a social outcast without offsetting qualities.

Khepri, the God of the Rising Sun, had given me no protection. But I loved Julia. I had continued to plot as to how I could get her. We went through classes together, field trips and museums. But underneath all my emotions were the very thought of Julia and how I could have her.

She was the prettiest thing I had ever seen. She had blonde hair reflecting her heritage from both parents. Her limbs were long — she was a tall girl. When she stood straight, she crossed her legs slightly. She understood the model's stance and their regal posture. Then, her back was straight. Her buttocks had just enough curve to call attention always. They projected slightly to the rear although they were definitely narrower than most. She held her head in just a certain way that was unforgettable. She was a knockout horse.

Her clothes were well put together. Everything looked like designer clothes but I believe they reflected good taste rather than money. The spikes on her shoes caused the legs to take a special shape. It is hard to accept these since we expect God to endow us with good looks. We should be so lucky. We are given the gifts of good looks. What we do with it is our business.

"Besides," she continued her previous thought. "I don't like ugly people. Why should I? I only like pretty people and I do not like to hang around people that are not pretty. To me, you are not a pretty person and I don't want anything to do with you. I know it is elitist and arrogant but that is the way that it is. So leave me alone, you creep."

Darn! Those things were expected but they still burned me.

Julia was a clotheshorse. She had a way of pulling out scarves or flimsy blouses and matching her clothes. She could make T.J. Max's minions look like expensive designers. She had a way of turning as she showed off a scarf or blouse so she looked like she was on a runway. Her mother did not have her imagination but she became a necessity in putting Julia together after suggestions by Julia. The two were an imaginative clotheshorse and a worker bee and that was a winning combination.

Julia's hair was always washed and set into place. She always had bottles of moisturizer, lotions and all kinds of beauty aids. Her smells were mesmerizing. She always wore spiked shoes that pulled her legs into exotic shapes. A stiletto heel is a long, thin, high heel found on some boots and shoes. It is named after the stiletto dagger, the phrase being first recorded in the early 1930s. These shoes are sometime in fashion or they sometimes are out. Right now, they are chic and in again.

She could have the same halo effect on all the accessories. She would be very good for business if she stayed with her enthusiasm. Even if she thought I was a bug, she seemed to like my hanging around. Having an admirer hanging about seemed to make her even more beautiful and desirable. Thousands of models on runways attest to how big the fashion industry really is. Julia had jumped into her new calling: that of the fashion industry. Her ravenous interests were grabbing at everything she could find on the subject. Each piece of clothing had long histories that followed trends around.

I needed some excuse to stay with Julia as long as I could. Actually, we were the best two in our classes. We were both pretty smart. Each expected it to stay that way. We enjoyed being the first in our classes.

"Julia," I asked. "Let's study together tonight?"

This often appealed to her since she had her best-in-class requirements in her own mind. It helped to have a study mate. I used this guise often. However, it did not always work.

I could tell that she was softening toward me. I liked that. This almost never mattered if her mother was around. Jane, her mother, would make some sort of cutting remark that was hard to take. After such a remark, I did not acknowledge her presence for the next several classes, but who did that hurt? Before long, we were back into our traditional roles. Julia was a pretty thing and I was a bug. Why would I persist?

However, nothing stays the same forever. Her mood seemed to change. She became a sweet thing, right off the peach tree. She was an ice cream cone dipped in honey. I could not believe my good fortune. We made arrangements to see each other often.

"Julia," I asked. "How did you change your mind so quickly?" It was springtime. We both had spread a napkin and we sat in the grass for a sandwich lunch.

She had a way of slinking with hand expressions and bypassing any question she did not want to answer. "Well, I don't know. Did you never change your mind?"

She began to take more of an interest in me. "What do archaeologists do?" This seemed to be of high interest to her.

"I don't know," I answered, but I certainly had an idea. I had better look that up.

"Well, how much money do they make?" Again, this seemed to be on her mind a lot. I don't think it is very much, but I do not want her to know that.

After a while, it became clear. She was considering a commitment to me but it came slowly. I was as crazy about her as I had always been. The blood rushed to my head every time I saw her. Please, God. Make her like me. It soon dawned on me that she liked me, wanted a commitment from me and wanted to confirm I could support her. There were far more complications than this but there is no point in bringing them up now. She was a ripe sweet thing and I could feel a victor.

I could see no way out, or not any conventional way. This caused me to join the Air National Guard. This was not well understood by my family nor hers. But, like I said, she was foot-loose and of her own mind. Training then kept me deployed often. After that, and after they had made a regular soldier of me, the deployments came often. I liked that since the Guard pays by the hour and they also pay travel expenses.

On top of that, I could work regularly and be paid twice. Well, not twice but often enough so that I could finance my continued education.

Somehow, I made this work. I recognized she was young and ready for a regular family. She wanted pretty clothes, a good apartment and a wardrobe that was new. I think all young girls want this. Yet, they are willing to wait until a stable family beckons. She was a lot more aggressive than that.

Julia lived with her mother. Her father had disappeared and I never saw him. They lived in a small apartment. Her mother did not like me. In fact, it was as if she wanted to do me in. She made hurtful remarks. "Why are you wearing summer clothes? Don't you know it is mid-winter?"

Sometimes I would show up just as they were about to go somewhere.

"Damn," her mother would say. "Does he have to come too?"

Her name was Jane. "Why do you make those nasty comments?" I asked. "Because I don't like you and I don't want you hanging around," she responded. "You are not for Julia. How much money do you make? How are you going to support her? Maybe you think she will support you."

Jane had a hard head and a stiff neck.

I tried to defend myself but that was beyond me. Those are rhetorical questions; they are not asked to be answered.

Julia often snapped at her mother but it did not have much effect.

In the end, like a little puppy dog, I went along with them to the movie.

Julia wanted to live the academic life, with diggings, museums, and scholarly papers. Perhaps there would be a book or two later. She did not seem to be a high liver. Yet, her mother worked on her night and day to be a high liver. According to her mother, she should appreciate the finer things of life and learn to live a life of luxury. Perhaps, after all this time, she had swayed Julia. Maybe she wanted to live that life for herself and she thought she could hang on if Julia made it. Maybe she was a stage mother without a client, without a child star that could make unlikely things come true.

Whatever the reasons, Jane was driven. There were no ends to her wants, and she thought she deserved them. Julia resented her and tried to slip away. But Jane hung on like glue. She knew where she wanted to go and how to get there. Julia was too big to run away from home, but she thought about it. But where would she go? She had no relatives. She had no money. After a long time considering it, she stayed the course.

"After all, Shaun, is not all that bad," she thought. "He is a grunt but she kind of liked him. She liked him more every day."

Julia seemed to fall more and more under the influence of her mother. Further, with each negative encounter, Julia withdrew further. Eventually, there was a deep chasm between her and her mother. At those times, Julia fell further under my influence. It was during this time that things became more serious and eventually, they became profound.

We then started to talk seriously about marriage. At first, it sounded reasonable. We could split the bills. Did I not say that it didn't make much sense to a reasonably sane person? These discussions slid on, still not making too much sense.

These discussions set the stage for our interest in the Vikings. Our passion for the Viking people was to come a thousand years later. Archaeology was in both our bloods but there was nothing to confirm this in our day-to-day activity. First, we need to define the archaeological environment that led to the phenomenal successes. These usually resulted from digging in the earth, usually 10-25 feet down. These early sites were the results of the Vesuvius volcano and Pompeii. The Neanderthal man was found and prompted everyone's ideas about ancient mankind to change. Ancient Egypt and their multi-millennium civilization prompted Lord Cardevon and Howard Carter to redefine our ideas about ancient dynasties. Then Heinrich Schliemann not only found Ancient Troy but also validated Homer's writings.

There are other tapestries that make a larger picture. The Hanseatic League provided some relief from raiders and internationalized trade. Then, the new world had to be swept clean if the Europeans were to run the world as the Vikings attempted with settlements in the Arctic regions, central Europe to the Volga, mortal conflict with Indians and their replacement with Iron Age weapons and tools.

From these and the whole panoply of antiquity and environment, the Trojan wars became real. Only then has the annals of history prepared us for the modern age. From this, we recognized that the Vikings were coming.

Pompeii excavation.

CHAPTER 2

Pompeii

As it turned out, I was a witness to the eruption of Mount Etna. After my sophomore year in college, I had joined the Air National Guard. This was for a temporary period. It gave me a great understanding of the world. That provided experiences and carried me to numerous sites that I would not have seen otherwise.

The Guard had been a lucky break for me. This separated me from the regular military. I was often on temporary assignment. This allowed me to be an expert on certain subjects and I was often called on for this expertise and interest. To some extent, it was like being an umpire in a war game. I did not make those kinds of decisions but the aircraft or ship personnel did not know that. I was fortunate in that many of my special assignments were as a part of an aircraft crew.

Soon, I was typecast as an expert in the general field of archaeology, volcanology and earthquakes. I was assigned to a staff position, reporting to Washington but seldom there. For this, one had to satisfy the government and requirements; yet, how deep one digs into the technology is up to the individual. Naturally, I had to dig deeper than my peers. That was an astounding opportunity so I soon excelled in several fields associated with archaeology.

Many of my assignments were in the fields of archaeology and volcanology. The National Guard had an interest in the digs themselves and the government's adjudication of conflicts over ownership and negotiations concerning the exhibition of artifacts. The National Guard had an interest in archaeology, volcanos, and earthquakes. They thought that gathering data or observations of both Mount Etna and Mount Vesuvius were of interest to them; both may provide visuals if they erupted while one of their experts were in the area. I fit that bill so they put me into the manifest for the deployment, based on little but a far chance that something of interest might occur. Mount Etna was showing signs of eruptions and quakes with many groans and sighs but never knew when it may provide fireworks. One always feared that groans on Etna might indicate activity on Vesuvius. Anyway, the groans might imply worthwhile observations.

This year saw considerable activity at the volcano on Mount Etna. Etna is an active volcano. It growls and sometimes roars but it has not caused great destruction so far. Once, my aircraft crew participated in war games in the Mediterranean. We became a 'casualty' so floated around in the air killing time. Etna was undergoing one of its many eruptions. It was early in the morning, before daylight. We then circled Etna for an hour or so. We watched the burning sky with infinite fascination; the fires of the mountain provided plenty of light. There were fiery bursts of lava reaching upward, presenting fiery circles with massive thrusts upward from time to time. We could get as close as we dared while the mountain presented almost a perfect cone, with roman candles at the top. But Italy and its volcanoes did not always show such a sanguine picture.

Although not connected directly with volcanoes, the work of volcanologists and archaeologists fit and overlap each other. Of great concern is the products ejected from an explosive volcano. The ejected material is looked at as tephra, ranging from boulders to shards to ash. The distribution of tephra following an eruption usually involves the largest boulders falling to the ground quickest and is usually closest to the vent, while smaller fragments travel further. Then, ash under some circumstances can often travel for thousands of miles, as it can stay in the stratosphere for days to weeks following an eruption. Large amounts of tephra sometimes accumulate in the atmosphere from massive volcanic eruptions or from a multitude of smaller eruptions occurring simultaneously. Ash can reflect light and heat from the sun back through the atmosphere, in some cases causing the temperature to drop. This can result in a temporary volcanic winter climate change.

This is one time that I would especially like Julia to be with me. She would enjoy the experience beyond belief. Her fascination with natural phenomena is real and consuming. I have come to terms over this. I know she has a barrier against me but I love her. She has reached my depths and I now always put myself with her all the time. This is especially true when I experience natural phenomena. The flaming ice cream cone grasps your attention and holds it. Mount Etna was rumbling and shooting fire into the sky.

"C'mon, Julia. Watch it with me."

"Eh?" Someone responded." I was immediately embarrassed. Here I am, talking to myself.

"It's just Shaun Rhodes here. I must be talking to myself." This mountain is so eerie I have to remind myself. Look at it. It is almost like daylight here. It is like beach bonfires but multiplied by thousands. We continued to watch as the sun blasted through the horizon and daybreak.

"Oh. It's you Georgio Moldavi."

The light was now creeping across the world in silhouette. When things had sharp edges, the sun outlined them. Even mountains responded to these edges.

As the sun asserted itself, Moldavi said to me, "So its you, Shaun."

"Look at you, Shaun. I do believe you are in love. You have that dawny look about you. And this is only sunrise. It is bound to get more obvious during the day."

"Nah. Nah," I'm just ready for a coffee. That is all."

"OK." Have it your way.

Mount Vesuvius had also been rumbling this year but it did not seem to be anything spectacular. Georgio and I saw the eruption in real time. Newspapers had reported rumblings and this aroused our curiosity. There was nothing to indicate that Vesuvius was correlated with Etna.

There had also been volcanic activity in a different real time on Iceland. These were not minor eruptions but the mountain spewed lava and a stream of hot, red lava crawled down the mountain and pushed on into the sea. Huge geysers resulted from this, with the sea boiling and churning and this fed great activity at the ocean interface. The hot lava was spectacular and some homes were destroyed. The 2010 eruptions in Iceland, although relatively small for volcanic eruptions, caused enormous disruption to air travel across Europe over an initial period of six days. History tells us that ash can spread around the world and pile up to several feet thick near the volcano, as had been the case in Pompeii. In recent days, modern aircraft may be grounded and ash can cause mechanical failures as occurred during the eruption on Iceland. Aircraft were grounded across Europe for several days. Fortunately, Vesuvius is generally a benign mountain.

The aircraft ride was eons after the great eruption of Mount Vesuvius in 79 CE or during the Common Era. In fact, there were about two thousand years between the two. This massive eruption followed a smaller eruption in 62 CE that killed thousands and drove many from their homes. Vesuvius is on the west coast of Italy. Mount Etna is on the east coast of Sicily, toward the mapped, mainland boot's toe. Vesuvius is best known because of the great eruption that destroyed the cities of Pompeii and Herculaneum in the 1st century. Vesuvius is an active volcano only a few miles from Naples. Vesuvius and Etna are about 200 miles apart.

The 62 CE eruptions killed about 1,000 people. Furthermore, over 2,000 people died in the great eruption of Vasuvius in 79 CE that killed thousands in Pompeii. Recent studies indicate that heat was the general cause of death rather than earlier estimates that it was asphyxiation. One's lungs burned up rather than shut down.

At Etna, we witnessed a benign volcano. Alternately, Vesuvius is only 200 miles or so from the Etna roaring mountain volcano but they act as though they are independent. Even so, Vesuvius can provide some of the worst characteristics of nature.

So there we were, two witnesses in modern time trying to visualize two different eruptions of the same mountain 17 years apart or almost 2,000 years ago.

Finally, Georgio and I had been witnesses to the Etna fireworks. The mountain had erupted and imitated almost a perfect ice-cream cone. The fact that we witnessed the eruption of Etna was almost a miracle in itself. Although there had been signs, our bosses in Washington had made the call and it was essentially perfect. They took the chance that one of the volcanoes would erupt and so it did. They had a lower priority than the war games but there was a good chance that if there was an eruption, the crew could observe it. After all, the war games were located in the Mediterranean and both volcanoes were in the right region.

After the eruption of Etna, the return trip to my home was uneventful and rather dull.

The Washington bosses were encouraged and decided to continue the observation of another volcano. After all, adding one more crew-member to the flight of a military plane was very inexpensive. They negotiated the trips where both the Guard units and the military aircraft units were on the same floor of the Pentagon. The orders were cut and sent me to Hawaii to observe the past volcanic activity there.

The more I read about Hawaii, the more I wanted to go. As described above, I had the opportunity to go on Guard business. Julie and I both went to Hawaii using my travel expense. We both loved it. I visited the Volcano on the big Island of Hawaii. They had laid wooden mats over part of the cone and it was hot to one's feet. As the Hawaiin volcano flowed downward, it froze and looked like a tube with a diameter of 8-10 feet. This is a special kind of flow, I understand. I have seen lava flows in Hawaii down to the sea on television. This is a dramatic scene. The Hawaii quake looked very much like the lava flow in Iceland I had seen on TV when it was erupting. Someone will have a hard time digging this one out, I thought.

I had invited Julia to Hawaii with me when my Guard business took me to Honolulu. She was happy to get away. We were having some problems anyway so the trip helped a lot.

The fun in this was moderated somewhat as I came to the hotel after business. Julia had three or four dresses that she modeled for me. "How much was that," I asked.

"What matter does that make?" she rejoined. "You want to spoil everything. Money! Money! That is all I hear about." She then carried on and on. The sweet cherry tree was looking more and more barren. "

"Let us not forget," she said. "I carry this team. I pay the bills. You try to make it up by telling me how hard you work but that does not play here. I know you really knock yourself out in these conferences. Well, how about me? I would like some of these goodies also."

"Now we have been all over this subject," I said. "We both agreed that you would work a couple of years and then I could support myself. Has that changed?"

"So what do we do when you graduate?" she said. "You think you are going to get a plush job and all will be okey-dokey. I don't think so; I'll be making more than you, all the way to the horizon. You think that I don't know this and that I don't see how unfair it is?"

"Georgio does not treat his wife like this! She is living well. She goes to ball games and the theater often. Why can't I tailgate at a football game once in a while? She does."

"What. What are you talking about? I see your sly looks at Georgio. Are you trying to make me jealous with your downcast eyes? I love you, you know that. I can't stand your looking around. Things will look different once I get a degree and go to work."

"Yeah, sure." she said..

We got closer before the Hawaii trip was over. In many respect, it was an idyllic time. We were confident that things would change for us. We would no longer disagree or have domestic fights.

But things did not change. If anything, they got worse. George and his new wife were tolerant. They continued to be the best of friends and took it all in like nothing was happening. Yet, things were happening.

There was always a schism between the two of us. She hated her simple life and I tried to blunt the criticism the best I could. Sometime I would get hostile and express muself in an intimidating way. As often as not, I threatened her. Then she retaliated. So far, both expressed only threats and ultimatums. We would walk up to the edge but both would back off.

I hated these outbursts. I tried to control myself better. I kept thinking things were going to settle down. I made promises to myself and made resolutions but none of it seemed to make things better. "Well," I would think. "I reached too far. I went for the beauty that was skin deep. But she told me that. None of this should come as a surprise. This would play on my consciousness and force my obligations to the forefront. I was responsible. I had chased her and this is what it is coming to. She was young and irresponsible. It had been up to me to show some restraint."

The silent soliloquy continued. I blamed myself for everything. It made my stomach hurt. I soon reached a familiar expression of mine. "We will see." I said.

That did not settle the issue.

I tried to shake off our differences and the acrimony that seemed to have taken over our relationship. However, it was becoming more and more difficult. Meanwhile, we continued to learn about Pompeii and Herculaneum as one of our most interesting classes.

The inhabitants of Pompeii were used to minor quaking. And indeed, the writer Pliny the Younger wrote that earth tremors "were not particularly alarming because they are frequent in Campania", but on 5 February 62 CE a severe earthquake did considerable damage around the bay. This was to recur in the year 79 CE at the Pompeii epicenter. By one account, these were very destructive. The lesser quake was at a magnitude 5-6 on the Richter scale while the 79 CE quake registered 7.5-8 on the same scale. To give one an idea of the size of the 79 CE earthquake, it was comparable to the 1906 San Francisco earthquake at 7.8 on the Richter scale. That quake caused 3,000 deaths and destroyed much of the city.

These were both minor events compared to the volcano eruption of Vesuvius in year 79 CE. After the earthquakes, a monster volcano eruption by Vesuvius occurred, causing massive destruction in Pompeii and Herculaneum. Clearly, the eruptions were at nearly the same time as the quakes causing everyone to assume they were connected. Pliny the Younger witnessed the 79 CE eruption from a distance. He saw the various events and described them many years later in letters to a friend. These revealed that he and his uncle, Pliny the Elder, were one of the few eyewitnesses to the eruption events. Pliny the Elder was an admiral commanding the fleet and Roman naval base that was on the Bay of

Naples. Vesuvius is only a couple of miles from the bay waters and is slightly behind the town of Pompeii.

Chaos followed the earthquake. Fires, caused by oil lamps that had fallen during the quake, added to the panic. Nearby cities of Herculaneum and Nuceria were also affected.

Temples, houses, bridges, and roads were destroyed. It is believed that almost all buildings in the city of Pompeii were affected. In the days after the earthquake, anarchy ruled the city, where theft and starvation plagued the survivors. In the time between 62 CE and the eruption in 79 CE, some rebuilding was done, but some of the damage had still not been repaired at the time of the 79 CE eruption. A considerable number of inhabitants moved to other cities while others remained and rebuilt, although it is unknown how many exactly.

The probable reason why these structures were still being repaired around 17 years after the minor earthquake was the increasing frequency of smaller quakes. These led up to the major quake of 79 CE. The minor volconic eruption of Mount Vesuvius occurred in 62 CE. The major eruption occurred in 79 CE. The events occurred over a period of several days. Meanwhile, the destruction continued with falling ash that was several feet thick, or some found the ash to be up to 82 feet depth, buildings collapsed, aqueducts fell, water works erupted and most wealth vanished. The inhabitants lost their lives on a massive scale.

Pompeii was one of a number of towns near the base of the volcano. Mount Vesuvius was renowned for its agricultural fertility.

A study of the eruption products and victims, merged with numerical simulations and experiments. These indicate that at Pompeii and surrounding towns, heat was the main cause of death. People previously believed that victims died mostly from ash suffocation. The results of the study, published in 2010, show that exposure to at least 482°F hot surges. These were known as pyroclastic flows. It was shown that only a distance of 6 miles from the vent was sufficient to cause instant death, even if people were sheltered within buildings.

Ash covered the people and buildings of Pompeii in up to 12 different layers of tephra, to a total of 82 feet.

"That is it, but that is the way volcanoes work. Nothing happens for a hundred years and then it happens. It comes to life and the world will never be the same again."

The ash rained down for about six hours. Pliny the Younger provided a first-hand account of the eruption of Mount Vesuvius from his position across the Bay of Naples at Misenum. He wrote a version 25 years after the event. His uncle, Pliny the Elder, with whom he had a close relationship, died while attempting to rescue stranded victims. As admiral of the Roman fleet in Naples Bay, Pliny the Elder had ordered the ships of the Roman Imperial Navy stationed at Misenum to cross the bay to assist evacuation attempts.

Here was a time that the National Guard and military experiences were well suited for each other. Pliny the Elder commanded the Roman fleet stationed across the bay from Naples. He became a national hero when he commanded the fleet to save all the lives that he could. He deployed the fleet and commanded it for that purpose. He became a national hero when this was found out. Unfortunately, he was killed during the eruption.

The eruption started on 24 August in 79 by the CE calendar. This relies on one version of the text of Pliny's letters. However, the archeological excavations of Pompeii suggest that the city was buried about three months later. This is supported by another version of the letter which gives the date of the eruption as November 23.

Beginning in 1757, the eight volumes of *Le Antichità di Ercolano* brought knowledge of Pompeii and Herculaneum to the fore. Charles VII, King of Naples, sponsored this book of engravings.

Following is a different description of the Vesuvius eruption relating more details or sometimes a larger overview.

Mount Vesuvius has not erupted since 1944, but it is still one of the most dangerous volcanoes in the world. Experts believe that another Plinean (or Pliny) eruption is due any day--an almost unfathomable catastrophe, since almost three million people now live within 20 miles of the volcano's crater.

The Vesuvius volcano did not form overnight, of course. In fact, scholars say that the mountain is hundreds of thousands of years old and had been erupting for generations. In about 1780, for example, an unusually violent eruption (known today as the "Avellino eruption") shot millions of tons of superheated lava, ash and rocks about 22 miles into the sky. That prehistoric catastrophe destroyed almost every village, house and farm within 15 miles of the mountain.

But it was easy to overlook the mountain's bad temper in such a pleasant, sunny spot. Even after a massive earthquake struck the Campania region in 62, a quake that scientists now better understand, offered a warning rumble of the disaster to come–people still flocked to the shores of the Bay of Naples. Pompeii grew more crowded every year.

Seventeen years after that telltale earthquake, in August 79, Mount Vesuvius erupted again. The blast sent a plume of ashes, pumice and other rocks, and scorching-hot volcanic gases so high into the sky that people could see it for hundreds of miles around. The writer Pliny the Younger, who watched the eruption from across the bay, compared this "cloud of unusual size and appearance" to a pine tree that "rose to a great height on a sort of trunk and then split off into branches." Today, geologists refer to this type of volcano as a Plinean (Pliny) eruption.

As it cooled, this tower of debris drifted to earth: first the fine-grained ash, then the lightweight chunks of pumice and other rocks. It was terrifying. "I believed I was perishing with the world," Pliny wrote, "and the world with me"–but not yet lethal: Most Pompeians had plenty of time to flee.

For those who stayed behind, however, conditions soon grew worse. As more and more ash fell, it clogged the air, making it difficult to breathe. Buildings collapsed. Then, a "pyroclastic surge" — a 100-miles-per-hour surge of superheated poison gas and pulverized rock — poured down the side of the mountain and swallowed everything and everyone in its path.

By the time the Vesuvius eruption sputtered to an end the next day, Pompeii was buried under millions of tons of volcanic ash. About 2,000 people were dead. Some people drifted back to town in search of lost relatives or belongings, but there wasn't much left to find. Pompeii, along with the smaller neighboring towns of Stabiae and Herculaneum, were abandoned for centuries.

Today, the excavation of Pompeii has been going on for almost three centuries, and scholars and tourists remain just as fascinated by the city's eerie ruins as they were in the 18th century.

After thick layers of ash covered Pompeii and that some say to a depth of 60 feet and others say to a depth of 82 feet, the occupants were abandoned and eventually their names and locations were forgotten. The first time any part of them was unearthed was in 1599, when the digging of an underground channel to divert the River Sarno, encountered ancient walls covered with paintings and inscriptions. The architect Domenico Fontana was called in; he unearthed a few more frescoes, then covered them over again, and nothing more came of the discovery. A wall inscription had mentioned a decurio Pompeii but its reference to the long-forgotten Roman city was missed.

Fontana's covering over the paintings has been seen both as a broad-minded act of preservation for later times, and as censorship in view of the frequent sexual content of such paintings, as he would have known that paintings of the hedonistic kind later found in some Pompeian villas were not considered in good taste in the climate of the counter-reformation.

Herculaneum was re-discovered in 1738 by workmen digging for the foundations of a summer palace for the King of Naples, Charles of Bourbon. The Spanish military engineer, Rocque Joaquin de Alcubierre, rediscovered Pompeii as the result of intentional excavations in 1748. These towns have been excavated to reveal many intact buildings and wall paintings. Charles of Bourbon took great interest in the findings even after becoming king of Spain because the display of antiquities reinforced the political and cultural power of Naples.

Karl Weber directed the first real excavations; he was followed in 1764 by military engineer Franscisco la Vega.

Giuseppe Fiorelli took charge of the excavations in 1863. During early excavations of the site, occasional voids in the ash layer had been found that contained human remains. It was Fiorelli who realized these were spaces left by the decomposed bodies and so devised the technique of injecting plaster into them to recreate the forms of Vesuvius's victims. This technique is still in use today, with a clear resin now used instead of plaster because it is more durable, and does not destroy the bones, allowing further analysis.

The discovery of erotic art in Pompeii and Herculaneum left the archaeologists with a dilemma — between the mores of sexuality in ancient Rome and in Counter-Reformation Europe lay a clash of cultures.

In the year 1738, Maria Amalia Christine, daughter of Augustus III married Charles of Bourbon. He was King of the two Sicilies. They then moved to Naples. The young queen appreciated the wealth of statuary in her garden. The beauty of the artifacts she observed was a delight. She begged her new husband to let her search for new statuary and artifacts. With government support, things moved swiftly. In 11 December 1738, a destroyed theater was discovered in the center of the city of Herculaneum. They found no gold or precious stones and they did not understand their luck in penetrating the center of the city. The debris of the digs were then covered up, delaying recognition until 1754. From that time until the present, digging has been near-continuous. In 1754, these, revealed both Pompeii and Herculaneum.

For 1783 years, the tephra from the volcano lay in its final resting place, without disturbance. A woman's search for beauty changed all that. The area now brings millions of people to look at it and try to put the legends together. They wonder at the history of Mount Vesuvius and the fragile time we have here on earth.

Pompeii is next to Egypt in the amount of wealth dug up from a dig. The tomb of Tutankhamun itself in the Valley of Kings was an incredibly rich find.

Herculaneum in our scenario is a second great dig, attracting archaeologists from all over the world. It is near Pompeii. Unlike Pompeii, the deep pyroclastic material which covered it preserved wooden and other organic-based objects such as roofs, beds, doors, food and even some

300 skeletons which were discovered in recent years along the seashore. It had been thought until then that the inhabitants had evacuated the town.

Herculaneum was a wealthier town than Pompeii, possessing an extraordinary density of fine houses with, for example, far more lavish use of colored marble cladding.

After the eruption of Mount Vesuvius in 79 CE, the town of Herculaneum was buried under approximately 60-82 feet of ash. It lay hidden and largely intact until discoveries from wells and underground tunnels became gradually more widely known. Excavations continued sporadically up to the present and today many streets and buildings are visible, although over 75% of the town remains buried.

Pliny the Elder's diary was found in Hurculaneum. In the long line of miracles that occur with excavations in archaeology, a miracle happened in modern Herculaneum. A farmer was digging in his field to find fresh water. He was hot and tired. Then he noticed that the edges of a note pad appeared in the mud and grime of the hole. His drill was a homemade contraption that was as likely to collapse and fill in the hole as to excavate it. But he carried on. He needed the water.

He became excited as he pulled the pad from the hole. It was a set of notes being made during the great volcano. Pliny the Elder in the panic kept the secretary or scribe next to him most of the time. The scribe copied down every comment or order from the Elder. The notes were almost intact, being frozen in time in the mud and ashes of the volcano. Pliny the Elder died in the volcano as he directed his navy to evacuate as many people as possible. This was reported, making him a national hero.

The scribe probably suffered the same fate as the Elder. The scribe was uneasy when on ships, but Pliny ordered him to stay close. No one ever found any notes after the eruption. In fact, we have no direct observations of the destruction of Pompeii. Our only eyewitness was strange. Pliny the Younger was in Misenum during the eruption, a small village near Herculaneum, and watched the events around Naples Bay from there. He was 13 years old. Our knowledge of the events is a letter by Pliny the Younger. He wrote hundreds of letters, of which 247 survive and are of great historical value. Some are addressed to reigning emperors. Pliny served as an imperial magistrate under Emperor Trajan and his letters to Trajan provide one of the few surviving records of the Pompeii events.

The farmer's find produced a real eyewitness and written record that survived the chaos.

This find reverberated around the world; not only the archaeological world but everyone celebrated this find. It was not quite of the caliber or popularity of the Egyptian Pharaoh, Tutankhamun, but it was close. The newspapers reported the diary finding with huge front page printing. This was a moment into our collective past that was 2,000 years old. Since this is a novel, liberties with the truth can be taken. This is illustrated by the Pliney Diary discovery.

CHAPTER 3

Neanderthal Man

In 1856, an explosive event took place for me and my fellow archaeologists. A cave in Dusseldorf, Germany, revealed the skeletal body of 'Neanderthal man'. It did take 50 years before the scientific community generally accepted the fact that this was a factual revelation in man's haphazard approach to understanding the human progression. The disorganized approach to understanding digs and saving their results weighed heavily on those who appreciated these things.

It is now accepted that early on Neanderthal man coexisted with Homo sapiens. A profound lesson was also taken more seriously. What was needed was a systematic organization of the facts being discovered. What was needed was a scientific organization for the data and theories. A new field was required. This field became archeology or the division of applied and theoretical archeology.

Archaeology is especially attractive to those committing fraud. Whatever makes a person think it is a big accomplishment to do this and to succeed in fooling people? One fraud is running tractors through a cornfield or other crop product and making it appear the broken stalks have some kind of code pattern. They then claim that this was a code made by Martians or some other unworldly claim to fool people. What in the world causes people to spend hours and hours in developing the hoax without gain or profit? One can claim that proof can be found but it is not very conclusive. If the hoax is well prepared, it may be years of digging to throw doubt on the hoax. Perhaps years are required to destroy the credibility of the hoax.

The cornfield hoax appeared over a period of a couple of centuries and it never was completely discredited. There are a huge number of people ready to believe or to support such beliefs. What causes such spoofs to be credible? Of course, we will never know whether the believers are buying into the hoax or do they truly believe and thereby become part of the hoax.

Probably the most common hoax is that of buried human giants, typically from 8 to 10 feet tall. These purportedly were sighted all over the world. Many books were published with numerous photographs. Even magazines were published monthly to satisfy the craze. These findings became commonplace. If your credulity meter is ringing, the most curious explanation I have seen is that giants come from a cross of women and angels.

The Cardiff Giant (or The Concrete Man) was one of the most famous hoaxes in United States history. It was a 10-foot-tall purported 'petrified man' uncovered on October 16, 1869, by workers digging a well behind the barn in Cardiff, New York. Both it and an unauthorized copy made by P.T. Barnum are still on display.

The giant was the creation of a New York tobacconist named George Hull. Hull, an atheist, decided to create the giant after an argument at a Methodist revival meeting about Genesis 6:4 stating that there were giants who once lived on Earth.

The idea of a petrified man did not originate with Hull, however. In 1858 the newspaper, Alta, California, had published a bogus letter claiming that a prospector had been petrified when he had drunk a liquid within a geode. Some other newspapers also had published stories of supposedly petrified people.

Hold on! What is a geode? It is a hollow rock with lots of sparkling crystals inside? Geodes start their lives as a hollow bubble inside a layer of rock. The bubble could be from air inside explosive volcanic rock or it could come from the hollow remains of animal burrows or tree roots. When these rocks form from air bubbles inside of volcanic rock it is pretty easy to picture. Think about the small air bubbles you see in pumice. Now, imagine just one of those bubbles completely surrounded by black or red volcanic rock. As rain pelts down on the hot bubble, the chemicals in the rock are slowly released into the water. Some of the water soaks through the hard, rocky outside of the bubble and is trapped for a moment on the inside. As the mineral-rich water moves on through the bubble, tiny crystals are left behind, clinging to the sides of the bubble. Millions of years pass while this in and out flow of water gradually builds crystals inside the empty space. The crystal formations might become large single crystals or tightly packed micro-crystals, so small that you can't even distinguish one from another.

As to the change in material from the dripping of water, think of stalactite and stalagmite elongated forms of various minerals deposited from solution by slowly dripping water. A stalactite hangs like an icicle from the ceiling or sides of a cavern. A stalagmite appears like an inverted stalactite, rising from the floor of a cavern. The resulting forms in caves and caverns are truly awesome.

Hull hired men to carve out a 10 foot long and 4 feet wide block of gypsum, or concrete, in Fort Dodge, Iowa, telling them it was intended for a monument to Abraham Lincoln in New York. He shipped the block to Chicago, where he hired a German stonecutter, to carve it into the likeness of a man and swore him to secrecy.

Various stains and acids were used to make the giant appear to be old and weathered, and the giant's surface was beaten with steel knitting needles embedded in a board to simulate pores. In November 1868, Hull transported the giant by rail to the farm of his cousin. By then, he had spent US $2,600 on the hoax (nearly $46,000 in 2015 dollars, adjusted for inflation). The man was purported by some to be made of concrete, others by different material. It was of terrible quality and instantly recognizable as a fraud, people said. P.T. Barnum made the man famous and sold a great number of tickets over several years. It was easy to make money from such a credulous public with a museum and exhibit, so his motives were clear.

Nearly a year later, in 1869 they found the giant. One of the men reportedly exclaimed, "I declare, some old Indian has been buried here!"

Newell set up a tent over the giant and charged 25 cents for people who wanted to see it. Two days later he increased the price to 50 cents. People came by the wagonload.

Archaeological scholars pronounced the giant a fake, and some geologists even noticed that there was no good reason to try to dig a well in the exact spot the giant had been found. Some called it 'a most decided humbug'. Some theologians and preachers, however, defended its authenticity.

Eventually, Hull sold his part-interest for $23,000 (equivalent to $436,000 in 2016) to a syndicate of five men. They moved it to Syracuse, New York, for exhibition. The giant drew such crowds that showman P. T. Barnum offered $50,000 for the giant. When the syndicate turned him down, he hired a man to model the giant's shape covertly in wax and create a plaster replica. He put his giant on display in New York, claiming that his was the real giant, and the Cardiff Giant was a fake. There you are! A fake of a fake!

As the newspapers reported Barnum's version of the story, David Hannum was quoted as saying, "There's a sucker born every minute," Over time, the quotation has been misattributed to Barnum himself.

In 1870 both giants were revealed as fakes in court. The judge ruled that Barnum could not be sued for calling a fake giant a fake.

In another example, in 1897, a petrified man was found downriver from Fort Benton, Montana. It was claimed by promoters to be the remains of former territorial governor and U.S. Civil War General Thomas Francis Meagher. Meagher had drowned in the Missouri River in 1867. The petrified man was displayed across Montana as a novelty and even exhibited in New York and Chicago.

Such tricks usually are very small in comparison but they show how credible people are. I can only offer one other perplexity. I look at the modern primary vote and see that it is nominally half the electorate. Judging from looking at the candidates, it is clear to me that half those voters will believe anything. They must be buying into the hoax because they don't know any better, or they do because they are sarcastically being a part of the fraud.

Thereby, archaeologists tend to attract the worst characters in ourselves. Their risks are not great, their artifacts do not have to be works of art, no one has been commissioned to debunk the claims and it may be years before decisive proof against the hoaxers is found. It is somewhat like disproving fake art but credible fake art artifacts are far more demanding.

Why do people fall for hoaxes? One suspects the reasons are greed, pride, revenge, nationalism, pranks, or gullibility.

Nevertheless, truth sometimes emerges even in this world of fakes and fraud. The Neanderthal man was the historical truth even if it took decades to accept it as such.

CHAPTER 4

The Trojan Legend

In one of the long conversations between Julia and I, it was clear that her heart had softened toward me. She agreed on most of the things I was saying on the subjects of our classes. We began to sit and explore the possibilities for the Vikings and the other archeological events that were happening. We also read the magazine articles that reported them. I tried to keep her interested but she was often in a different world and I did not appreciate all she was interested in. Nevertheless, our interests truly did run parallel to each other's. Even George could see a 'case' developing and he teased both of us about it. He made us mad but he did have redeeming qualities.

The next myth in our mythology takes one back about 3,000 years, until the year of about 900 BCE. The Classical Period or Golden Age of Greece, from around 500 to 300 BCE, has given us the great monuments, art, philosophy, architecture and literature, which are the building blocks of our own civilization and culture. The two most well-known city-states during this period were the rivals: Athens and Sparta.

In Greek mythology, Helen of Troy was the daughter of Zeus and Leda, and was a sister of Clytemnestra, Castor and Pollux. In Greek myths, she was considered the most beautiful woman in the world. By marriage to King Menelaus, she was Queen of Laconia, a province within Homeric Greece. Her elopement with Prince Paris of Troy brought about the Trojan War. Dares Phrygius described her thusly, "She was beautiful, ingenuous, and charming. Her legs were legendary and the best; her mouth was the most voluptuous." Elements of her biography come from classical authors such as Aristophanes, Cicero, Euripides and Homer (in both the *Iliad* and the *Odyssey*). Her story appears in Book II of Virgil's *Aeneid*.

She was abducted by Theseus in her youth. A competition between her suitors for her hand in marriage sees Menelaus emerge victorious. An oath sworn beforehand by all the suitors required them to provide military assistance in the case of her abduction; this oath culminates in the Trojan War. When she marries Menelaus, she was still very young; whether her subsequent involvement with Paris is an abduction or a seduction is ambiguous.

The legends recounting Helen's fate in Troy are contradictory. Homer depicts her as a wistful figure, even a sorrowful one, who comes to regret her choice and wishes to be reunited with Menelaus. Other accounts have a treacherous Helen who simulates Bacchic rites and rejoices in the carnage. Ultimately, Paris was killed in action, and in Homer's account Helen was reunited with Menelaus, though other versions of the legend recount her ascending to Olympus instead. A cult associated with her developed in Hellenistic Laconia, both at Sparta and elsewhere; at Therapne she shared a shrine with Menelaus. She was also worshipped in Attica and on Rhodes.

Her beauty inspired artists of all time to represent her, frequently as the personification of ideal beauty. Christopher Marlowe's lines from his tragedy '*Doctor Faustus*' (1604) are frequently cited: 'Was this the face that launched a thousand ships and burnt the topless towers of Ilium?' However, in the play, this meeting and the ensuing temptation are not unambiguously positive, closely preceding death and descent to Hell.

Images of her start appearing in the 7th century BCE. In classical Greece, her abduction by Paris—or elopement with him—was a popular motif. In medieval illustrations, this event was frequently portrayed as a seduction, whereas in Renaissance painting it is usually depicted as a rape by Paris. The fact that the terms rape and elopement were often used interchangeably lends ambiguity to the legend.

Regardless of all this, there appears to be a mass collection of ships or boats for the invasion of the European mainland. Our minds have been conditioned to think of huge fleets to support the army and often to operate independently as a navy.

CHAPTER 5

Troy and Schliemann

Heinrich Schliemann, even today, warrants our attention and respect. He was not one of the Greek gods but deserves to be. He formed a lasting belief in the story of the Trojan wars and stuck with it all his life. This stiffened his backbone every time he or his concepts of the Trojan wars came up. In many cases, this German was correct in his beliefs.

He was successful in his career before his successes with the Trojan episodes. This included forming a company in the California gold fields. He then moved to Russia and met success there. He was worth millions before undertaking his findings in Greece and Turkey. He claimed to be an expert in languages, boasting that he could become proficient in any language in 6 months. He met challengers often to prove his point. He had a genius for languages. He spoke and wrote many of them, more than seems possible.

Julia and I both liked him and he became one of our heroes. Adamant in his beliefs, well studied in forming his beliefs, willing to spend from his own pockets and an abiding faith in his own judgment made him a man of great consequence. Just following him was both entertaining and informative.

It is generally asserted that Heinrich Schliemann was a pioneer of modern archeology. His knowledge and treasures from digs surpassed anything known at the time. He was thought to have made a million dollars by 1830. This would increase due to inflation to be worth about $27 million today. He was therefore able to determine how he approached various digs and could influence how he appeared to the public.

Schliemann did not live in a fairyland world but he truly was a dreamer. One of the dreams that he had was about the Trojan War. He studied Homer's book, *Iliad,* and Virgil's *Aeneid,* that he held reflected historical events exactly and without embellishment. He held his unpopular beliefs until his dreams were converted into reality for him. His father, a poor clergyman, told stories to him of an earlier time. These were about fables, fairy tales and legends. These were mostly about Homer's heroes as recounted in the *Iliad* and the *Odyssey*. His head was filled with the exploits of Paris, Helen, Achilles, and Hector. The Greek hero Odysseus was a legendary Greek king of Ithaca and the hero of Homer's epic poem, the *Odyssey*. Odysseus also plays a key role in Homer's *Iliad.* The setting was mighty Troy that, in defeat, was burned and leveled. In 1829, Schliemann acquired Jerrer's *Illustrated History of the World* and this was a further influence on his life."

"Is that the way Troy looked?" Schliemann asked his father, while studying the pictures in the book. The young boy wanted verification of his ideas about Troy from someone he respected.

"Yes," his father answered.

Schliemann then asked, "And it is all gone, and nobody knows where it stood?"

"That is true," his father confirmed.

"But I don't believe that," Schliemann said. "Someday I will find the real Troy."

His life was then filled with adventure for another 36 years. These included working in the California gold fields, in Russia and many other places.

He then took up languages, for which he had a genius. He claimed he could learn to speak any language in six weeks. He proved this by learning to speak and write fluently in that time. He swore to this. He claimed that, using his own method, he had learned English, French, Dutch, Spanish, Portuguese and Italian. Other languages were picked up along the way. He became unbelievably successful in the world of finance. He acquired over a million dollars before taking on the Trojan War challenge. This wealth gave him a certain amount of independence.

Troy was known to be located beside the Dardanelles. The Dardanelles was also known in classical Greek antiquity as the Hellespont or Hellespont Narrows.

This historic waterway connects the Black Sea of central Europe to the Aegean Sea on the Mediterranean. Smyrna was the classical or biblical name, changed in modern times to the city of Izmir. This is a narrow strip of water dividing Europe from Asia. It is about 38 miles long and about one-third mile wide at its narrowest. It averages 180 feet deep with a maximum depth of 338 feet at its narrowest point abreast the city of Çanakkale. It therefore accommodates deep draft ocean-going ships and connects the commercial goods from Russia and several eastern European nations past the Rock of Gibraltar to the rest of the world. It empties the Black Sea down through the narrow Bosphorus past the famous Golden Horn and the exotic city of Istanbul. After transitioning the Bosphorus and Dardenelles, the waterway continues southward through the Greek Islands of the Aegean, the Mediterranean and to the deep ocean of the North Atlantic.

It was believed on the academic world that Troy was located near a small village called Bunarbashi, near the Dardanelles. Schliemann was doubtful that this could be true since there were many clues where the academic scholars took one interpretation and he took another. There were many cases he discovered where the physical evidence contradicted the notions of the Trojan Plain. His interpretation held that a village further north and further from the waterway contradicted the traditional belief. Schliemann hired workers for digging under his direction

He weighed his interpretations against those stated by Homer. The accounts that were accepted by scholars described Bunarbashi as the location of Troy whereas Schliemann believed the correct location was next to Hassirlik, a different village that was several miles away. He believed that Homer gave exact and literal descriptions of the true location. A number of clues convinced him that Hassirlik was the site he was looking for. Then he dug. This was Schliemann's triumph, and also Homer's triumph.

He and his diggers found ivory, gold and other priceless treasure. It was the legendary King Prium's treasure. King Prium was one of the mightiest kings of prehistory. Just before Schliemann's death, it was learned that Troy lay not in the second or third level as celebrated by Schliemann. There were two more layers. The treasure he had found belonged to a king who antedated Prium by a thousand years. But, this was not to distract from Schliemann's heroic discoveries.

Schliemann's work was not completed here — his legacy continued for the rest of his life. "As a boy steeped in the Trojan War, I felt a glorious sensation every time I heard parts of the story of Helen and Troy. He gave me a reason for rejoicing with each archeological success."

The golden artifacts found by Schliemann were of indescribable value. His findings were not exceeded until Carnarvan and Carter's finds in ancient Egypt. Schliemann himself boasted that, "All the museums of the world taken together ... do not have one-fifth as much [as I have]!"

Schliemann pursued his archeological passion for the rest of his life. The Trojan plains always called to him, even when he excavated the ancient prehistoric royal palace at Knossos on Crete where the Minoan bull culture held sway.

An *Art Review* report by Michael Kimmelman in 1996, *Priam's Treasure* display.

> After decades of intense mystery and speculation as to its whereabouts, the storied gold of ancient Troy is back on view. And its exhibition here at the Pushkin Museum has inflamed tensions between Russians, Turks and Germans over who should own it.
>
> The collection of jewelry and other lavish objects was unearthed by Heinrich Schliemann, the German entrepreneur and pioneering archeologist who stunned the world in the 1870's with his discovery of the steep and windy city Homer had described. Digging deep within an eight-story mound at Hissarlik in Turkey, at the mouth of the Dardanelles, hard by the Aegean coast, he found a cache of gold pendants, rings, bracelets and other articles that he ceremoniously and optimistically dubbed "Priam's Treasure."
>
> In 1881, Schliemann donated the treasure to Germany, where it remained until the end of World War II, when it disappeared from a Berlin bunker during the

war's chaotic last days. Rumors were that it had been destroyed by bombs or melted in the fires engulfing the city. For half a century, no one, it seemed, knew what had happened to it.

In fact, a precious few people did. Not long ago, the treasure was rediscovered, so to speak, when the Russian authorities finally acknowledged that Soviet troops occupying Berlin had spirited the gold back to Moscow, along with hundreds of thousands of other works of art. For decades, a handful of Soviet officials, sworn to silence, were the only ones allowed to know that the treasure was here, stored in the bowels of the Pushkin Museum. Even the head curator of ancient art at the museum, Vladimir Tolstikov, learned the secret only by chance in 1975, and he wasn't permitted to see the gold until 1993.

Occupying a single room in the museum, it consists of about 260 mostly tiny objects, miraculously preserved in mint condition and theatrically lighted. The finest of the lot are large jadeite and lapis lazuli ritual axes and opulent diadems of feathery gold, including the one that Schliemann, with his Barnum-like flair, said might have belonged to Helen of Troy.

In truth, it didn't. The treasure is a millennium older than the city Homer described. Schliemann realized his miscalculation shortly before he died in 1890: in his initial haste, he had dug right past the layer of Helen, Hector and Andromache to find the gold from a much earlier, Bronze Age Troy, which dates to around 2450 BCE. Homer's Troy, such as it may ever have been, dates to around 1200 BCE contemporaneous with the Mycenaean empire in Greece that Schliemann also unearthed.

In sum, "Trojan Treasures" is a beautiful, modest-size exhibition of the most spectacular remains from a rich and important city on the edge of Europe during the third millennium BCE. Trojan artifacts are spread among 50 or so locations around the world.

CHAPTER 6

Ancient Egypt

A guardsman and I were assigned to do some work in Israel that took several days. This trip was left open-ended so we could determine our travel loosely. After our work in Israel ended, we decided to go to Egypt and Germany.

The *Book of the Dead,* also known as *The Papyrus of Ani,* dates from 1240 BCE. It was stolen from an Egyptian government storeroom in 1888 by Sir E. A. Wallis Budge, as described in his two-volume *By Nile and Tigris*, for the collection of the British Museum, where it remains today. Before shipping the manuscript to England, Budge cut the 78-foot scroll into 37 sheets of nearly equal size, damaging the scroll's integrity at a time when technology had not yet allowed the pieces to be put back together. This text yields a sense of the Egyptian's view of life and the afterlife.

The *Book of the Dead* is the common name for the ancient Egyptian funerary texts. The name "Book of the Dead" was the invention of the German Egyptologist Karl Richard Lepsius, who published a selection of some texts in 1842.

Religion guided every aspect of Egyptian life. Egyptian religion was based on polytheism, or the worship of many deities. The Egyptians had as many as 2,000 gods and goddesses, each representing characteristics of a specific earthly force combined with a heavenly power. Often gods and goddesses were represented as part human and part animal. They considered animals such as the bull, the cat, and the crocodile to be holy.

Their two chief gods were Amon-Ra and Osiris. Amon-Ra was believed to be the sun god and the lord of the universe. Osiris was the god of the underworld and was the god that made a peaceful afterlife possible. The Egyptian *Book of the Dead* contains the major ideas and beliefs in the ancient Egyptian religion. Because their religion stressed an afterlife, Egyptians devoted much time and energy into preparing for their journey to the "next world."

The text was initially carved on the exterior of the deceased person's sarcophagus, but was later written on papyrus, now known as scrolls, and buried inside the sarcophagus with the deceased, presumably so that it would be both portable and close at hand. Other texts often accompanied the primary Book of the Dead, and constituted a collection of spells, charms, passwords, numbers and magical formulas for the use of the deceased in the afterlife.

This described many of the basic tenets of Egyptian mythology. They were intended to guide the dead through the various trials that they would encounter before reaching the underworld. Knowledge of the appropriate spells was considered essential to achieving happiness after death. Spells or enchantments vary in distinctive ways between the texts of different "mummies" or sarcophagi, depending on the prominence and other class factors of the deceased, and were usually illustrated with pictures showing the tests to which the deceased would be subjected.

The most important was the weighing of the heart of the dead person against Ma'at, or Truth (carried out by Anubis). The heart of the dead was weighed against a feather, and if the heart was not weighed down with sin (if it was lighter than the feather) he was allowed to go on. The god Thoth would record the results and the monster Ammit would wait nearby to eat the heart should it prove unworthy.

The earliest known versions date from the 16th century BCE during the 18th Dynasty (1580 BCE–1350 BCE). It partly incorporated two previous collections of Egyptian religious literature, known as the Coffin Texts (ca. 2000 BCE) and the Pyramid Texts (2600 BCE-2300 BCE), both of which were eventually superseded by the *Book of the Dead.*

The text was often individualized for the deceased person — so no two copies contain the same text. However, "book" versions are generally categorized into four main divisions — the Heliopolitan version, which was edited by the priests of the college of Annu (used from the 5th to the 11th dynasty and on walls of tombs until about 200); the Theban version, which contained hieroglyphics only (20th to the 28th dynasty); a hieroglyphic and hieratic character version, closely related to the Theban version, which had no fixed order of chapters (used mainly in the 20th dynasty); and the Saite version, which has strict order (used after the 26th dynasty).

Amenhotep IV was the first ancient to believe in one god, and he introduced this through his reign. He changed his name to Akhenaton. He was an ancient Egyptian pharaoh of the 18th Dynasty who ruled for 17 years and died in about 1334 BCE. He is noted for abandoning traditional Egyptian polytheism and introducing worship centered on Aten, the one true god. Akhenaton tried to bring about a departure from traditional religion, yet in the end it would not be accepted. After his death, his monuments were dismantled and hidden. He was all but lost to history until the discovery of Tutankhamun's tomb during the 19th century.

Tutankhamun was nine years old when he became Pharaoh, and he reigned for approximately ten years. In historical terms, Tutankhamun's significance stems from his rejection of the radical religious innovations introduced by his predecessor and father, Akhenaten. His tomb in the Valley of the Kings was discovered almost completely intact — the most complete ancient Egyptian royal tomb ever found.

The mask of Nefertiti is still at the Berlin Museum. It remains one of the most valuable and popular artifacts.

In 1897, Napoleon Bonaparte paced his room filled by unrequited ambition. He wrote, "Paris weighs me down like a cloak of lead! This Europe of ours is a molehill. Only in the East, where six hundred million human beings live, is it possible to found great empires and realize great revolutions."

On May 19, 1798, Napoleon sailed from Toulon with a fleet of 328 vessels carrying 38,000 men on board — a force almost as large as the one he commanded when he embarked on the Eastern campaign. The goal of this army was Egypt. Behind this goal, however, was far beyond the Nile Valley — the enormous peninsula of India.

Napoleon's expedition had the long-range result of politically and economically awakening Egypt. It set in motion the modernization of Egypt that continues to this day. He implemented this by taking 170 learned civilians and experts to Egypt.

"Egypt was old, older than any other culture known at the time. It was already old when the political policy of the future Roman Empire was being framed in the first meetings on the Capitoline Hill. It was old and blighted when the Germans and Celts of the north European forest were still hunting bears. The first dynasty came into power about five thousand years ago. So, fixing Egyptian history in calendric time, and describing marvelous cultural forms, had already been evolved in the land of the Nile. And when the 26th Dynasty died out, still five hundred years separated Egyptian history from our era. The Kybians ruled the land, then the Ethiopians, the Assyrians, the Persians, the Greeks, the Romans — all before the star shone over the stable at Bethlehem."

I had seen the environs of the star, in front of the village of Bethlehem. There is a long, sweeping valley covered in short green grass. One end rises to the steps of the manger, it is said. The valley then falls away, declining perhaps by 500-1000 feet. I was there during summer and saw the green grass of the valley. There is a small village around the cathedral where tourist items are sold. This is considered to be the old town. Near the cradle, horses were quartered. Above the stable today, stands a huge cathedral. In the past, the structure was financed by all Christian nations, each now claiming their share of the Church of the Nativity. The doors are foreshortened, so that Moslem horsemen cannot ride inside the church, it is said. The visitors are the devout, the rich Russians, the rich Europeans and those just wanting to get a glimpse of eternity. Today, one can only imagine the manger housing the baby Jesus with the wise men standing guard over the valley.

Is the Israeli-Palestine conflict real? Rowdy young boys during the Intifada conflict were glad to respond by nicely answering one's question of, "Where's the old city?" they were asked. They gave explicit instructions on how to get there.

As we would expect, their answers directed one to nonsensical places. They merged fun and confusion. They had done their duty.

"Of course, the stone marvels of the Nile had been known to some, but knowledge through them was more or less legendary. Most Egyptian monuments had been carried away to museums in foreign lands and were accessible to public view. In the Napoleonic period, the tourists in Europe gaped at the purloined lions, on the steps of their capitols. One could also see the statues of some of the Ptolemaic kings — that is, very late works finished during a period when the splendor of ancient Egypt had been replaced by the new glories of Alexandrian Hellenism. Some monuments that were truly representative of ancient Egyptian times were still in Egypt but they were few. The most famous twelve obelisks had all been removed to museums around the world. Not one remained in Egypt.

Even so, several ancient writers had mentioned the hieroglyphs. These ancients included the Roman Herodotus as an example, and the Greeks, Strabo and Diodorus. They gave several fanciful interpretations of how to approach translations and what they mean. All refer to the hieroglyphs as an unintelligible form of picture writing.

Egyptians point out that Europeans have stolen the George Washing monument concepts, at least the 500 foot obelisk memorializing it and all the real obelisks like the Washington monument. These artifacts have been stolen by museums until not a single large obelisk stands in Egypt today. One can only find them in the British Museum and similar national museums. This is a pity. It is such a phenomenal representation that it is wondrous when seen alone, but what it could have been in their original placement.

Meanwhile, ancient buildings and monuments had hieroglyphs; they appeared everywhere, on buildings, on columns, on shards strewn everywhere in the vicinity of ruins, on bas-reliefs. Hieroglyphs appeared on every conceivable flat or curved surface. Millions of people saw these picture graphics but not a living soul could read or write them. Not a single person could transcend from the extremely constraining social limit they represented.

After years of study or sometimes a lifetime of effort, someone found and translated the Rosetta stone. This stone was found near the village of the same name. This was a revelation. It had a king's story in three different languages including Greek. The side-by-side comparison yielded perhaps the single greatest intellectual achievement that we have known. To this we owe our gratitude to Jean-Francois Champollion and to a soldier whose identity will never be known that was the custodian of the stone. The Rosetta stone was the key to it all, branching out from the Greek hieroglyphs to the carvings on formal temples, on architectural surfaces, on broken shards scattered around the mounds of antiquity.

Even this section was over-simplified. The language like everything grew, became more complex and evolved to totally different forms. The linguistic abilities of archaeologists had to be at their maximum, and the challenges were continuous. The cuneiform version of the language reached a plateau, hesitated, and then moved on. As always, Herodotus the traveler, documents Darius and finds he was at the height of his power in about 500 BCE. Hammurabi often shows up where his power dates at about 1700 BCE. One might run into Harun al-Rashid, the caliph, who was at his maximum power in about 800 CE. This is about the year that Charlemagne reached his powers in northern Europe where kingdoms tended to roam around a lot. The players answered loosely to the Pope in Rome and they conspired to promote Christianity and unite northern Europe.

"Today, Cairo's street cars carry one almost up to the pyramids as I experienced. We can then climb to the top of the Pyramid of Cheops, highest and largest of them all. To the south we see another whole group of Pharaonic monuments rising in the distance. There is the sphinx, naturally. The proportions of all these are unbelievably huge, from the Pyramid of Cheops to the lion-headed Sphinx. One can climb to the burial room in the pyramid of Cheops. This is a small tunnel that rises from ground level to the burial chamber. The tunnel requires one to stay bent over while climbing the three-by-four foot rising tunnel. A long line is often required to enter the tunnel. Then, a series of electric lights, with bare bulbs, leads the visitor upwards. The long line in the tunnel is constraining, uncomfortable and very claustrophobic.

About three- quarters the distance from Cairo to Aswan, one finds both ancient cities of Lexor and Karnak. This is the same Karnak that has a huge set of carved lions and other animals for entrance and a number of massive columns surrounding the forepart of the entrance. Naturally, most of the figures have been stripped and find themselves in many European museums.

The ancient city of Thebes is located here on the east side of the Nile. Further, the nearby region holds the Valley of the Kings.

In the first year of WWI, the concession for excavating in the Valley of the Kings was transferred to Lord Cornarvon and Howard Carter. This pair worked together, Carnarvon supplied the finances and Carter the background knowledge. They set out to discover the tomb of Tutankhamen. They succeeded beyond anyone's wildest imagination. Their work represents the very summit of success in archaeological effort.

I have been in the Valley of Kings during the summer. There are digs of several graves that are no further than 10 or 20 feet apart. The ground is barren with rocks, pebbles and dusty powder consistency. This is up to a mini-ridge steep climb. One must be aware that geography and structures change often. What was there in some year might be totally changed a few years later.

There is a hole in the ground sufficient for a man to enter with a fragile hand rail. One climbs down through the opening. There are massive stones here and there in the passageway. After traps, or what appears to be traps, one comes to a couple of rooms. Behold, we reach Tutankhumen's tomb. Many of the objects are covered in gold. There have been efforts to make the tomb dramatic so there are Egyptian hieroglyphs pasted to the walls. There is a tomb with a proclaimed mummy therein. Even so, the tomb is dramatic. The Egyptian artifacts, or their replicas are impressive. The tomb is filled with golden chariots, divans, and all those items he will need in his unearthly travel.

Nefertiti was the queen of Egypt and the wife of the famous Pharaoh Akhenaten during the 14th century BCE. Her name means, "a beautiful woman has come." The famous sculpture of her face, which is on display at the Neues Museum in Berlin, is one of the most recognizable icons of Egyptian art with its high cheekbones, almond eyes and long graceful neck.

The family tree was a little bit tangled and confusing. Nefertiti had six daughters with Akhenaten, who then went on to take other wives — including his own sister. He fathered King Tut with his sister.

Akhenaten and Nefertiti ruled together during a tumultuous time in religion. They rejected polytheism and proclaimed that there was only one important god — Aten, the god of the sun.

If for no other reason than their monotheism, they deserve a special place in our pantheon of heroes.

The archeological work of picks and small brushes continued. Sooner or later, other kingdoms were laid bare, mounds were invaded, and the desert was dug up, sifted and interpreted. The kingdoms of Assyria, Babylonia and Sumeria became part of our known heritage.

There has usually been a fight over who really owned the artifacts being dug up by all archaeologists. This continues to escalate. Many countries and museums make the claim that the countries where the artifacts are found should own them. There are many lawsuits to enforce this attitude.

Germany was always very active in funding digs and putting the results on display in Berlin. This made the East German museum one of the richest in the world. This strange ownership question resulted because there was a contentious division of artifacts in Germany after WWII. Probably the most valuable artifact was the beautiful head of Queen Nefertiti and this question that surrounded most artifacts. Julia and I wanted to take a trip to Germany and see this exhibit.

As luck would have it, I got the opportunity to visit Berlin as part of my job. I jumped at the chance. Unfortunately, Julia was unable to arrange her schedule and she did not go with me.

We would have to wait until another time to go together. Meanwhile, I had to take the opportunity without her.

I am a tourist at heart. There was no place I did not want to go.

Tangier was a tourist place. It sits on the northwest corner of Africa in what used to be Spanish Morocco and French Morocco. It was one of those places that attracted me. My bosses sent me to Spain from Germany. There were many digs in Spain or it was rich in antiquities.

The history of Tangier is very rich due to the historical presence of many civilizations and cultures starting from the 5th century BCE. Tangier was a refuge for many cultures. In 1923, Tangier had international status by the agreement of foreign colonial powers, and became a destination for many European and American diplomats, spies, writers and businessmen. In 1912, Morocco was effectively partitioned between France and Spain, the latter occupying the country's far north, while France declared a protectorate over the remainder. Tangier became an international zone in 1923.

The multicultural placement of Muslim, Christian, and Jewish communities in pre-war Tangier made it a Mecca for art and literature. The immigrants attracted writer and composer Paul Bowles. The same was true for playwright Tennessee Williams, the 'beat' writers William S. Burroughs, Allen Ginsberg and Jack Kerouac, the painter Brion Gysin and the music group 'The Rolling Stones.' These all lived in or visited Tangier during different periods of the last century. The writer George Orwell and his wife visited Tangier in 1938.

It was after Delacroix that Tangier became an obligatory stop for artists. In the 1940s and until 1956 when the city was an International Zone. The city served as a playground for eccentric millionaires, a meeting place for secret agents and all kinds of crooks, and a Mecca for speculators and gamblers, an Eldorado for the fun loving. During World War II, the Office of Strategic Services (OSS) operated out of Tangier for various operations in North Africa. It was only a two-hour or so ferry ride from Tangier to Algeciras, Spain, and it was only two hours from Africa to Europe by way of Gibraltar.

It was surprising that around the same time, the important circle of writers emerged. These were to have a profound and lasting literary influence. After WWII, the artists and spies all disappeared and Tangier became a plain old town.

At this time, I and another guardsman were ordered to Israel on National Guard business. After our business was completed, we decided to return home on a trip through Egypt. Egypt was after all the birthplace of our culture. It would help round my knowledge of North Africa and the Maghreb area. Until the time of Columbus, it included Moorish Spain. It now comprises essentially the Atlas Mountains and the coastal plain bordering on the Mediterranean Sea. Morocco, Algeria, Tunisia, and Libya host this plain. Some say the Mahgreb also extends south of Morocco down through Western Sahara and Mauritania.

The native peoples of the Maghreb have resisted successive Punic, Roman, and Christian invasions. This accounts for all the walled villages stuck into cliffs and caves. It was as if a huge ledge had been carved into the cliff and a medieval village and fort placed in it. Not until the 7th and 8th centuries was the Maghreb conquered by Arabs and the new arrivals from the East. The Arabs then imposed the religion of Islam

These points in history are what make the Mahgreb so exotic. When flying along the Atlas viewing these villages carved into the lower hills of the Atlas Mountains, the spotter planes we used became magic carpets. Our imagination transported Ali Baba and the Forty Thieves from the sands of Arabia to the Maghreb. We could see in our imagination their loaded asses hauling gold and treasure from the 'Open Sesame' cave to the village. The fecundity of our imaginations brought forth visions unsurpassed in natural experience.

The Guardsman and I were then to take a boat down to Cairo in large river boats from Aswan. My friend and I were finishing our business in Tel Aviv so we hurried for diplomatic people to get visas; we were then to meet busses that would take us across the desert to Cairo. After enough time, these things usually work out but nothing is for sure. We crossed at the border of the Sanai and Gaza Strip. A small commercial bus picked us up and carried us across the Sanai Desert. We were the only passengers. The only thing of note was that the Egyptians provided a two-motorcycle police escort that whole distance of 300 miles or so. The motorcycles kept the emergency lights and their sirens on all the way across the Sanai. All the little children ran out to meet us and cheer us on as we passed. After an interminable period we passed over the Suez Canal that showed us a couple of ocean ships moving along this barren strip of seawater. The Suez Canal was a celebration of man's many extraordinary accomplishments, only to be surpassed by the Panama Canal.

From the High Dam, we boarded a cruise boat that took us after several days down the Nile to Cairo and the Great Pyramid.

Finally, I had to return home.

The Cold War was heating up at this time. The Wall had been built and the two Germany's faced each other through barbed wire and machine guns. By 1960, the combination of World War II and the massive emigration westward left East Germany with only 61% of its population of working age. On August 13, 1961, the Communist government of East Germany began to build a barbed wire and concrete wall between East and West Berlin. Khrushchev had been emboldened by U.S. President John F. Kennedy's tacit indication that the U.S. would not actively oppose this action in the Soviet sector of Berlin. In August the leaders of the GPU signed the order to close the border and erect a wall.

The Berlin Wall stood until November 9, 1989, when the head of the East German Communist Party announced that citizens of the GDR could cross the border whenever they pleased. That night, ecstatic crowds swarmed the wall. Some crossed freely into West Berlin, while others brought hammers and picks and began to chip away at the wall itself. To this day, the Berlin Wall remains one of the most powerful and pathetic symbols of the Cold War.

I often related a story about the wall when I visited Berlin once. I had always heard of Unter den Linden Boulevard. It was the continuation of the Charlottesburg Strasse past the Brandenburg Gate and that straddles

Unter den Linden. I struck out walking through the Tiergarten in the general direction of the street. The walk was long, being a mile or two. I stopped a West Berliner and asked him in halting German how to get to Unter den Lendin. The German looked startled. He finally pointed in a direction but he was reluctant for me to walk there.

I continued. Suddenly, I broke out of the forest to a wide zone with no houses or trees. Just before me was the wall of concrete and barbed wire about six or seven feet high with a guard post about 25 feet high. In it, there were three Vopos holding machine guns across their chests, watching me with binoculars while they fingered their triggers.

"Whoa!!!"

That was scary. Just to the left was the Russian headquarters along with the French, British and American. Entangled barbed wire was everywhere, so you could not just walk to where you wanted to go. There were 2 very high pillars of 150 feet or so in front of the Russian headquarters. On top of each was a T-62 (I guess) tank pointing to the horizon across Berlin.

These were massive machines. That must have rankled the Germans to no end.

On 12 June 1987, U.S. President Ronald Reagan spoke to the West Berlin populace in a speech at the Brandenburg Gate,

Addressing the Soviet Union leader, Mikhail Gorbachev, President Reagan said in a speech, "Mr. Gorbachev, tear down this wall!"

There were perhaps 10-20 busses in the departure courtyard at Check Point Charlie. The Vopos, or East German Police, had machine guns across their chests with their hands on the triggers. The first stepped aboard our bus and glared at us with great hostility. He then chose each person to give a personalized stare. The passengers looked straight ahead without flinching. No cameras were in sight. For all the world, the passengers could have been on their way to Auschwitz or at least to a hanging.

Julia had been undergoing a change in heart about me. She began to see my better points, and we even thought of marriage. It was not long before the trip was over and I returned home. By this time, a wedding was in the works.

I found East Germany to be a dull, lifeless, police state with hardly anyone on the beautiful promenade, Unter den Linden, with Linden trees along the street and sidewalk as far as the eye could see. The Brandenburg Gate was originally the last of several city gates. That wonderful victory arch exhibited the 4-horse chariot sitting on top of the gate. This is the center of Berlin.

Fortunately, the division into East and West Germany no longer exists. The Unification Day, 3 October 1990, saw East and West Germany combined along with East and West Berlin. The Germans in the east no longer had to fear the volpes or East Berlin police.

When I returned home, Julia's and my relationships seemed to be much better than before. The planning for the wedding became very serious. It was not long before it took place in her mother's apartment in the US.

Most of the wedding guests were Julia's friends from the school.

Things kept on more-or-less as they had been. Money was short. Her mother was sharp. We both were extremely ambitious. As all bridegrooms believe, it will work itself out. We had infinite faith in this. Things would work themselves out.

The head of Nefertiti had a large room in the museum to itself. The exhibit focused on the head where colors seem maintained. It was a wonderful exhibit. I was glad I went.

Julie looked teasingly to me. She said, "That was great. Now, what are you going to do for me?" I looked puzzled toward her. She had a way of teasing that was supposed to be funny but somehow it was a piece of barbed wire. It was certainly not funny. "Do you know what I mean?"

I looked at her, blankly. I said, "I know exactly what you mean." Judging by her facial muscles tightening and his chin projecting outward, I did know exactly what she meant. It was clear that Jane had paid for the trip. One more time she lorded it over that it was her that provided the money for their living expenses.

Julia wanted to be near her mother. She became the one that planned our life, that decided what in life was important and what was not.

Over the years, her mother exhibited changes. Her face became sharp with angular features. Her lips became sharp and tight. One could say they were even thin lips. Those features that I thought were nice were now becoming negatives. My mother always told me that women with thin lips were quick to exhibit anger and outrage. I think my mother might have been right.

Once again, Jane had a stiff neck and a hard head. I tolerated her remarks but I certainly did not like it.

CHAPTER 7

Hanseatic League

This chapter is about the 11th to 17th century trade group, the Hanseatic League. This was also known as the Hansa. It was a commercial and defensive confederation of merchant guilds and their market towns. Growing from a few North German towns in the late 1100s, the league came to dominate Baltic maritime trade for three or more centuries along the coast of Northern Europe. It stretched from the Baltic to the North Sea and inland during the Late Middle Ages and declined slowly after 1450.

Hansa, was the German word for a convoy, and was applied to bands of merchants traveling between the Hanseatic cities whether by land or by sea. The league was created to protect the guilds' economic interests and diplomatic privileges in their affiliated cities and countries, as well as along the trade routes the merchants visited. The Hanseatic cities had their own legal system and furnished their own armies for mutual protection and aid. Despite this, the organization was not a state, nor a confederation of city-states; only a very small number of the cities within the league enjoyed autonomy and liberties comparable to those of a free imperial city.

The Hanseatic League was a commercial and defensive confederation of merchant guilds and their market towns. Growing from a few North German towns in the late 1100's, the league came to dominate Baltic maritime trade for three centuries along the coast of Northern Europe. It stretched from the Baltic to the North Sea and inland during the late middle Ages. Thus, its operation from about 1100 to 1450 provided a trade convoy system for trade and protection, or a defense system lasting about 350 years following the Viking Age.

A major economic advantage for the Hansa was its control of the shipbuilding market, mainly in Lübeck, Danzig and Bremen. We remember 'the musicians of Breman' from the Grimm Brothers *Fairy Tales*. The familiar symbol of Bremen is the donkey, dog, cat and rooster as they rode on each other's back in that order. Bremen was also a member of the Hansic league. The Hansa sold ships everywhere in Europe, including Italy. They drove out the Dutch, because Holland wanted to favor Bruges as a huge stable market at the end of a trade route. When the Dutch started to become competitors of the Hansa in shipbuilding, the Hansa tried to stop the flow of shipbuilding technology from Hanseatic towns to Holland. Danzig, a trading partner of Amsterdam, attempted to forestall the decision. Dutch ships sailed to Danzig to take grain from the city directly, to the dismay of Lübeck. Hollanders also circumvented the Hanseatic towns by trading directly with north German princes in non-Hanseatic towns. Dutch freight costs were much lower than those of the Hansa, and were excluded as middlemen.

The Hanseatic League was a commercial and defensive confederation of merchant guilds and their market towns. Growing from a few North German towns in the late 1100s, the league came to dominate Baltic maritime trade for three centuries along the coast of Northern Europe. It stretched from the Baltic to the North Sea and inland during the late Middle Ages and declined slowly after 1450. Hansa was the word for a convoy, and this word was applied to bands of merchants traveling between the Hanseatic cities.

Before the age of the Vikings, starting about 700 until about 1100, the Huns had the spotlight from about 200 until about 700. Then, after the Vikings age, the world belonged to the League. It briefly belonged to Genghis Kahn until his premature death in 1227. This left the Khans in control, some for centuries. This Horde legacy is remembered as the

Golden, the Blue and the White Hordes. The Stan legacy remains even today in the exotic names that end in 'khan' or 'stan', such as Kazakhstan, Uzbekistan and Turkmenistan. The Hanseatic League was in existence from about 1159 until the renaissance in about 1400. They were unique in many ways and their own architects gave the towns of the League their own unique distinction. These tended to be the largest buildings in town so had the most influence.

Historians generally trace the origins of the Hanseatic League to the rebuilding of the north German town of Lubeck. North German Architecture raised extraordinary red brick buildings of unique concept and design. These can be seen on the German side of the Baltic today. Exploratory trading adventures, raids, and piracy had occurred earlier throughout the Baltic region—the sailors of Gotland sailed up rivers as far away as Lake Ladoga and the Rus city of Novgorod, a powerful city a hundred miles south of Saint Petersburg—but the scale of international trade in the Baltic area was limited. Lübeck became a central node in the seaborne trade that linked the areas around the North and Baltic seas. The hegemony of Lübeck peaked during the 15th century.

Lübeck and Hamburg were about 20 miles south of Bergen. They became a base for merchants from Saxony and Westphalia trading eastward and northward. Well before the middle of the 12th century, merchants in different cities began to form guilds. This area was a source of timber, wax, amber, resins, and furs, along with rye and wheat brought down on barges from the hinterland to port markets. The towns raised their own armies, with each guild required to provide levies when needed. The Hanseatic cities came to the aid of one another, and commercial ships were often used to carry soldiers and their arms.

In 1241, Lübeck, which had access to the Baltic and North Sea fishing grounds, formed an alliance—a precursor to the league—with Hamburg, another trading city, that controlled access to salt-trade. The allied cities gained control over most of the salt-fish trade. Cologne joined them in 1260. In 1266, Henry III of England granted the Lübeck and Hamburg Hansa a charter for operations in England, and the Cologne Hansa joined them in 1282 to form the most powerful Hanseatic colony in London. Even today, Lubeck is the center for ship and submarine design and construction which is sold all over the world.

Starting with trade in coarse woollen fabrics, the Hanseatic League had the effect of bringing both commerce and industry to northern Germany. As trade increased, newer and finer woolen and linen fabrics, and even silks, were manufactured in northern Germany. The same refinement of products out of cottage industry occurred in other fields, e.g. etching, wood carving, armour production, engraving of metals, and woodturning. The century-long monopoly of sea navigation and trade by the Hanseatic League ensured that the Renaissance arrived in northern Germany before it did in the rest of Europe.

The league primarily traded timber, furs, resin (or tar), flax, honey, wheat, and rye from the east to Flanders and England with cloth (and, increasingly, manufactured goods) going in the other direction. Metal ore (principally copper and iron) and herring came southwards from Sweden.

Another similarity involved the cities' strategic locations along trade routes. At the height of its power in the late 14th century, the merchants of the Hanseatic League succeeded in using their economic clout, and sometimes their military might—trade routes required protection and the league's ships sailed well-armed—to influence imperial policy.

The Hansa also waged a vigorous campaign against pirates. Between 1392 and 1440, maritime trade of the league faced danger from raids. Most foreign cities confined the Hanseatic traders to certain trading areas and to their own trading posts. They seldom interacted with the local inhabitants, except when doing business. Many locals, merchant and noble alike, envied the power of the league and tried to diminish it.

CHAPTER 8

Marriage and Whose Country Is It, Anyway?

By this time, I was just coming to understand the restrictions of marriage. Julie had pulled the trigger earlier. Even a little bit of softening had been encouraging to me. Julia had begun to discuss marriage. All those things I had considered in the past suddenly didn't matter anymore. Somehow, it would all work out, I thought. The wedding took place in Jane's apartment. The guests were mostly friends of Julia from the school. Almost before I realized it, Julia and I got married.

I loved Julia and that was all that mattered. I still felt my heart flutter every time she gave me the slightest attention.

Now, that was in the past. We were married. Things remained sweet and nice for a while. Meanwhile, Julia finished her archaeology degree. She had decided by this time that she wanted to go to fashion school, and she enrolled. She also started graduate school. She was carrying a heavy load. She earned a few dollars here and there. I also was able to earn a few dollars through graduate school. It was a tough road.

By this time, Julia and I had a certain respect for each other's passions and fields of knowledge. The truth is, I thought I could help her by relating things that I know and she doesn't. This made me a pedantic and she hated it. On the other hand, it helped me to organize my knowledge and this fed my passion for the whole archaeology field. Besides, in those days, I was steaming with ambition and thought this made me more knowledgeable and she could profit from this. Was I wrong, or what?

"Shaun," she said. "I hate you when you get into that pedantic mode. You are talking down to me. Besides, who got the better grades in school?"

"Well," I said. "I could do some disliking myself. You activist women don't just advocate a position, you use your position as a movement. Spare me from that. In fact, let's have a truce."

Julia had adjusted her scheduling and decided to meet me in Spain. She found a cheap ticket and accommodations in Costa del Sol. We met there. We intended to take tour busses from there since we only had a few days to stay there. Things went off exactly as planned.

One evening, we sat on the hotel veranda and made small talk. "I am working on a paper and I love it." I said. "It is just a bunch of notes now but one can tell where I am going from these. "I can use all the help I can get. If I can get this thing published, it means a great deal for me. It will enhance my reputation and people will start taking me more seriously. You have been reviewing this as we go along and you make it much better than it would otherwise be. Please help me."

"Good." She said. "I love it when you beg."

I said, "I know I help you. I try to guide you and I hope you realize that."

I ignored her tease and said, "I am trying to see or visit all kinds of places that relate to my work. That means tourist places, digs, museums and other such places. In fact, I am working on a little segment that I may use. It is about Gibraltar. Would you like to see it?"

"She answered positively."

"These are my notes that have not been organized so far. I hope you can make something of them. It is intended for a technical audience. North Africa is germane since the Vikings were not strangers to the Strait. They made many raiding trips to Spain and even to Italy. They also traded with the Eastern Roman Empire in Constantinople. Their paths to Constantinople and the Byzantines were either through the Mediterranean or the Dnieper and Volga Rivers.

The written segment, showed mostly the Atlas Mountains. These separate the Mediterranean from the Sahara Desert. They extend about 1,600 miles around Morocco through Tunisia and Algiers through Libya. The maximum height is over 13,600 feet. "These are respectable mountains. They are mostly snow and ice covered. They have the cooling north side and the hot desert south side so it is a dynamic environment. The mountains drop down to form the Mediterranean Strait where Gibraltar and Spain are on the north gate and Morocco is on the south gate. Spain has claimed the caves and tunnels of the Gibraltar rock for centuries with no resolution in sight. They remain in British hands."

Western Sahara bounds Morocco in the south, the Atlantic Ocean and Canary Islands in the west, Tangier in Spanish Morocco and French Morocco in the north and Algeria in the east. The Atlas Mountains hold back the Sahara.

During the 19th and 20th centuries, the French colonial empire was one of the largest in the world, behind the British, Russian and Spanish. The French had the largest empire in the 17th century and the second in 1929.

It became a moral mission to lift the world up to French standards by bringing Christianity, French culture and language to the colonies. This was said in 1884 by the leading exponent of colonialism, Jules Ferry, who declared; "The higher races have a right over the lower races; they have a duty to civilize the inferior races." The colonials offered full citizenship rights although in reality "assimilation was always being denied and the colonial populations were treated like subjects, not citizens." France sent large numbers of settlers to North Africa, trailing behind Lafayette and they in turn became a powerful political force in Paris.

Julia continued reading the unorganized notes. From these, Julia proposed to generate a peer-revue technical paper to be submitted to a technical journal.

CHAPTER 9

Moors of North Africa

She continued to read. The Moors of North Africa inhabited the lower half of Spain before their expulsion in 1492, Columbus's year. The mountains were then pockmarked with walled villages and fortresses drilled into the mountain cliffs. They looked like Moorish fantasies, clinging to the walls and caves. When sun light fell on those maintains in the right way, they elicited what was almost a religious experience. They were reddish gold with bright sunshine reflecting the sandstone architecture. It was the land of 'Sinbad', of 'Ali Baba and the Forty Thieves'. It was hard not to conjure up these images, these multi-tiered sand mirages across the dunes.

The Moors reached a high level of architecture, science and technology between about 700 and 1492. This means there was overlap from the Huns, through the Viking age and onward through the Byzantine Empire embedding the eastern Holy Roman Empire. This preserved the learning of the Europeans. This was a gift to the West through Spain and Italy and sea commerce generally. Even our numbering system came from the Moors and Arabs. Most people think there has been little progress with them since that time. Yet, the architecture and natural world remains. There certainly has been little progress since 1895 when the French took them over as part of their empire. The number of Arab high school graduates under the French was less than one's fingers and toes.

The Atlas Mountains held numerous villages and walled cities in mountain valleys. These all conformed to similar architectural patterns and conventions. These are beautiful to see.

I'll tell you one thing, he said to no one in particular. When the time is right, I'm coming back here and explore this whole area adequately. You need to be in a small airplane to do it properly. "Absolutely," was the response, again to no one.

This paper was a little segment about the trip we took together. Gibraltar is mentioned a thousand times in Greek and Roman times, not to mention its prominence in all western literature. Gibraltar guards the Strait. In ancient times, this was by Phoenician sailors, by Greek sailors, by Romans, those scattered after the Trojan wars, and many others.

When the ancient Vikings were in both their trading and raiding days, they also knew Gibraltar and it was not too unusual for them to sail down the west coast of Europe. They could divert their activity from the west into the Mediterranean Sea or trade down the Dnieper and Volga rivers to enter the Byzantine capitol by the Black Sea and Rus territory.

Gibraltar is located on the southern end of the Iberian or Spanish Peninsula. It has an area of 2.6 square miles and shares its northern border with Spain. The Rock of Gibraltar is the major landmark of the region. At its foot is a densely populated city of 30,000 people. On the African side of the Mediterranean right by the port lies the city of Tangiers. This used to be Spanish Morocco after about 1912. Further on south lie the cities of Rabat and Casablanca that was French Morocco from 1912 until after WWII. These both were combined after WWII to constitute the country of Morocco. It has been an important base for the British Royal Navy as it controlled the entrance and exit to the Mediterranean Sea, which is only eight miles wide at this naval "choke point" and remains strategically important to this day. Half the world's seaborne trade passes through the strait every year.

Since I am on the trail of the Vikings, I naturally wanted to see this area. I did not have the ideas put together at this time as you can see with this segment. I am still talking to Julia.

The sovereignty of Gibraltar is a major point of contention in Anglo-Spanish relations as Spain contests Great Britain for this. The British counter this with Spanish plebiscites choosing to remain with Britain.

She continued the Gibraltar notes. Gibraltar is famous for its dozens of wild monkeys, its small shopping and tourist area, its caves and tunnels and its impregnability as the entrance into the Mediterranean Sea.

The monkeys seem to be everywhere. They jump from cable to cable and bridge structure to structure. The thing I don't like about it is they also jump onto you. They try to steal your food if you have a candy bar or other edible. Most tourists seem thrilled by this. Not me! I think they are dirty and, God knows what kind of diseases they carry. They pop on your shoulder and grab your food. They search your coat to find quick food. I don't like them. I had rather watch and let the tourist pay the price if there is one.

Julia and I took a ferry trip from Algeciras, Spain to Tangiers, Morocco. We were to take a ferry from Algeciras, Spain, across the Gibraltar strait and then Tangiers. In the long morning trip to Algeciras, the rain was furious. A storm must have been just off the land causing a really rough sea to roll through the straits. Later in the day, the rain let up and we decided to continue on our planned trip by ferry to Tangier. There was an Arab woman passenger with a tiny baby that cried all the way across the 8 mile strait. The mother tried to comfort the baby, but the baby was sick. The mother was sick. The mother was seasick, as were many of the passengers. The mother took the baby to the back of the ferry. She was terribly embarrassed and there was no respite. It was a relatively small boat and provided little protection from the ocean on our starboard side. The baby screamed and cried and about everyone got sick.

Tangier was not such a clean place. The road stretches on with refuse here and there. The rain continued to gully down where mud formed in the street. Malcom Forbes was having some kind of to-do on this date at his museum in Tangiers. Glory! The rain felt like the waters of W. Sumerset Maugham in the short story of that name, "*Rain*", where he pictured the decadence of Miss Sadie Thompson and her flawed minister. I hope they made it but the museum was wet and all the visitors were wet. All of it just made for more wetness. Thank Goodness, we were not lashed by heavy winds as in Maugham's prolonged South Pacific drenching. It had been a similar jog between Julia and the Gibraltar notes. She jogged forward but she was not liking it. She needed a more finished document to critique.

I could not wait to get out of there. Unfortunately, when we left this place, we had to wind back up the hill in the pouring rain. "Oh, give me respite," I cried!

The history of Tangier is very rich due to the historical presence of many civilizations and cultures starting from the 5th century BC. This was before the Viking Age in America and continued long afterwards. Tangier was a refuge for many cultures. In 1923, Tangier had international status by the agreement of foreign colonial powers, and became a destination for many European and American diplomats, spies, writers and businessmen. In 1821, the Legation Building in Tangier became the first piece of property acquired abroad by the U.S. government.

In 1912, Morocco was effectively partitioned between France and Spain, the latter occupying the country's far north and far south, while France declared a protectorate over the remainder. Tangier was made an international zone in 1923.

Spanish troops occupied Tangier in June 1940. The territory was restored to its pre-war status on October 11, 1945. Tangier joined with the rest of Morocco following the restoration of full sovereignty in 1956 as Morocco. The exotic French and Spanish Morocco disappeared. The mundane and pedestrian trump exotica.

The multi-cultural placement of Muslim, Christian, and Jewish communities in pre-war Tangier made it a Mecca for art and literature. The foreign immigrants attracted writer and composer Paul Bowles, playwright Tennessee Williams, the 'beat' writers William S. Burroughs, Allen Ginsberg and Jack Kerouac, the painter Brion Gysin and the music group The Rolling Stones, who all lived in or visited Tangier during different periods of the 20th century. The writer George Orwell, one of my favorites, and his wife visited Tangier in 1938. It was after Delacroix that Tangier became an obligatory stop for artists seeking to experience the colors and the light that he spoke of for themselves. There were varying results in this. Matisse made several sojourns to Tangier. "I have found landscapes in Morocco," he claimed, "exactly as they are described in Delacroix's paintings." The Californian artist Richard Diebenkorn was directly influenced by the haunting colors and rhythmic patterns of Matisse's Morocco paintings.

In the 1940s and until 1956 when the city was an International Zone, the city served as a playground for eccentric millionaires, a meeting place for secret agents and all kinds of crooks, and a Mecca for speculators and gamblers, an Eldorado for the fun loving. During World War II the Office of Strategic Services (OSS) operated out of Tangier for various operations in North Africa. Malcom Forbes owned a museum there to house his huge collection of toy soldiers.

Around the same time, a circle of writers emerged which was to have a profound and lasting literary influence. This included Paul Bowles, who lived and wrote for over half a century in the city, Tennessee Williams and Jean Genet as well as Mohammed Mrabet and Ahmed Yacoubi. Among the best-known works from this period is Choukri's '*For Bread Alone*'. Tennessee Williams described it as "a true document of human desperation, shattering in its impact." Independently, William S. Burroughs lived in Tangier for four years and wrote '*Naked Lunch*' there. After several years of gradual disentanglement from Spanish and French colonial control, Morocco re-integrated the city of Tangier in 1956. Then, the city had its reputation as an international city. The spies all disappeared and it became a plain old town. Tangier remains a very popular tourist destination for cruise ships and day visitors from Spain and Gibraltar but its color has been long gone.

Cork oak forests are a characteristic of the Morocco region wherever you look. It is a medium-sized, evergreen oak tree. It is the primary source of cork for wine bottle stoppers and other uses, such as cork flooring and non-squeak shoes. Mostly, the area produces the wine corks for the entire world. The tree has a thick, insulating bark that may have been the cork oak's evolutionary answer to forest fires. After a fire, many of the other tree species merely regenerate from seeds or re-sprout from the base of the tree. The cork oak branch, protected by cork bark quickly re-sprouts and recomposes the tree canopy. The quick regeneration of the tree seems to be an advantage compared to other species. The tree forms a thick, rugged bark. Over time, a layer of bark can develop considerable thickness (probably more than an inch) and can be harvested every 9 to 12 years to produce cork for various applications, especially wine cork material. The harvesting of cork does not harm the tree; in fact, no trees are cut down during the harvesting process. Only the bark is extracted, and a new layer of cork re-grows, making it a renewable resource. The tree is cultivated from Spain, to Tunisia. This seemed contrary to my biology classes in my schools since that taught that the nourishment for the tree was in the veins running up the bark. If you kill the bark, the tree would die. That is what they taught. It is tough to find universal truths.

We got off the ferry and walked toward town. We had no more than started and the rain started again. It was as if the morning thunder-bursts in European Gibraltar had moved over to African Tangiers. We made dashes back to the ferry landing. It was not to keep dry. We were soggy and wet from the morning. The streets of Algeciras had been flooded in the cloud bursts of the morning.

We all stood in the knee-deep water that reached up from the bottom while rain fell precipitously from the top. That causes the description of wet from top to bottom. The return trip was just a replay of the earlier trip. We were miserable until we sat down in the hotel. Well. All my memories of great literary writings in Tangiers were forgotten. Great art that was made there and the setting of all those spy operations of WWI and WWII were no longer of interest. It was just another North African town that had lost its glamour.

By this time, both Julia and I were tired and hungry. We decided to have an afternoon tea and try it again. I did most of the talking here.

I then related a little of the story of the new world. "When Columbus announced he had found India, he made a monumental mistake. He landed in a few isolated islands in the Caribbean chain. This was not an empty land. There were a huge number of "Indians" spread across the whole of North and South America. Even the Anuit or Eskimo tribes inhabited the far polar region. These and other tribes presented a monumental question. This was what to do about those Indians that were already here."

"I know," Julia responded. "By the time Columbus arrived in 1492, Europe was in its renaissance period. Kingdoms had risen and fallen, Egypt and its pharaohs had strewn its culture across 3,000 years or so.

Homer had made famous the Trojan wars with its heroes. Greece and Rome had had their day. Constantinople had prospered for well over a thousand years and finally began serious break-ups. They reached their peak in 1453 with the invasion of the Muslim Ottomans then held power for another 500 years. Their Ottoman architecture was best expressed by the Taj Mahal. This and many other examples are located in India, and other Ottoman places. It was always punctuated by Mosques and Minarets."

"You hit the nail on the head." I said. "We have a right to ask, 'What happened?' "How did Europeans clear all opposition, even if a minor Indian problem is still with us? How did Columbus and the Spaniards defeat a continent full of Aztecs, Toltecs, Mayans and Indians? How did the Americans clear opposition in South America?" We knew the Indians had to be wiped out. The continents had to be cleared.

CHAPTER 10

The Slate Had to be Cleared

"Yeah," she said. "Within a period from 1492 until the 17th century, the Europeans finished off multiple tribes and cultures and established themselves as the dominant force throughout North and South America. We can only appreciate this feat by looking at those factors that had to be changed if Indians were to be removed and Europeans were to displace the Indians across both continents. The new Americas had to bow to this new reality.

The Spanish conquistadors had to be accommodated in South and Central America. The Spaniards cleansed their area spectacularly and left dead cultures. The Toltecs, Aztecs and Mayans were erased. The American Indians roamed across all of the US and the West at the start. Canada and even the high polar regions were inhabited by Indians in the beginning."

I said, "Montezuma could have destroyed the Spanish at any time, but he did not. Why? The worst defeat of all was that of the Aztecs. The Indians had a chance with these Mexican Indians but they squandered it. We know a great deal about the Aztecs and how they became extinct. These are itemized below.

1. Montezuma, the leader of the Indians, thought that Cortez was the God Quetzecoatl. The Spanish were invited into the inner circles of the Indians. Warfare to the Indians was to capture, not kill. The Spaniards did not see it that way. The Indians also practiced human sacrifice. This horrified the Spanish. It was fair

game after that for any outrage by the Spaniards. The priests and monks profited from this situation, as did the Catholic Church. Any outrage was acceptable after that.

2. The Spaniards had better weapons. The Aztecs had clubs, bows and arrows, spears and rocks. The explosive weapons of the Aztecs were light years ahead of the Stone Age Indians. Further, the Spanish were heavily armored to protect themselves. They used leather and steel to wrap their bodies and deflect the primitive Indian weapons. The iron age weapons will trump stone age weapons at any time.
3. The Aztecs thought the horse was a god. This animal had size, speed, strength and power. The Spanish, armored and decorated, sat high in the air on the horse, projecting a God-like appearance. The Indians had never seen anything like this.
4. The Spanish were cruel. The Indians of both North and South America could not understand the cruelty of the Spaniards. The European thirst for gold and riches could not be satisfied. The conquistadors that came to America were independent men with no family ties. Most were criminals escaping the inevitable imprisonment and execution. The Spanish had emptied their prisons to provide sailors. There was no remorse.
5. Indian neighbors on the edge of the Aztec empire hated the Aztecs. Cortez played them against each other.
6. When Cortez started their campaign in 1519, there were about 25 million Indians living in what is now Mexico. A hundred years later, only 1.2 million Indians had survived.
7. Cataclysmic epidemics had swept through the Mexican highlands taking as many as 17 million lives. European germs and diseases killed more Indians than any army could have.

This was a clash between high European cultures that would soon be living through their industrial revolution and their enemy, the indigenous people that were stuck in the Stone Age with little vision of modern lives. The outcome of such a clash is inevitable. Even so, the Indians would lose in so many ways that it is difficult to describe them all. Further, Indians died by the millions during this time. It was death by diseases, the death of cultures, death by warfare, death by inferior weaponry, death by land migration and far more mortal vulnerabilities.

Below, several crucial factors are listed that destined a new America that was favorable to the Europeans. Nay, these factors caused the outcome of Americanization to be inevitable.

CHAPTER 11

Horses Supply the Energy

First of all was the question of energy for the new world. Throughout history, horses have been used for riding and for pulling carriages, chariots, plows, and carts. They played a significant role in warfare by carrying soldiers into battle. Because the first domesticated horses are thought to have been quite small, it is more likely that they were used to pull carts than for riding.

Horses lost their place in history when gasoline engines were invented. Rigs for horses provided harnesses to convert the pulling power of the animals to linear motion. Horses could provide impressive sprints, they could pull heavy loads for a long time and they could provide this power for long distances. They had long distance capabilities and they could exist with low maintenance.

There is a continuing argument of whether the mule or the horse is the most practical in terms of pulling power, required feed quality, travel per day and similar specifications. The answer is not conclusive.

Europeans had the horse culture. Europeans discovered early on that horses were faster than ox, rain-deer, goats and other animals. Ox, mules, donkeys and horses provided the muscle power that fueled the new world. Horses could eat mundane grasses and they were hardy animals. Further, saddle horses could efficiently pass through the narrow Indian trails of the wilderness areas of America that could not accommodate four-wheel carts or even two-wheel carts. The colonies had only a primitive road system and this fact counted decisively for the ridden-horse. American horses could be broken and domesticated rather easily. This culture could not have succeeded had the Europeans not had the horse where the Indians in both North and South America had no horses. Although a lengthy dissertation, it is crucial to understand horses and their role in this revolution.

A further revolution swept the horse cultures. The saddle, harnessing, and stirrups were invented, all in the deep Mongol lands of central Asia. These converted the saddled horse from a helter-skelter of powerful muscles to a well-coordinated, efficient machine that converted the horse's power to linear motion. One more breakthrough was the invention of the stirrup. This allowed the rider to stand on his stirruped feet and shoot straight and fast. Further, he could ride for very long distances standing on stirrups that favored such motion, again better matching the horse to the mechanics of linear motion.

Horses that live in an untamed state but have ancestors that have been domesticated are not truly "wild" horses — they are feral horses. For instance, when the Spanish reintroduced the horse to the Americas, beginning in the late 15th century, some horses escaped, forming feral herds; the best-known being the mustang. Similarly, the brumby descended from horses strayed or let loose in Australia. Isolated populations of feral horses occur in a number of places, including Portugal, Scotland, and a number of barrier islands along the Atlantic coast of North America from Sable Island off Nova Scotia, to Cumberland Island, off the coast of Georgia. Even though these are often referred to as "wild" horses, they are not truly "wild" in the biological sense of having no domesticated ancestors. Of course, every movie-watcher knows that Indians became robbers and looters across the western plains, but that was later, after the issue had been decided. Horses tamed the West.

CHAPTER 12

Indian Hostility

Second, there was the hostility of the Indians. At the start, Indians befriended the Europeans and showed the settlers how to hunt, fish, preserve food and introduced them to crops, they showed them the use of some irrigation, and they even helped the settlers stay alive. Shortly thereafter, the Indians in both Americas realized they were being cheated and lied to.

The Indians turned against the Europeans. That is, the attitude of the Indians was friendly at first but soon turned hostile. The Indians were rounded up and sent to reservations. This was similar to the Chinese Long March with all its tragic consequences. The Americans became corrupt neighbors. This caused the Indians to fight the settlers. That encouraged the settlers to decimate and eliminate the Indians.

CHAPTER 13

Superior European Weapons

Third, the Europeans had superior weapons. The Europeans had explosive guns consisting of hand guns, blunderbusses, rifles and canon.

The Europeans were past both the Bronze Age and the Iron Age. The use of these materials to produce weapons gave an enormous advantage to the Europeans. The Europeans in the south and the Vikings in the north, on the other hand, knew about metals and their formulation. What they could not produce, they had access to European bronze and to iron as they traveled back and forth to the new land. Thus, they had metal for their arrow tips, they had nails for fastenings, and they had iron weapons and defensive armor generally.

The Indians had neither and that relegated them to the Stone Age with stone-tipped arrows, stone axes, non-explosive weapons and other disadvantages. The Indians made do with bows and arrows. It was a rout.

The Inuit are the descendants of what anthropologists call the Thule culture, that emerged from western Alaska around 1000 CE. They had split from the related Aleut group about 4,000 years ago and from northeastern Siberian migrants, still earlier. They spread eastwards across the Arctic They displaced the related Dorset culture. Inuit legends speak of the displaced people as "giants", people who were taller and stronger than the Inuit. Less frequently, the legends refer to the Dorset as "dwarfs". Researchers believe that the Dorset culture lacked the dogs, larger weapons and other technologies of the Inuit society, which gave the latter an advantage. By 1300, Inuit migrants had reached west Greenland, where they settled, moving into east Greenland over the following century.

Faced with population pressures from the Thule and other surrounding groups, such as the Algonquian and Siouan to the south, the Tuniit gradually receded. They were thought to have become completely extinct as a people by about 1400 or 1500.

The Sadlermiut population survived up until winter 1902–03, when exposure to new infectious diseases brought by contact with Europeans led to their extinction as a people.

In the early 21st century, mitochondrial DNA research has supported the theory of continuity between the Tuniit and the Sadlermiut peoples. It also provided evidence that a population displacement did not occur within the Aleutian Islands between the Dorset and Thule transition. In contrast to other Tuniit populations. Inuit legends recount them encountering people they called the Tuniit, or Sivullirmiut, "First Inhabitants". According to legend, the First Inhabitants were giants, taller and stronger than the Inuit but afraid to interact and "easily put to flight." Scholars now believe the Dorset and the later Thule people were the peoples encountered by Norsemen who visited the area. The Norse called these indigenous peoples Skræling, as first named by the Greenlander Vikings in their early explorations, over 1,000 years ago. The Greenland Inuit circulated almost exclusively north of the "Arctic tree line", the effective southern border of Inuit society.

In the south, the descendants of the southern Labrador Inuit continued their traditional semi-nomadic way of life until the mid-1900s. The people usually moved among islands and bays on a seasonal basis. They did not establish stationary communities. In other areas south of the tree line, native American cultures were well established. The culture and technology of Inuit society that served so well in the Arctic were not suited to subarctic regions, so they did not displace their southern neighbors.

Inuit had trade relations with more southern cultures; boundary disputes were common and gave rise to aggressive actions. Warfare was not uncommon among those Inuit groups with sufficient population density. Inuit who inhabited the Mackenzie River delta area, often engaged in warfare. The more sparsely settled Inuit in the central Arctic, however, did so less often.

Their first European contact was with the Vikings who settled in Greenland and explored the eastern Canadian coast. The Norse sagas recorded meeting what they called Skrælingars (the ugly men with weird sounds). This probably was an undifferentiated label for all the indigenous peoples whom the Norse encountered.

After about 1350, the climate grew colder during the period known as the Little Ice Age. During this period, Alaskan natives were able to continue their whaling activities. But, in the high Arctic, the Inuit were forced to abandon their hunting and whaling sites as bowhead whales disappeared from Canada and Greenland. These Inuit had to subsist on a much poorer diet, and lost access to the essential raw materials for their tools and architecture, which they had previously derived from whaling. The changing climate forced the Inuit to work their way south, forcing them into marginal niches along the edges of the tree line. These were areas which Native Americans had not occupied or where they were weak enough for the Inuit to live near them. Researchers have difficulty defining when Inuit stopped this territorial expansion. There is evidence that they were still moving into new territory in southern Labrador when they first began to interact with Europeans in the 17th century.

The lives of Paleo-Eskimos of the far north were largely unaffected by the arrival of visiting Norsemen or Vikings except for mutual trade. Labrador Inuit have had the longest continuous contact with Europeans. After the disappearance of the Norse colonies in Greenland, the Inuit had no contact with Europeans for at least a century. By the mid-16th century, Basque whalers and fishermen were already working the Labrador coast and had established whaling stations on land, such as the one that has been excavated at Red Bay. The Inuit appear not to have interfered with their operations, but they raided the stations in winter for tools and items made of worked iron, which they adapted to their own needs.

Martin Frobisher's 1576 search for the Northwest Passage was the first well-documented post-Columbian contact between Europeans and Inuit. Frobisher's expedition landed in Frobisher Bay, Baffin Island, not far from the settlement now called The City of Iqaluit, which was long known as Frobisher Bay. Frobisher encountered Inuit on Resolution Island where five sailors left the ship, under orders from Frobisher, and became part of Inuit mythology. The homesick sailors, tired of their adventure, attempted to leave in a small vessel and vanished. Frobisher brought an unwilling Inuk to England, possibly the first Inuk ever to visit Europe. The Inuit oral tradition, in contrast, recounts the natives helping Frobisher's crewmen, whom they believed had been abandoned.

In the final years of the 18th century, the Moravian Church began missionary activities in Labrador, supported by the British who were tired of the raids on their whaling stations. The Moravian missionaries could easily provide the Inuit with the iron and basic materials they had been stealing from whaling outposts. These materials had no real cost to Europeans, but their value was enormous to the Inuit. From then on, contacts in Labrador were far more peaceful.

The European arrival tremendously damaged the Inuit way of life, causing mass death through new diseases introduced by whalers and explorers, and enormous social disruptions caused by the distorting effect of Europeans' material wealth. Nonetheless, Inuit society in the higher latitudes had largely remained in isolation during the 19th century. The Hudson's Bay Company opened trading posts such as Great Whale River (1820), where whale products of commercial whale hunts were processed and furs traded. The British Naval Expedition of 1821–3 led by Admiral William Edward Parry, which twice over-wintered in Foxe Basin, provided the first informed, sympathetic and well-documented account of the economic, social and religious life of the Inuit. Parry stayed over the second winter.

American Admiral Robert Peary (not to be confused with British Admiral William Edward Parry) and his Afro-American aide, Mathew

Henson struck out to reach the North Pole. Both had relationships with Inuit women outside of marriage and fathered children with them. Peary appears to have started his relationship with his Inuit wife when she was about 14 years old, this was before the Mann Act.

After several failed attempts, 23 years of effort, and a lifetime of obsession with the Arctic, Admiral Robert Peary led in April 1909 what was then believed to be the first successful expedition to the North Pole. His stalwart crew was shown at his announcement of success. A photo of several members of the crew included the American Matthew Henson and 4 Intuits. Peary was sled-ridden and unavailable for pictures. This shows how dependent Peary was on Intuits

During the early 20th century a few traders and missionaries circulated among the more accessible lands. After 1904 they were accompanied by a handful of Royal Canadian Mounted Police (RCMP). Generally, the lands occupied by the Inuit were of little interest to European settlers. To the southerners, the homeland of the Inuit was a hostile hinterland. Southerners enjoyed lucrative careers as bureaucrats and service providers to the north, but very few ever chose to visit the lower Canada. With its more hospitable lands largely settled, they began to take a greater interest in Canada's more peripheral territories, especially the fur and mineral-rich hinterlands. By the late 1920s, there were no longer any Inuit who had not been contacted by traders, missionaries or government agents. In 1939, the Supreme Court of Canada found, in a decision known as *Re Eskimos*, that the Inuit should be considered Indians and were thus under the jurisdiction of the federal government.

World War II and the Cold War made Arctic Canada strategically important for the first time and, thanks to the development of modern aircraft, accessible year-round. The construction of air bases and the Distant Early Warning (DEW) Line in the 1940s and 1950s brought more intensive contacts with European society, particularly in the form of public education, which traditionalists complained instilled foreign values. They believed these were disdainful of the traditional structure of Inuit society.

In the 1950s, the Government of Canada undertook the High Arctic relocation for several reasons. These were to include protecting Canada's sovereignty in the Arctic, alleviating hunger (as the area currently occupied had been over-hunted), and attempting to solve the 'Eskimo problem', meaning the assimilation and end of the Inuit culture.

CHAPTER 14

European Diseases Killed the Indians

Four factors decided the fate of the Indians: horses, neighbor hostility, superior European weapons and European diseases destined the Indians in America to oblivion. These factors were only operational details for eradicating all things Indian from the Americas. This included the native population.

If the Europeans were to totally conquer the Americas, it remains clear today that the Indians and their culture had to be swept clean. That was not too hard because of the of the disadvantages of the new world Indians. It was a contest of stone age Indians versus iron age Europeans. The natives were totally mismatched.

The Americas represented a virgin territory. We know we rid the new world of millions of Indians sprinkled in most all the areas of the Americas. Compared to the Indians, the Europeans represented a doomsday machine; it was an infinitely wide eating maw, a threshing machine bringing in all the sheaves of the new land. It turned out not to be Europeans that had advantages over the Indians, it was an Armageddon for them. Of the 5% or so that survived, the doomsday machine kept its work into modern times by the malevolent miracle of DNA. Following the doomsday machine, there were a plethora of lesser evils for the Indians that accomplished the inevitability requirement.

CHAPTER 15

Diseases Between Cultures

"Julia" I said. "It was all about demographics. The Europeans roamed far and wide killing as often as not. However, nothing changed of any consequence compared to European diseases." We kept on talking until we were both weary eyed. In the end, however, we had hardly touched on the original question about the Vikings moving further south than Newfoundland.

Contact between Europeans and Native Americans led to a demographic catastrophe as described by Google ("diseases killed Indians", "Native American disease and epidemics" — Wikipedia). Many of the epidemic diseases that were well established in the Old World were absent from the Americas and Indians before the arrival of Christopher Columbus in 1492. The catastrophic epidemics that accompanied the European conquest of the New World decimated the indigenous population of the Americas. Influenza, smallpox, measles, and typhus fever were among the first European diseases imported to the Americas. European diseases, seeds, weeds, and animals irreversibly transformed the original biological and social landscape of the Americas. By 1518, the Native American demographic catastrophe and the demands of Spanish settlers for labor led to the importation of slaves from Africa. Thus, the

Americas quickly became the site of the mixing of the peoples and infectious agents of previously separate continents.

There is doubt about the time of the arrival in the Americas of the first humans. Some scholars believe that wandering bands of hunter-gatherers first crossed a land bridge from Asia to the New World about 10,000 years ago. Other evidence suggests that human beings might have arrived much earlier, but the earliest sites are very poorly preserved.

Centuries before Europeans arrived in the Western Hemisphere, advanced cultures and great cities had developed in Guatemala, Mexico, and the Andean Highlands. These areas were not free from disease, but accounts of pre-conquest epidemics were generally associated with famines. Archeological evidence suggests that there were several periods of significant spurts of population growth and sudden declines in the Americas long before European contact. However, the impact of European diseases and military conquest was so profound and sudden that other patterns of possible development were abruptly transformed. Contact events involving the Aztecs, Mayans, and Inca civilizations were especially dramatic, primarily because Mexico and Peru had the highest population densities and the most extensive trade and transport networks in the Americas. Such factors provide ideal conditions for the spread of epidemic diseases.

Initial European reports about the New World speak of a veritable Eden, populated by healthy, long-lived people, who could cure illness with indigenous medicinal plants, and did not know the diseases common in other parts of the world. Of course, the New World was not really a disease-free utopia. Smallpox, measles, chicken pox, whooping cough, diphtheria, scarlet fever, trachoma, malaria, typhus fever, typhoid fever, influenza, cholera, bubonic plague, and probably gonorrhea and leprosy were unknown in the pre-contact period. The pre-Columbian distribution of syphilis and yellow fever were rampant. Most physicians believe that Europeans carried syphilis to the New World. Because yellow fever can be confused with malaria, dengue fever, or influenza, early accounts of such epidemics are unreliable. Modern immunological and entomological studies seem to have eliminated earlier claims that Mayan civilization was virtually destroyed by yellow fever, or that epidemics of this disease occurred in Vera Cruz and San Domingo between 1493 and

1496. Some epidemiologists contend that yellow fever was brought to the New World from Africa and that the first known epidemic occurred in Cuba in the seventeenth century.

Although a precise determination of the population of Indians in the Americas in 1492 is probably impossible, there is no doubt that contact with Europeans resulted in a massive demographic collapse of the Native American population. The magnitude of the collapse and its causes remain controversial. Assessing the impact of European contact is not a simple matter because changes in population are the result of complex forces. Some scholars have argued that the devastating population decline in the New World was due primarily to imported diseases, while others have argued that the demographic catastrophe was the result of the chaos and exploitation that followed the conquest. The rapid decline in the numbers of native American peoples and the demands of Spanish settlers for labor, led to the establishment of the transatlantic slave trade by 1518. The Americas became the site of an unprecedented mixing of peoples and infectious agents from previously separate continents.

Although it is impossible to quantify with any certainty, estimates of the pre-contact population of the Americas or Indians have ranged from 8 to 30 million. Between 1492 and 1650 the Native American population may have declined by as much as 90% as the result of virgin-soil epidemics (outbreaks among populations that have not previously encountered the disease), compound epidemics, crop failures and food shortages.

The first Spaniards to reach the Caribbean islands found at least four distinct Indian cultures. Some recent estimates suggest that the pre-Columbian population of Hispaniola (modern Dominican Republic and Haiti) was close to 4 million. By 1508, fewer than 100,000 Indians remained. By 1570, almost all of the Caribbean Indians had disappeared, except for the Caribs in a fairly isolated area of the eastern Caribbean. A similar pattern occurred in Cuba, which was conquered in the year 1511.

Even before the first appearance of smallpox in the Caribbean, some epidemic disease seems to have swept through the islands and devastated the Indians of Hispaniola, Cuba, and the Bahamas. The first epidemic disease to attack the Caribbean Indians might have been swine influenza, brought to the West Indies in 1493 with pigs that Columbus had obtained from the Canary islands on his second voyage. Typhus may also have attacked the islands before the first known smallpox outbreaks in Hispaniola in 1518 and Cuba in 1519. Smallpox decimated the Arawaks of the West Indies, before making its way to Mexico with the Spaniards, and preceding them into the Inca Empire. The Spanish estimated that death rates among Native Americans from smallpox reached 25 to 50%. A similar death rate occurred in Europe, but the disease had essentially become one of the common childhood diseases. Therefore, most adults were immune to the disease. Other European diseases seem to have reached the islands before the measles epidemic of 1529. More recent examples of virgin soil outbreaks suggest that the mortality rate for swine influenza is about 25%, smallpox about 40%, measles about 25%, and typhus between 10 and 40% of the affected population.

"God," said Julia. "That was awful. I know the slate had to be swept clean if the Europeans were to succeed. But think about it. Was it worth all that. A whole race killed. In fact, several races were killed to satisfy Spain's lust for gold and silver.

"In fact," she said. "When they started the slave trade, more than one race was wiped out. How could they do such a thing?"

"They were not always responsible," said Shaun. "The Europeans did not always know they were transporting the diseases."

"That's a poor excuse," she spoke forcefully. "They had hundreds of years to figure it out. Would the Europeans go back home if they did find out?"

With the establishment of the transatlantic slave trade by 1518, diseases from Africa were added to the epidemic burden imposed on Native Americans. The virus for yellow fever probably appeared in San Juan, Puerto Rico by 1598. Better-documented outbreaks occurred on Barbados and Guadeloupe, Cuba, and the Gulf coasts of Mexico and Central America in 1647. Soon after the original human inhabitants of the islands were gone, the native plants and animals were forced to compete with Old World invaders. The peoples of the present day Caribbean trace their ancestry principally to Asia, Europe, and Africa. Slaves were imported as early as 1502, but by 1518 the decline in labor supply had become so acute that King Charles I of Spain approved the direct import of slaves from Africa. However, the Africanizing of the islands was the result of the sugar demands that began in the seventeenth century, along with the importation of epidemic yellow fever.

The Empire of the Aztecs was the first American civilization to encounter the Spanish and the first to be destroyed. Several factors, including devastating epidemics of smallpox, which killed many Aztec warriors and nobles, facilitated the Spanish capture of the Aztec capital in 1521. Native Americans came to see this smallpox epidemic as a true turning point in their history. The time before the arrival of the Spanish was remembered as a veritable paradise, free of fevers, smallpox, stomach pains, and tuberculosis. When the Spanish came, they brought fear and disease wherever they went. Mayan civilization had already experienced a long period of decline by the time it encountered European explorers and invaders, but the Inca Empire was at its peak when the Spaniards conquered it in 1532.

European diseases probably preceded European contact in the Andean region. A catastrophic epidemic, which might have been smallpox, swept the region in the mid-1520s, killing the Inca leader Huayna Capac and his son. Subsequent epidemics struck the region in the 1540s, 1558, and from the 1580s to 1590s. These waves of epidemic disease might have included smallpox, influenza, measles, mumps, dysentery, typhus, and pneumonia. The precise impact of smallpox and other European diseases throughout the Americas is difficult to document or comprehend. However, studies of more recent and limited virgin soil outbreaks clearly demonstrate how small a spark is needed to create a great conflagration in a native population.

CHAPTER 16

The Indian People

In 1492 the native population of North America north of the Rio Grande was seven million to ten million. These people grouped themselves into approximately six hundred tribes and spoke diverse dialects. European colonists initially encountered Native Americans in three distinct regions. Eastern Woodland tribes included the Five Nations of the Iroquois Confederacy, Abenakis, Shawnees, Delawares, Micmacs, Mahicans, and Pequots. Some of these tribes were sedentary hunter-gathers while others grew maize (corn), beans, and squash.

In the Southeast white settlers came into contact with Powhatans, Catawbas, Cherokees, Creeks, Natchez, Choctaws, and Chickasaws; these people were primarily agriculturalists. Pueblos, Zunis, Navajos, and Hopis represented some of the adobe-dwelling bands in the arid Southwest. Regardless of their differences, these groups shared some common characteristics. For Native Americans the family, clan, and village represented the most important social groups. In addition, religions revolved around the belief that all of nature was alive, pulsating with spiritual power.

As to contact, when the various European nations reached the New World the encounters were predictably diverse. Culture, climate, and the location and timing of the contact all affected the nature of the experience. One common factor was disease, as large numbers of native peoples succumbed to the microbes that the Europeans unwittingly carried with them in virtually every encounter. Massive population declines undoubtedly placed great stress on economic, social, political, and religious systems of native peoples. From 1492 until the Revolutionary War, trade was a central theme of interaction between natives and Europeans. This relationship shifted over time, transforming native life by drawing North America into a web of global economic connections. The process began when the first traders offered textiles, glass, and metal products in exchange for beaver pelts and buffalo robes. The transactions did not end until Europeans had virtually dispossessed the native people of the land that produced the goods the foreigners desired. Relations between the different European nations and native peoples were often complex and contradictory. Spanish colonists developed a reputation for harsh treatment, but because the Spanish sent almost no women to the New World, Spanish men often intermarried with native women. The French have been portrayed as sensitive to the culture of native peoples, but under the Spanish and French influence, the Indians were all but destroyed.

There you go. The Europeans, including the Vikings had a clear slate. The natives in America swept the continents of people. In 1800, there were approximately 5.3 million Americans. After this, there is no doubt who owns the Americas today. Diseases were the decisive factor among the many. Perhaps this was inadvertent; however, the weighting of several factors were conclusive for any one of them. The Europeans took the new world and decisively converted its rich resources to their ends. The continents were swept clean. The Americas were ready for a new chapter.

CHAPTER 17

The Vikings Come

In about the year 800, the Vikings fell out of the north on Ireland, Britain and Scotland. They were originally traders and moved their wares throughout Asia, Europe and North Africa. After about a hundred years or so, they changed their strategies. They became brigands and highwaymen. They became robbers and the terror of the north. In doing this, the Vikings began to change. They were soon taking on many of the characteristics of their prey.

Many of the Vikings were staying in Ireland, Britain or elsewhere. They were often marrying into the culture they were conquering. Their strategy was to make arms and train during the winter and then to raid. Their least favorite activity was to farm. But, it did support the raiding and slaughter. They were soon raiding Ireland, England, Germany, France and all the way east to the Volga river in Russia. All of Europe came under assault.

The trading Vikings started the Viking Age. These traders and marauders dominated Europe for over 300 years. The fleets that the Vikings managed to put to sea are surprising. They used a large number of ships and they had a large number of men on them. Before they became marauders, about 830 or so, the Vikings had confined their attacks to coastal waters.

After 830, they began to force their way ever-deeper inland. This probably was a prelude to larger and more organized raiding. That was probably also an investigation of the possibilities of settlement or colonization. Land acquisition appears the motivation for most of the Vikings, especially since many returned to their farms after raiding. In 837 they formed 2 fleets of 60 ships each. These accommodated 3,000 to 4,000 men that served as warriors and fighter once the fighting started. This indicates an average of about 33 men per ship.

These ships were often up to 88 feet long and about 42 feet wide. They had to accommodate warriors with their shields and body armor of steel and leather and their weapons. Attachments were on the gunwales to hold their oars so the shields could present a uniform wall to their enemies.

They had to transport their plunder and loot on the return voyage. Sooner or later, their plunder challenged the capacity of their boats. They plundered the Plain of Life and the Plain of Brega, including churches, forts and dwellings. Church's were their favorite targets since the priests and believers stored valuable vestments and various religious vessels of silver and gold.

In another attack in 848 by the Danes, they mounted 160 ships in a ferocious sea battle. The Danes were triumphant. In 4 separate battles in that year 2,600 men were reported as killed. Assuming an average of 33 men per boat, about 25% of the warriors must have been killed. Life was hard in those days. Of course, this is miniscule compared to the killings in modern skirmishes.

As stated, the attacks became more profound. Somewhat typical was the siege of Paris in 885. This was a part of a Viking raid on the Seine, in the Kingdom of the West Franks. With hundreds of ships, some say upwards of 700 longships, and possibly tens of thousands of men, the Vikings arrived outside Paris demanding tribute. This was denied despite the fact that the defenders could assemble only a couple of hundred soldiers to defend the city.

The Vikings attacked with a variety of siege engines, but failed to break through the city walls after some days of intense attacks. The siege was upheld after the initial attacks, but without any significant offence for months after the attack. As the siege went on, most of the Vikings left Paris to pillage further upriver. The Vikings made a final unsuccessful attempt to take the city during the summer.

The trading Vikings divided their territories like a modern sales organization. These territories tended to be the North Atlantic, Northern Europe, Southern Europe and Russia to the Volga.

During that period, the Vikings traveled across the north Atlantic often. It was a regular trading route. There were long periods where settlements were made and often lasted for hundreds of years. These periods included the Shetland Islands in northwestern England, the Faroes near Norway, Iceland, Greenland, Newfoundland and almost certainly further south.

We know there were settlements across the north by the Norsemen at least in the 8th century. There was also contact with Indians. Why then, did the local populations not succumb to the European diseases as happened with the Columbus contacts. We know there were contacts with the Anuits or Eskimos. I postulate that there was more spreading out of the populations than we know about. This would certainly have spread and caused epidemics among the Indians. Our only response is that there were not enough contacts to cause epidemics.

We believe they could have settled as far south as New York. Maybe further! Only time and archaeology will tell.

Fundamental to all this, is man's infinite capacity for curiosity and exploration.

"Look!" I said to Julia. "The question we pose for history is one of navigation. Without the ability to navigate, there could be no Viking Age. With no such age, the other necessities fall into place, as either supportive or negating. For this, there are several sections included here. As man has struggled for navigation, the similar question is posed here. From this viewpoint of time, it looks as if the problem is solved with the Global Positioning System or GPS satellites. We have seen the explosive growth in the 21st century that has reduced the size of GPS units being close to a single chip. In fact, the basic navigation technology is included in essentially every cell phone unit. It is truly a miracle.

The history of navigation is messy. The GPS defining book of background and history states that man has been using every clever trick to navigate for the past 6,000 years. We do not disagree. Just as man has gnawed on that old bone for centuries and millennia, the data here relates several navigation techniques. One might take the position that it has all been done now and no further breakthroughs need occur. Yet, if history teaches us anything, it teaches that technology threads are long and wide. We don't know what is now being proposed. But, you can bet there are thousands of engineers and technologists working on such problem. And we must also say this includes other facilitators, that are championing ideas that would make us shake in our boots if we could comprehend even a small piece of the future.

Some of the ideas here are merely suggestions of the technology behind them.

As stated above, navigation is crucial to man's climb through our cultural milieu. There were several critical Viking states that forged ahead until they dominated our world. These included navigation, infinite curiosity, the urge for resettlement with the acquisition of land, a revolution in boating design and operations and the compulsion for archaeological digging to validate the claims suggested above.

CHAPTER 18

Viking Traders and Silk Road

It is a mystery as to how the Europeans landed in north America and then cleared away almost all opposition. In about 800, Iceland had been explored and permanent settlements established there. It was a difficult land. The Norsemen from Scandinavia owed their existence to trade early on. Materials traded included fur pelts, amber, wood products and other goods from the north, while the Norsemen acquired silks, and various other exotic goods.

Needless to say, Vikings were partial to boats. Their longships could carry heavy tonnage that facilitated trade. Their bellicose nature also helped their security. These were designed to sail in heavy seas. When capsized, they were designed to be relatively easy to recover. They also were made to operate in the rivers and streams in shallow water. Easy access to shallow water allowed multiple boats to go far toward river sources. This was necessary to transport their trading goods and access river sources. This supported trade operations. Being light, they accommodated portages. The light boats also favored deep penetrations of the countryside's rivers and streams.

Central Asia has always seemed like the other side of the moon to most people. Few people had firsthand experience with the Silk Road or the peoples that traded up and down Asia. Much of the area is covered in mystery and romance. The Silk Road was not central to the history of the Steppes, but it was very prominent. Tatars and Slavs were often traders in Central Asia. They followed the Steppes of Russia and helped spread culture throughout the region.

The Norsemen were soon operating through the western Mediterranean and across the North Country, all the way east as far as the Volga River. The Scandinavians traded heavily with the Russians between the northern Baltic Sea and the southern Caspian Sea. Transitioning from the Caspian to the Black Sea then put the Vikings in touch with Constantinople and the Mediterranean. The Black Sea allowed the Swedes to open trade routes in the far north.

Soon, the Norwegians extended this to Denmark and especially to the British Isles. From here, they had settlements in Norway, Ireland, the Shetlands, Scapa, the Faroes, Iceland and Greenland. We know the Vikings had settlements on Labrador and Newfoundland. They also established settlements south of this, in a place called Vineland. This was a mysterious land. We continue to wait for archaeologists to locate Vineland for us.

Silk, the magic fabric of the mulberry worm, reached eastern Rome in the second century BCE. This added to a long list of goods making their way in both directions on the long and tortuous journey between China and Europe. Trade included wool, bronze, porcelain, cobalt, and a hundred other things. They made their way from Changan to Constantinople, Kashgar to Samarkend.

The great trade routes across Asia have become known as the Silk Road. It has served over two millennia, since the Christian era, as a conduit for ideas, science, technology, language, and literature, as well as trade. It is a mistake to consider these claims as justifying the travel of a single person. The movement was of goods and products. A trader of silk may hand off goods to a trader in Kiev, then he trades it for goods in Sweden. The movement addresses the goods, not necessarily the traders.

The Han people of China traded with the nomads beyond their borders since time immemorial. By the second century BC, they were purchasing not only animal products from the Huns but sufficient quantities of jade from Khotan had passed into China to give the primary route the sobriquet of "Jade Road." This route passed from Changan (Xi'an) to Yumen and Anhsi, then south past the Lop Nor dry lake to Keriya, Khotan and Kashgar. Kashgar is at the far western reaches of the Tarim Basin in Sinkiang Province. From there, the route continues over the passes of the High Pamirs to Samarkand. It then went west to Antioch on the Mediterranean.

In later times, it went to both Antioch and then north of the Caspian Sea into Russia and Europe. Constantinople and the other major cities were on the routes. There was also a northern route of this east-west artery. This separated from the southern route at Anhsi and meandered northerly through Hami, Turfan, Kucha, and Aksu before rejoining the other route at Kashgar. From Khotan and Kashgar, routes passed southward through the Karakoram passes into India via the Indus Valley. All these routes became known loosely as the Silk Road, again reflecting the chief goods being traded.

Silk was China's main export, and was enormously desired in the courts of Europe and the Middle East. In addition to silk and jade, jewels and pearls from India were traded in return for gold from the Greek east. This occurred early on, and later from the Eastern Roman Empire.

So important did silk become that Romans used rolls of it as currency in official trade with foreign courts. The Romans were particularly fond of it for their togas or robes. The balance of trade became very adverse to Rome as its gold and silver flowed to China, India, and Arabia to pay for its indulgences of these fineries. It is said that by the fourth century CE, two-thirds of all the gold and silver of the Roman Empire had flowed eastward. Silk and eastern trade had bankrupted Rome just as surely as Britain's Indian opium bankrupted China in the nineteenth century.

The Silk Road saw porcelain, lacquer-ware, silk, jade and other goods flow from China. Inventions sent to the West included the wheelbarrow, harnesses for draft animals, the crossbow, deep-drilling and mining techniques, porcelain making, cast iron, gunpowder, the compass, papermaking, and printing. China acquired jewels, pearls, coral, amber, damasks, rugs, asbestos cloth, spices, incense, fine steel, bronze, and other things.

These great overland trading routes were augmented by sea traffic, or such traffic was sometimes a part of the journey. A century before the Common Era, seafarers discovered that the monsoon season winds in the South Asia regions of the Indian Ocean blew west to east in the spring and in the reverse direction in the winter. By following these known patterns, heavily laden ships could travel across the Indian Ocean with goods and treasure, between the Roman world and that of India and China and beyond in the spring, then depend on returning in the winter, both on favorable winds.

The Huns were a group of nomadic herdsmen, warlike people from the steppes of North Central Asia who terrorized, pillaged, and destroyed much of Asia and Europe from the 3rd through the 5th centuries CE. The invention of the stirrup gave the Huns a technological advantage over other warriors of the time. Stirrups support a horse rider's feet; these let the Huns brace themselves on their horses while wielding swords or shooting arrows. Attila the Hun was an infamous, vicious barbarian King who attacked the Roman Empire and was so fierce he was named "The Scourge of God"!

Attila the Hun was the legendary king of the Huns - a Mongoloid people who began invading the Roman Empire in the 300's CE. The Huns were originally from a tribe of Mongolians from Central Asia, who settled in the area known later as Hungary.

Attila was born in 406. In 434, at the age of 28, he succeeded his uncle as leader of the Huns. Attila at first ruled with his brother, Bleda, but murdered Bleda in 445 to take complete control. By the 5th Century, the Roman Empire was almost totally disintegrated and the Huns ruled a large empire. From 435 to 439, Attila conquered, pillaged and attacked his way through eastern and central Europe. The Emperor of the Byzantine Empire was paying Attila an amount to keep the Huns from attacking his empire. But the emperor could not keep up the payments and Attila invaded the Byzantine Empire in two attacks in 441 and in 447. In 447, he led his horsemen to take over the Balkan Land, attacking Greece and threatening Constantinople, which was the center of the Holy Roman Empire in the east.

Attila then moved onto the Western Roman Empire and in 450, he demanded that Honoria, sister of the Western Emperor, Valentinian III, marry him and also receive half of the Western Roman Empire as her dowry. Valentinian refused. To enforce his demand, Attila then attacked Gaul (France), but the Romans and barbarians stopped his attacks in 451. In 452, Attila and his horsemen crossed the Alps to invade Italy which caused Pope Leo I to pay money to Attila to save Rome from total attack. Attila devastated the western half of the Roman Empire between 451 and 452 and controlled a region from the Danube River to the Baltic Sea and from the Rhine River to the Caspian Sea. Attila the Hun died unexpectedly in 453 at the age of 47, on his wedding night.

The Chinese built their Great Wall to defend themselves against the Huns. By this time, any feared leader such as Goths, Visigoths, the Huns, and others adopted the name and reputation of the Huns. The people of India, Persia (what is now Iran) and Eastern and central Europe were invaded by separate hordes of Hun warriors attacking on horseback. In Europe, groups of Huns defeated the Goths (Germans) of eastern Europe, the Slavs, the Franks, the Roman Empire, and many others. The Huns had pillaged similar to the Vikings as much as a century or two later.

Chinese trade traveled west to the Caucasus, to Constantinople, Venice, and beyond. The trade and travels were long and hazardous. Nevertheless, the Silk Road provided a tenuous path between cultures, races, and ethnic groups for two thousand years.

Traders frequented the Asian steppes. The Asian steppes were a part of this east-west transportation corridor. There has always been an ebb and flow of people migrations, horsemen seeking booty and conquest, trade caravans, and desultory trading among wandering tribes. Thereby, goods, trinkets, things, and technology flowed across the far reaches of Asia. The trading goods of Greek and Roman times would later find their way into Russia, such things as Chinese ceramics, sheer silks, exotic spices, things of art, and fabulous jewelry.

Slowly and erratically, these things found their way across the Great Plains, and eventually into Russia and the Baltic countries. Similarly, Western trinkets, such as amber, gold, weapons, and metal goods found their way east. Usually, the goods traveled by short steps, from hand-to-hand, or sometimes by more formal trade caravans, or other times by great caravans consisting of hundreds or sometimes thousands of pack animals and people.

In addition, there were north-south cross-trails or routes. The Scandinavians boated down the Volga, Dneiper, and other great rivers of Europe until the Byzantines of Constantinople, and later the Ottoman Turks, had small but distinct Norse ethnic characteristics. Their bellicose nature often made them prized above all men as mercenary fighters. Their amber and other things gave them trading chips for their long southern odysseys. Caravans found their way northward around the Caucasus and along the Caspian toward the Urals. Indians, Pakistanis, Afghans, and Iranians all found their way northward, as did the Mongols and Tatars into Siberia.

The steppes-men supported the caravans, provided succor, defended against other steppes-men, showed the way, and retailed the goods to various tribes, groups, and localities. Into time immemorial, they became the traders, the intermediaries, the movers of goods across Asia. They formed a vast network of traders.

This trader class was not homogeneous. It consisted of all sorts of men; Tatars, Bashkirs, Kazaks, Turks, Mongols, Chinese, Jews, Byzantines, Russian Slavics, Viking Norsemen, and on and on. They had distinct but mixed tongues, religions, cultures, dress, technology, art, written script, and math for record keeping.

This vast network lubricated international exchange. It provided books of history and knowledge to the ignorant, and provided an exchange of cultures, languages, ideas, methods, and art up until modern times. Chance did not maintain this network; China supported it by high state policy until a few centuries ago. It was sponsored or advocated by the Khanates, by the various states along and peripheral to the routes, and by the Europeans. It brought wealth and power to the Khanates and desirable things and ideas to the others.

CHAPTER 19

Little Ice Age

The Little Ice Age occurred in the early part of the 20th century. Vikings and other marauders were not the only worries from the Scandinavian north. Western Europe experienced a Little Ice Age with general cooling of the climate between the years 1150 and 1460 and a very cold climate between 1560 and 1850 that brought dire consequences to its peoples. The overwhelming majority of international climate scientists agree that humans are causing global warming.

The impact of regional climate change on the Viking civilization and Europe during the Little Ice Age is due to a natural cycle. The climate change being observed today is unprecedented in modern times and can only be explained by the rapid increase of greenhouse gases by human activities. There are no known natural forces that could have caused the modern climate change. The colder weather impacted agriculture, health, economics, social strife, and emigration.

Lamb, a noted researcher, attracts our attention and in 1966 points out that the growing season changed by 15 to 20 percent between the warmest and coldest times of the millennium. That is enough to affect almost any type of food production, especially crops highly adapted to use the full-season warm climatic periods. During the coldest times of the Age, England's growing season was shortened by one to two months compared to present day values. The availability of varieties of seed today that can withstand extreme cold or warmth, wetness or dryness, was not available in the past. Therefore, climate changes had a much greater impact on agricultural output in the past.

Each of the peaks in prices corresponds to a particularly poor harvest, mostly due to unfavorable climates with the most notable peak in the year 1816 — "the year without a summer." One of the worst famines in the seventeenth century occurred in France due to the failed harvest of 1693. Millions of people in France and surrounding countries were killed.

In Norway, many farms located at higher latitudes were abandoned for better land in the valleys. By 1387, production and tax yields were between 12 percent and 70 percent of what they had been around 1300. In the 1460's it was being recognized that this change was permanent. As late as the year 1665, the total Norwegian grain harvest is reported to have been only 67–70 percent of what it had been about the year 1300.

There was a considerable impact on forests during the Little Ice Age. A study of the tree populations in forests of Southern Ontario by shows how the tree population in Europe might have been changed by the Age. Their analysis of pollen demonstrated that after the year 1400, beech trees, the formerly dominant warmth-loving species, were replaced first by oak and subsequently by pine. Further, the forest under study appears to have remained in disequilibrium with the prevailing climate of today. That suggests that tree population distribution takes hundreds of years to recover from major climate changes

The cooler climate during the Age had a huge impact on the health of Europeans. As mentioned earlier, famine killed millions and poor nutrition decreased the height of the Vikings in Greenland and Iceland. Cool, wet summers led to outbreaks of an illness called St. Anthony's fire. Whole villages would suffer convulsions, hallucinations, gangrenous rotting of the extremities, and even death.

Grain, if stored in cool, damp conditions, may develop a fungus known as ergot blight and also may ferment just enough to produce a drug similar to LSD. In fact, some historians claim that the Salem, Massachusetts witch hysteria was the result of ergot blight. Malnutrition led to a weakened immunity to a variety of illnesses. In England, malnutrition aggravated an influenza epidemic of 1557-8 in which whole families died. In fact, during most of the 1550's deaths outnumbered births

The Black Death (Bubonic Plague) was hastened by malnutrition all over Europe.

One might not expect a typically tropical disease such as malaria to be found during the Age, but Reiter (2000) has shown that it was an important cause of illness and death in several parts of England. The English word for malaria was ague, a term that remained in common usage until the nineteenth century.

In sixteenth century England, many marshlands were notorious for their ague-stricken populations. William Shakespeare (1564-1616) mentioned ague in eight of his plays. Oliver Cromwell (1599-1658) died of ague in September 1658, which was one of the coldest years of the Age.

Cod fishing greatly decreased, especially for the Scottish fisherman, as the cod moved farther south. The cod fishery at the Faeroe Islands began to fail around 1615 and failed altogether for thirty years between 1675 and 1704.

English fisherman benefited by the southern movement of herring normally found in the waters off Norway. This increase in deep-sea fishing helped to build the maritime population and strength of the country. The failure of crops in Norway between 1680 and 1720 was a prime reason for the great growth of merchant shipping there. Coastal farmers whose crops failed turned to selling their timber and to constructing ships in order to transport these timbers themselves.

One group in particular suffered from the poor conditions — people thought that weather-making was among the traditional abilities of witches. During the late fourteenth and fifteenth centuries, many saw a great witch conspiracy. Extensive witch hunts took place during the most severe years of the Age, as people looked for scapegoats to blame for their suffering.

CHAPTER 20

The Developing Vikings

Ancient history is a record of societies rising from pastoral activity to agriculture, followed by metalworking and trade. The hunters, gatherers, and nomadic tribes develop a culture of the plough and become sedentary. They become stationary, and their culture develops rapidly. They worry about rain, water for their crops, irrigation, predictions of the seasons, trade, and soon comes a monetary system, followed by writing and numbers as a means of keeping accounts, and then mercantilism. Thus, the edges of Europe and central Asia have grown as sedentary people expanded their territory. It has happened with the Romans, Gauls, Germans, Scandinavians, Slavs, Greeks, Persians, Indians, Chinese, and a thousand others.

But, the Vikings appear to have left little literature. These warriors are relatively unique in this respect. They left primarily rune sticks made of stone, bone or wood with scraped messages. Sagas that teased the reader who tried to make sense of them were also left. Each of the sagas did leave messages but there were only a few of these and their messages were few and simple. These are about the only things left of them.

When the sedentary people settled down to farming, it left a void. It was seen that the edges of civilization were vulnerable. Some, like the latter day Vikings and the Norsemen, were happy to provide marauders. The Vikings traded in the north Atlantic but this became a breeding ground for robbery. In time, the marauders became organized bandits. Their boats became navies. These longboat fighting ships terrorized Ireland and England at first. But they grew in size and organization until they looked like a navy of hundreds of ships. The Viking terror fleets had arrived. They were marauders during part of the year that trained and made their weapons. Then they farmed. They soon found it more rewarding to become predators throughout the year. The Vikings became brigands and soon practiced their arts, sometimes with hundreds or thousands of boats.

Like the American Indians, herdsmen are hardy people. They are primitive in a sense but specialized knowledge such as navigation is crucial. Yet, they had to have vast knowledge of the seas. Remember Iliad where Helen's face launched a thousand ships. They had to be navigated.

People sailing along the extensive European coasts, and Vikings must know the seas and they must have navigation skills using stars and whatever other information they can glean from the local waters or birds. Their notions of the supernatural are simple; they tend to be shamans and animists, finding spirits in the trees, rocks, and those things around them. Vast numbers did accept Christianity and Islam over a thousand years ago or in the eighth century. At the time of the Viking Era, Christianity and Paganism were in a deathly struggle.

The steppe and Scandinavian northlands are lands of the horse and sailing ships. These peoples must range far and wide with their herds; their animals. The Asian use of the horse goes far into antiquity. The horse provided transportation and a way of domesticating and controlling other animals. These included the herds of caribou, sheep, goats, cattle, camels, and whatever other animals could be domesticated and brought into the pastoral cycle. Yet, the Vikings depended primarily on longboats. With these, the Vikings rowed or sailed into battle with horses on board. They then wore thick leather and steel armor as they rode their enemies down from horseback using circular armor, steel swords, battleaxes and pikes.

We in recent times consider the domestication of the horse to be a necessary step toward high culture. It gives a mobility and vitality to a culture that is unique. When Columbus or the Vikings arrived, the American Indian did not have the domesticated horse. These had crossed the Bering Strait land bridge eons ago. People then spread across Europe. They became extinct after the last ice age. There were no horses with the

Aztecs, Toltecs or Mayans, until the Spaniards arrived from Europe with horses.

For eons, the sedentary peoples, particularly in Ireland and England but in all Europe, tended and cultivated their fields. Still, they feared the Vikings with their high sails and high-masted longships attacking the sedentary peoples. The farmers watched in trepidation, for who knew when some horsemen or Viking could come marauding? They could see the masts or horsemen in the far distance, and their hearts would seize in fear. Who knew what sightings might mean? Even if they had never experienced the wrath of the Vikings, they knew the stories that passed from mouth to mouth and generation to generation. They knew the stories of the ship masts over the horizon that appeared before hordes of barbarians swept down on their farms and villages, killing, pillaging, raping, and taking the women and children as slaves. Alternatively, they simply impaled them or slit them wide, and burned everything or put it to the sword.

The sedentary people shuddered and felt dread. They came to know stark terror when the masts appeared on the horizon, regardless of the cause. There was some congenital fear passed through the uterine walls, or had it become programmed into their genes in some mysterious way as they took to the tilling of land? For millennia, the sedentary people eyed the horizon for masts, which might signal the onslaught of the barbarian, and they lived in mortal dread. It may mean the murder of every man, woman or child of a village. Or worse, spare them but only to serve as slaves for the rest of their lives.

A major goal of marauders was to capture slaves. The Arabs specialized in this and specialized in "marketing these goods". Life was tough. The Vikings had rowing positions and they had to have manpower for this. Slaves were the answer. One may also consider the alternative. Roman slaves were chained to their seats. They provided the manpower for fighting ships. These oarsmen were never unchained. When nature called, they accommodated this in their clothing rags. These rules applied or continued through rain, ice, and snow. Food was given while they still sat there, in their eternal station. The slaves were literally chained there for the rest of their lives, which was not long. The life of slaves was hard, depending on the master, of course.

The Vikings were brought under control nominally after 1200. Their primacy was over. However, alas, around the year 1700, more or less, the horseman was emasculated finally. The spread of gunpowder put guns and artillery in the hands of the soldiers and, after millennia, the era of the Viking and horseman was over. Herders could live next to farmers, but it was at the farmer's sufferance. The gun ended the ability of primitive man to exist side by side and compete with advanced man. The pastorals were subjugated or killed. The steppes were tamed only five centuries ago!

The tale of the Varangians continues. It took the form of the Varangian Guard, a prominent and selective Byzantine army arising in the tenth century. It was composed of the Scandinavian marauders in the beginning. The Varangian Guard survived until the thirteenth or fourteenth centuries as the Byzantine Emperor's elite sentinels. Dressed in battle armor of blue tunics and crimson cloaks, with raised battle-axes gilded with gold. The bright colors of the Varangian Guard did nothing to quell the terrible Berserker power (as in going berserk; where Old Norse warriors fought as unchecked, frenzied shock troops who, when deployed, appeared so mad that neither "fire nor iron" frightened them.) There was reason to believe some were mad on natural drugs.

Much of what is known about the Varangian Guard comes down through the centuries from scholars such as Princess Anna Komnene, daughter of Emperor Alexios I, and Michael Psellos, a monk from Constantinople—both writing in the eleventh century CE. It is believed that the Varangian Guard had been formed around the year 874 when a treaty between the Rus and Byzantine Empire dictated that the Rus had to send warriors to the aid of the Empire as necessary. This was dutifully carried out over centuries. This had to be backed up with axe and sword.

Horses became critical assets for raids. The longships often carried horses, pigs, dogs and the whole family including wives, mothers and children. There is evidence that they also participated in the terror. Looking further back, it was not too long before horses were looked on as critical resources.

It appears that all kinds of animals crossed the Alaskan land bridge and spread throughout the Americas. Both North and South America then had a plethora of domesticated animals. For whatever reason, all the horses or domesticated large animals (horses, oxen, mules, donkeys, etc.) had been eradicated or became extinct before the last ice age, about 12,000 years ago. These are absolute necessities for advanced cultures.

Horses did not generally exist in the Americas before Columbus. There is evidence that horses were traded by England and Iceland in about 900. Although traded, there does not seem to be many of them and trading was in Europe with no evidence that the Vikings took them to America.

In 1493, on Columbus's second trip to America, he had about fifteen horses aboard. Soon thereafter, some of the horses were placed ashore for breeding. Later, many of the Spanish ships sank with horses aboard and the horses swam ashore. It was not too long before horses appeared in the hands of Indians. Soon, the American plains Indians had horses, the South American cultures had horses and horses appeared across both North and South America.

With the domesticated horses, one could ride the ancient Indian trails that could not be done with wide carts. Wheeled carts were not convenient for the rider. Good roads were not available in the Americas but the horse and rider traversed the wooded trails easily.

Modern horses, zebras, and asses belong to the genus *Equus*, the only surviving genus in a once diverse family. Based on fossil records, the genus appears to have originated in North America about four million years ago and spread to Eurasia (presumably by crossing the Bering land bridge) two to three million years ago. Following that original emigration, there were additional westward migrations to Asia and return migrations back to North America, as well as several extinctions of *Equus* species in North America.

The last prehistoric North American horses died out between 13,000 and 11,000 years ago, at the end of the Pleistocene, but by then *Equus* had spread to Asia, Europe, and Africa. In recent years, molecular biology has provided new tools for working out the relationships among species and subspecies of horses.

These recent findings have an unexpected implication. It is well known that domesticated horses were introduced into north America beginning with the Spanish conquest, and that escaped horses subsequently spread throughout the American Great Plains. Customarily, such wild horses that survive today are designated "feral" and regarded as intrusive, exotic animals, unlike the native horses that died out at the end of the Pleistocene. Indeed, domestication altered them little, as we can see by how quickly horses revert to ancient behavioral patterns and feral conditions in the wild.

CHAPTER 21

Navigation Imperatives

I often joked when I lived in eastern North Carolina and was asked, “How do I get to New York?” My respose was, “Go to I-95 and turn right.” This masterpiece of brevity sent one on I-95 not only to New York but to Nova Scotia, in Canada, over 750 miles north of NC as the crow flies.

The Vikings began their discovery phase after the 8th century. The world was expanding its knowledge and navigational skills at that time. In the next 300 years or so, the north Atlantic became a traffic lane for trade. That is, Vikings put settlers on several islands that acted as stepping stones to the north Atlantic islands. These included all of Scandinavia, Norway, Denmark and the ill-defined Sweden. The trading voyages included Scotland, Ireland, Scapa, Faroes, Iceland, Greenland, Labrador, Newfoundland, Shetland and a mysterious ‘Vineland’. All agreed that Vineland existed but they were never quite sure where it could be found. Does this sound a bit like Camelot to you? Can you conger up the round table and heroic knights?

Those who move on either land or water are faced with the problems of navigation. This is so fundamental to travelers that it must be addressed to the extent possible with little information, usually not enough for decisive conclusions. This will not attempt a conclusive undertaking but just enough information to suggest ways of looking at it.

CHAPTER 21

Maximum Visible Range Estimate

I have flown numerous times along the northern trade route of the Vikings. In fact, that is now the great circle route for most commercial airlines crossing the north Atlantic. A number of observations can be made based on these modern flights and on what is known of the Vikings during their explorations of the same routes. I segment the modern era of about 1950 and the ancient era of about 1,000.

Navigation was a critical factor as recognized by the Vikings, the south Sea Islanders and all seafaring peoples. Surprisingly, in the modern age centering in about 1950 or the post-WWII time, a number of Americans were strewn across the north Atlantic and the northern islands. There were several navigation ships permanently anchored across the north Atlantic and islands that provided navigation services and weather reports. The weather always reached the north prior to its reaching Europe so it was critical to predictions in the European war theater. Many of the islands across the north housed very small contingencies that provided weather and general lookout information. Treaties defined our responsibilities in patrolling the north Atlantic that were implemented in response to the sinking of the Titanic. The US was a signature nation that committed to providing iceberg tracking and reporting information as the icebergs floated through the shipping lanes. Germany initially contested these soldiers and facilities but were rebuffed across the North Atlantic which denied the Germans this vital weather information.

This work differs in some respects with the discovery issues. For instance, most historians advocate a discovery date for the Faroes or Iceland to be about 900. It seems to require an intentional sighting. It does not take into account a sighting after a heavy storm blew some ships off course. It does not take account of a Viking trying to satisfy his curiosity. It does not take into account volcanoes where some salvoes experience large lightning bolts that would provide large electrical activity identifying the presence and bearing of possible islands. It also discounts identifiable phenomena that might cause investigation although it might just feed rumors that something strange is occurring in an identifiable direction. Rumors may move one to action.

The table below reports these numbers and the equation to determine the maximum visual range (MVR) between two points on a map, one for the observer and one for a target distance. The maximum visual range is predictable using the two target map locations with their two postulated altitudes. It is obvious that sighting a target can be made from higher observation points. An example is the Faroe and Iceland Islands. The maximum visual range can be computed and is achievable on a day with good visibility. A very curious person might then climb a high point in the Faroes, look in forward directions and see the mountains of Iceland far away. Alternatively, he might move his boat as if in a storm and do a search along a latitude in a grid pattern.

CHAPTER 23

Exploiting Latitude

It is well known that the North Star gives latitude. A North Star 60 degrees above the horizon indicates the observer latitude is likewise always 60 degrees above the equator. That is, the North Star angle above the horizon indicates the observer is almost at the same latitude as the star. Once the latitude of 60 degrees for the Faroes is known, one only has to go north to 60 degrees latitude, then follow a constant latitude line to the west until the Faroes are reached.

If a navigational error is made, it can be corrected by doing a grid search to find the latitude.

Longitude, on the other hand, is not so easily found. Navigators often find this by observing fish travel, the course of birds, or dead reckoning using water speed and air speed. I have tried this with a little water wheel with good results. I have also tried this with a wind sensor. From this, I saw Damascus about 80 miles away. It was not clear but I could see a scarred blemish on the earth in the right direction. Damascus was a scar on the horizon. This helped to confirm the claims above although they are well known. Further, this requires a clear day. If the horizon is hazy or cloudy or stormy, then this does not work out to the horizon. In other words, it has to be a clear day for observations. That is to say, a measurement of angle has to be accurate. Measurements on a ship's deck in a rough sea also limits the visual range. As the Polynesians would tell you, one has to be careful. The penalties for error are often dire.

How does one get from eastern NC to New York? I answer, "Go to I-95 and turn right." I don't mean to make a correct turn although that is ambiguously correct. It means to follow your right arm and that is not ambiguous.

This is not a throwaway line although it sounds so. Ancient navigators certainly had this strategy in their bag of tricks.

This navigation example covers the Pythagoras Method, Beijing to Perth. The end points of Beijing to Perth has no significance. It is only an example from the referenced internet that shows the complexity of the navigator's task. It is otherwise to be ignored.

CHAPTER 24

Pythagoras Method, Beijing to Perth

The following method is meant to show the complexity of computing a navigation route. This is one example only to show complexity.

Example: What distance does a plane fly between Beijing and Perth. The Pythagoras Theorem provides angles in radians as seen below.

Beijing. P_1=39° 54' N=0.696386; Q_1=116° 24' E=2031563
Perth P_2=31° 57' S= –0.557633; Q_2=115° 52' E=2.022255
Beijing x_1= 6371 cos 0.6963896 cos 2.0316 = -4377.9
y_1= 6371 cos 0.686380 sin 2.0316 = 4864.3
z_1 = 6371 sin 6963896 = 4086.7
Perth x2 6371 cos -0.5576 cos 20223 =-2358.5
y_2 = 6371 -.5576 sin 20223 =4864.3
z_2 = 6371 sin -0.5576 =3371.4
Sqrt = square root; ^sq = square;
Direct Distance strait line through earth. Central angle theta
Central angle = phi, and 6371 km is the average of earths diameter with correction,
D1 = sqrt [(-2358.5 - -2173.2)^2 (4864.3-4377.9)^2 — (3371.4 -4086.7)^2] = 7476.2 km
Since sin (theta=(3738.11/6371) and central angle is twice that,
phi=2((arcsin(3738.11/6371))=2(0.6270249 = 1.254049 radians
For the great circle route,
s=r(theta)=6371(1.254049) km

This gives the direct path chord, and the great circle route distance. See Google 3-d earth geometry, compute maximimum radar range.

CHAPTER 25

Iceland and Latitude

Reykjavik, Iceland is at latitude and longitude coordinates as shown: 64.1265° N, 21.8174° W. Through these coordinate types one can fly the great circle route around the world and experience lesser distances than by other tracks. Norwegian navigators knew that the travel time was generally longer so they investigated this and found they expected smaller distances than they were experiencing because of the great circle route.

They soon found the great circle was much shorter and they adopted those techniques. They approximated the great circle route by sailing north to Reykjavik's latitude and then turned left. They got to Reykjavik that way but it was still longer than they desired. In other words, they knew the latitude of their destination. As long as they were sailing due north, they were on a great circle route to Iceland. Unfortunately, they were on a great circle route but it was the wrong one. The correct one was their run west. But who do we believe?

Vikings scratched their history on runes that were little more than splinters of wood. There were sagas and epics but these were all totally inadequate for carrying a dynamic culture. We just have to take someone's word even if they are not identified. We are told that one man discovered Iceland. Soon they say they planted a settlement there filling 25 ships with passengers and cargo. Faroes was a waypoint for Iceland.

It was estimated that the map distance between them is 300 miles on a map and 155 miles maximum range prediction. It would be incredible to think they launch a sailing from the Faroes to a point 155 miles away without implementing some kind of search pattern to close the 300-mile distance, which is only 145 miles in deficiency. This would be a 14.5-hour sail at 10 knots or a 7.25-mile sail at 20 knots. Some of the literature speculates the longboat might sail at 20-knot speeds.

The wanderlust of the Vikings is not very impressive to be within 14 or 15 hours sail for millennia without discovery. One must postulate storms, high winds, rough seas and fast currents, particularly in the North Sea during the winter. Might their trip be postponed but curiosity was their main characteristic. Surely adventurous souls would have given it a go during such long periods. We believe they did.

North Sea in winter. Might their trip be postponed but curiosity was their main characteristic. Surely, they would have given it a go during such long times. We believe they did.

Furthermore, I wonder if we are not imposing science with necessary attribution. Is our self-imposed confirmation not too restrictive?

CHAPTER 26

Lewis and Clark Navigation Method

Another hint of navigation is that practiced by Lewis and Clark as they made their way across the west or the Louisiana Purchase. According to them, meridian altitude observations of the sun could be taken without the use of a timepiece; almost all other celestial observations were dependent on knowing the correct apparent local time to within a few seconds. To take the altitude of the sun, the observer watched the progress of the sun as it neared its daily apex, then sighting with the sextant, tracked it. One then reads the angle observed. This is the sun's meridian altitude above the horizon.

Local apparent time is the time as shown by the sun at your location. When it is at the local apparent noon the sun is due south of you, which is to say, on your meridian, and is at its highest point in the sky. The time given by the chronometer for local apparent noon, after a correction made for the sun's changing declination and subtracted from 12:00:00, gives the error of the chronometer on local apparent time for that particular noon. This time check observation was called an Equal Altitudes Observation of the Sun. This concludes the Lewis and Clark method.

I believe the north was developed logically. It only makes sense that the Norsemen as well as the other explorers acted logically. They pursued their dreams logically and when they reached a dead end or impasse, they backed off and sought a new path. I can't believe they ran into an impasse and then gave up. I can't believe they rounded Greenland and then abandoned their dreams as soon as they reached north and south Newfoundland. They knew that they could be sustained there. They knew that the Denmark Straits and the Davis Strait held some of the best fishing grounds in the world. There was reason to believe that these fishing grounds could have been exploited to maintain themselves.

CHAPTER 27

Roman Water Clock for Navigation

A water clock or clepsydra is any timepiece in which time is measured by the regulated flow of liquid into (inflow type) or out from (outflow type) a vessel where the amount is then measured. Water clocks are some of the oldest time-measuring instruments. Where and when they were first invented is not known, and given their great antiquity it may never be. The bowl-shaped outflow is the simplest form of a water clock and is known to have existed in Babylon and in Egypt around the 16th century BCE. Other regions of the world, including India and China, also have early evidence of water clocks, but the earliest dates are less certain. Some authors, however, claim that water clocks appeared in China as early as 4000 BCE.

Some modern timepieces are called "water clocks" but work differently from the ancient ones. Their timekeeping is governed by a pendulum, but they use water for other purposes, such as providing the power needed to drive the clock by using a water wheel or something similar, or by having water in their displays.

The Greeks and Romans advanced water clock design to include the inflow clepsydra with an early feedback system, gearing, and escapement mechanism, which were connected to fanciful automata and resulted in improved accuracy. Further advances were made in Byzantium, Syria and Mesopotamia, where increasingly accurate water clocks incorporated complex segmental and epicyclic gearing, water wheels, and programmability, advances that eventually made their way to Europe.

Independently, the Chinese developed their own advanced water clocks, incorporating gears, escapement mechanisms, and water wheels, passing their ideas on to Korea and Japan.

Some water clock designs were developed independently and some knowledge was transferred through the spread of trade. These early water clocks were calibrated with a sundial. While never reaching a level of accuracy comparable to today's standards of timekeeping, the water clock was the most accurate and commonly used timekeeping device for millennia, until it was replaced by more accurate pendulum clocks in 17th-century Europe.

A water clock uses a flow of water to measure time. If viscosity is neglected, the physical principle required to study such clocks is Torricelli's law. There are two types of water clocks: inflow and outflow. In an outflow water clock, a container is filled with water, and the water is drained slowly and evenly out of the container. This container has markings that are used to show the passage of time. As the water leaves the container, an observer can see where the water is level with the lines and tell how much time has passed. An inflow water clock works in basically the same way, except instead of flowing out of the container, the water is filling up the marked container. As the container fills, the observer can see where the water meets the lines and tell how much time has passed.

When viscosity can be neglected, the outflow rate of the water is governed by Torricelli's law, or more generally, by Bernoulli's principle. Viscosity will dominate the outflow rate if the water flows out through a nozzle that is sufficiently long and thin. Approximately, the flow rate is for such design inversely proportional to the viscosity, which depends on the temperature. Liquids generally become less viscous as the temperature increases. In the case of water, the viscosity varies by a factor of about seven between zero and 100 degrees Celsius.

Thus, a water clock with such a nozzle would run about seven times faster at 100°C than at 0°C. Water is about 25 percent more viscous at 20°C than at 30°C, and a variation in temperature of one degree Celsius, in this "room temperature" range, produces a change of viscosity of about two percent. Therefore, a water clock with such a nozzle that keeps good time at some given temperature would gain or lose about half an hour per day if it were one degree Celsius warmer or cooler.

To make it keep time within one minute per day would require its temperature to be controlled within 1⁄30°C (about 1⁄17° Fahrenheit). There is no evidence that this was done in antiquity, so ancient water clocks with sufficiently thin and long nozzles (unlike the modern pendulum-controlled one described above) cannot have been reliably accurate by modern standards. Note, however, that while modern timepieces may not be reset for long periods, water clocks were likely reset every day, when refilled, based on a sundial, so the cumulative error would not have been great.

Man has puzzled over how to navigate for thousands of years. Most scientists agree that the Global Positioning System (GPS) with satellites has solved the navigational problem for once and for all. In the book, *Global Positioning System: Theory and Applications*, Vol. 1, Paul Zarchan as Editor-in-Chief, pays homage to those who tried before. He states, "For six thousand years, humans have been developing ingenious ways of navigating to remote destinations. A fundamental technique developed by both ancient Polynesians and modern navies is the use of angular measurements of the natural stars."

An hourglass (or sandglass, sand timer, sand watch, or sand clock) is a device used to measure the passage of time. It comprises two glass bulbs connected vertically by a narrow neck that allows a regulated trickle of material (historically sand) from the upper bulb to the lower one. Factors affecting the time interval measured include sand quantity, sand coarseness, bulb size, and neck width. Hourglasses may be reused indefinitely by inverting the bulbs once the upper bulb is empty.

There are no records of the hourglass existing in Europe prior to the Early Middle Ages. That date began with the fall of the Western Roman Empire in 476. The first supported evidences appears from the 8th century CE, crafted by a Frankish monk named Liutprand who served at the cathedral in Chartres, France. But it was not until the 14th century that the hourglass was seen commonly, the earliest firm evidence being a depiction in the 1338 fresco *Allegory of Good Government* by Ambrogio Lorenzetti.

Use of the marine sandglass has been recorded since the 14th century. The written records about it were mostly from logbooks of European ships. In the same period it appears in other records and lists of ships stores. The earliest recorded reference that can be said with certainty to refer to a marine sandglass dates from 1345, in a receipt of Thomas de Stetesham, clerk of the King's ship La George, in the reign of Edward III of England. Translated from the Latin, the receipt says: "In 1345: marine sandglasses were very popular on board ships, as they were the most dependable measurement of time while at sea. Unlike the clepsydra, the motion of the ship while sailing did not affect the hourglass. The fact that the hourglass also used granular materials instead of liquids gave it more accurate measurements, as the clepsydra was prone to get condensation inside it during temperature changes. Seamen found that the hourglass was able to help them determine longitude, distance east or west from a certain point, with reasonable accuracy."

The hourglass also found popularity on land. As the use of mechanical clocks to indicate the times of events like church services became more common, creating a "need to keep track of time," the demand for time-measuring devices increased. Hourglasses were essentially inexpensive, as they required no rare technology to make and their contents were not hard to come by, and as the manufacturing of these instruments became more common, their uses became more practical.

Hourglasses were commonly seen in use in churches, homes, and work places to measure sermons, cooking time, and time spent on breaks from labor. Because they were being used for more everyday tasks, the model of the hourglass began to shrink. The smaller models were more practical and very popular as they made timing more discreet.

After 1500, the hourglass was not as widespread as it had been. This was due to the development of the mechanical clock, which became more accurate, smaller and cheaper, and made keeping time easier. The hourglass, however, did not disappear entirely. Although they became relatively less useful as clock technology advanced, hourglasses remained desirable in their design.

Not until the 18th century did John Harrison and his son James, come up with a marine chronometer that significantly improved on the stability of the hourglass at sea. Taking elements from the design logic behind the hourglass, they made a marine chronometer in 1761 that was able to accurately measure the journey from England to Jamaica accurate within five seconds.

CHAPTER 28

GPS Navigation

Various mechanisms improved the accuracy of timepieces until the Global Positioning System (GPS) came available in about the 1970s.

From the book, '*GPS*', the fundamental technique for GPS is to use one-way ranging from the GPS satellites that are also broadcasting their estimated positions. Ranges are measured to four satellites simultaneously in view by matching (correlating) the incoming signal with a user generated replica signal and measuring the received phase against the user's (relatively crude) crystal clock. With four satellites and appropriate geometry, four unknowns can be determined; typically they are: latitude, longitude, altitude, and a time correction to the user's clock. If altitude or time is already known, a lesser number of satellites can be used. Further, the time of day is generated to incredible accuracy and sent to the satellites for downloads.

Each satellite's future position is estimated from the ranging measurements taken at worldwide monitoring stations. These ranging measurements use the same signals that are employed by a typical user's receiver. Using sophisticated prediction algorithms, the master control station forms estimates of future satellite locations and future satellite clock corrections. For the uploads, which occur daily or more frequently, the combined predictions for satellite clock and position have been measured to have an rms error of 2-3 meters.

In time, the concepts were improved. There also were launched many more than 4 GPS satellites. Thus, the accuracy improved. The rms error is now purposely controlled and may have the accuracy of inches. The Air Force puts in a controlled error so enemies are limited in what accuracy they can depend on for their weapons. The Russians and several other nations design and control their own constellation of satellites so each can introduce accuracies of their own choosing. Modern cellphones incorporate GPS receivers, which are now only a couple of chips.

Although GPS tells you where you are, one must still have a methodology of incorporating the information into the discipline of 'Navigating'. Remember, we are taking samples from a moving track.

This completes the examples for maximum visual detection ranges, navigational examples and history.

The Vikings certainly knew that the environment was more benevolent as one sailed south. I believe that settlements might have been made as far south as the Hudson River. There was fishing, a potential lumber industry; however, Indians were prevalent in many tribes on Long Island. Nevertheless, they had soon dwindled. They were not congenial to the Norsemen but the two seemed to tolerate each other.

CHAPTER 29

Julia Siezes Dr. Ahmed and His Company

Julia Hopkins loved archaeology but she was not happy. She and I talked about history and digs a lot. She had gone to work for the Los Angeles County Museum of Art (LACMA). This was within her field. She considered herself very lucky. She had to take a job at first as an unpaid apprentice. However, she was at the top of her class in university so it did not take long for her to assert herself. She also studied relentlessly and that showed in her rapid rise.

Her unhappiness led her to go a different route. She had decided she wanted to become a part of the fashion industry but she was totally unprepared for this. To her credit, she took the bull by the horns, so to speak. She applied to the Fashion School in Manhattan to work towards an advanced degree. She needed the money so asked for a scholarship. The woman in charge that I later learned was Irene Burns, seemed to take a liking to Julie. She was also impressed by her undergraduate work and her work at LACMA.

"I will tell you what," Ms. Burns said. "You take the courses and I'll keep my eye on you. If you work out, perhaps you can go to work for me in some capacity. I'm not promising you anything, but we will see how it works out."

"Great!" Julia responded.

"Now," Ms. Burns continued. "As to the scholarship, I'll see what I can do." That was good enough for Julia. She had depended on lots of promises that were a lot less binding than that. Some worked out and some didn't.

Julia was extremely ambitious once she set her goals. In fact, one could say she was aggressive towards her ends. She was not first in class for nothing. She worked very hard and she had a native ability. She was impressive.

Several months later, she got a call from Irene Burns asking her to lunch. They went through what amounted to a revue of Julie's work. It was handled with aplomb or certainly better than it appears by my description. "Fine, fine." Ruthie said. "You are doing splendidly." Ruthie then made arrangements for lunch once every month or so. Julie could not have asked for a better climate for her to exhibit her talents. Of course, she had a lot of juggling to do to use the airlines frequently. However, she pulled it off.

The next time I saw Julie, she had made the transition from a pretty woman to a fashion model. The change was striking. Her clothing was chic and dramatic. Somehow, she made it subdued at the same time. It was a lunch setting so the clothes had to recognize that. However, clothes are not the only thing that strike an imposing figure. She had obviously been working out for some time and had rearranged where her muscles showed. Her body had improved remarkably. It was not just the pose and how she handled herself, it was the overall presence of Julia, her body, her gestures, her clothes and the whole picture.

For some reason she wanted to talk. She said the owner of the school was a man named Dr. Ahmed. He did not spend time with any student and very little with the faculty. Julia, in her sly but aggressive way, learned his habits through Irene Burns, his executive assistant. There were rumors that he and she had a relationship. Julia had learned everything she needed to know about the tall grass protecting a tigress on the hunt. She focused on Dr. Ahmed. She winnowed down all her actions to concentrate on him. There was nothing she would not do to attract him.

We all know about that. Once a woman concentrates her wiles on one, the man hardly stands a chance. Nature is with her. She thinks the strategy through. She can select clothes that he favors. She can apply perfumes, again to please him. Even her body exudes attractive and beguiling scents to accentuate her natural endowments. Someone said,

"A tigress on the hunt is the most dangerous animal in the jungle." I am a witness to that.

"There you have it," she said triumphantly. "Like a fish, he was mine to hook and reel in." This seemed a most inappropriate discussion between her and me. She wanted to talk and I no longer threatened her.

"Like you say, you've got him. So what are you going to do with him?" I asked.

"That I don't know. The opportunities are rife. I have plenty of time to figure that out. Meanwhile, I have him."

I was anxious to change the subject. This sounded like an unseemly conversation in any event. Conquest is not a pretty subject. Julia asked me, "Why do you think the Vikings came further south than Newfoundland?"

"We have been over this so many times."

I responded. "I know your arguments and you know mine. Is that not right?" I asked.

CHAPTER 30

Faroe Islands

The Faeroe Islands are an archipelago between the Norwegian Sea and the North Atlantic, about halfway between Norway and Iceland, about 200 miles north-northwest of Scotland. The islands are an autonomous country within the Kingdom of Denmark. The Faroes area today is about 541 square miles with a population of 50,000 people.

The Faroes' terrain is rugged, and the islands have a sub-polar oceanic climate: windy, wet, cloudy, and cool. Despite this island group's northerly latitude, temperatures average above freezing throughout the year because of the warming effect of the Gulf Stream. The Gulf Stream has a profound effect on northern Europe. It warms the British islands with Ireland and Scotland, it warms Norway and even the north country around the Baltic as far as Sweden and Finland. It also warms Greenland and the Atlantic islands. Although, it is hard to believe that sometimes when you are surrounded by ice. When ice covers an anchored ship in the north Atlantic, one on the ship is not easily convinced this ship is also warmed by the Gulf Stream.

In this modern day, the main islands are connected by roads, bridges and tunnels. Government owned shipping provides public bus and ferry service to the main towns and villages. There are no railways.

By sea, there is a regular international passenger, car and freight service linking the Faroe Islands with Iceland and Denmark. Some 80 percent of the population of the islands is connected by tunnels through the mountains and between the islands, bridges and causeways

By air, a government owned company provides helicopter service to each of the islands. There are also international flights.

The Faroe Islands had a problem that bedevils all small demographics. It was certainly a problem for Greenland when it was populated and many other sites. The government of the Faroes recognized this problem and is helping to solve it. They help in the recruitment, making their lives simpler and making them more amenable for the women. Today's Faroes have too many women that migrate to Europe and elsewhere. This causes a deficit of childbearing women that must be addressed.

This interview highlights the problem that is occurring with sparse populations. The hunt for balance between man and wife is a universal struggle. It occurs with small islands, with remote settings, with population sprawl that puts people far away from city centers and from unbalances due to other remote challenges. First, it attracts women for work, then for education, then for child care, and finally for what has become any urban sprawl. This is not to say that men do not succumb to the same forces. They do and for the same reasons.

The response of several women on the Faroes is recounted here. This was actually the result of an interview by a fellow Faroe Islander in which many subtle points on this problem were made. This is an interview by Tim Ecott in a local paper. The wife is a transplant from Thialand.

Because of the shortage of women in the Faroe Islands, local men are increasingly seeking wives from further afield - Thailand and the Philippines in particular. But what's it like for the brides who swap the tropics for this windswept archipelago? When Athaya Slaetalid first moved from Thailand to the Faroe Islands, where winter lasts six months, she would sit next to the heater all day." People told me to go outside because the sun was shining but I just said: "No! Leave me alone, I'm very cold."' Moving here six years ago was tough for Athaya at first, she admits. She'd met her husband, Jan, when he was working with a Faroese friend who had started a business in Thailand.

Jan knew in advance that bringing his wife to this very different culture, weather and landscape would be challenging. "I had my concerns because everything she was leaving and everything she was coming to were opposites," he admits. "But knowing Athaya, I knew she would cope."

"There are now more than 300 women from Thailand and Philippines living in the Faroes. It doesn't sound like a lot, but in a population of just 50,000 people they now make up the largest ethnic minority in these 18 islands. Many small or isolated locations across the world increasingly have this problem.

In recent years the Faroes have experienced population decline, with young people leaving, often in search of education, and not returning. Women have proved more likely to settle abroad. As a result, according to Prime Minister, the Faroes have a "gender deficit" with approximately 2,000 fewer women than men. This, in turn, has lead Faroese men to look beyond the islands for romance. Many, though not all, of the Asian women met their husbands online, some through commercial dating websites. Others have made connections through social media networks or existing Asian-Faroese couples.

For the new arrivals, the culture shock can be dramatic. Officially part of the Kingdom of Denmark, the Faroes have their own language (derived from Old Norse) and a very distinctive culture - especially when it comes to food. Fermented mutton, dried cod and occasional whale meat and blubber are typical of the strong flavours here, with none of the traditional herbs and spices of Asian cooking.

The Faroe Islands were a major hurdle for the Vikings. It was a matter of sailing about 200 statute miles northward from Shetland to Norway, turn left, and then head to the Faroes. Both were well traveled routes. There are many islands in northeast England, Scotland, Ireland and Scapa Flow. The elevation of Norway is about 1,700 feet and Shetland is 1,181 feet. There are 18 fingers or spits of land making up the Faroe Islands. This is but a tiny spot between Norway, Scotland, Iceland, Ireland and Greenland

CHAPTER 31

Iceland

"I believe discoveries happened far more often and much earlier than reported. I also don't believe that anybody knew anything before about 700, and then the discoveries came crashing down on us. Then we discovered wholesale. We loaded our ships heavily. We found hordes of people willing to take the risks of settlements in far places. Our knowledge everywhere increased explosively. And, our skill sets increased exponentially. I can't explain our inadequacies any more than I can explain our explosive successes.

I for one do not believe this view of the world. A culture does not change overnight. Change comes slowly. The recognition of change may come suddenly but the underlying process takes time.

"Look at Iceland. Do air-breathing animals blow as seals, whales and porpoises and not give clues for navigation. How about birds taking and releasing as aids to navigation? Sometime currents reach as high as 6 knots, we read in the literature. Do navigators not track birds and interpret their flights?"

CHAPTER 32

Greenland: Or is it Vineland or Newfoundland

Julia, of course knew the story of the Arctic trade of the Vikings. I asked her did she not hunger to join the diggers and make discoveries. She said, "Are you kidding me? I applied when I first got out of school but their pay is miniscule. I may have been first in my class, but that does not mean I have to live like a pauper. I am beyond that."

"Okay," she said. "I would love to join them at a dig for a short time anyway."

I asked her, "Do you think you could finance a couple of weeks for me to join a dig?"

"Well go ahead," was her answer. "You do not make enough money to matter anyway."

"Come on," I said. "I do the best I can. You don't want me to give up archaeology altogether, do you? Or do you?"

"Ooh," she said. "That was really cruel."

"Do we have to go through that again?" she asked.

Her attitude has softened immeasurably since she was promoted. She lets things pass. However, it can't last. It is not a temporary attitude anymore, I fear. It has gone deeper. I have to recognize she has a mean streak. Sooner or later, that meanness in her heart will surface. I can only hope for the best.

Vikings were confused about their destination when they went to settle Greenland. They saw a shore of slate, not green grasses. They continued on to what people now think was a place they called Vinland. This was probably Newfoundland. We know the Vikings had at least two settlements in Newfoundland but they seemed to be temporary or waypoints. Likely places for diggings have been found and conclusions about the settlements have been reached. The settlers had glowing reports about Vinland but our knowledge of these settlements is distressingly incomplete. We also do not know what happened next. Was Newfoundland the end of their explorations, or were there far more to be found?

The Vikings living in Iceland knew all about the existence of Greenland long before any settled there. A Norwegian named Ulfsson had visited it although it was because of a storm in 900. The country's highest peak is 12,000 feet high. The existence of Greenland probably was common knowledge to Icelanders since one could see it from Iceland's tallest peak on a very clear day. Seafarers blown west of Iceland would have seen Greenland's ice sheet or glaciers.

A major problem was between Iceland and Greenland. The treacherous Denmark Strait lay between them on the east side of Greenland. During summer, a current of cold water carries pack ice and icebergs southwards. This is a challenge even for modern shipping. Further, the Davis Strait lying on the west coast of Greenland, between that and the Baffin Islands gives the same problem with calving ice spewing icebergs and prolific marine life down south of the southern end of Greenland.

"High. This is Shaun speaking with first hand knowledge of some of these areas. My experience dates back to WWII."

"The US signed a treaty after the Titanic disaster where they and several European countries would monitor ice bergs drifting into and through the shipping lanes. Ice through both straits threatened similar catastrophes. The Navy had the responsibility after WWII using ships but this was changed to planes later.

The responsibility later fell to the Coast Guard with their aircraft. I would sometimes fly with the crews. I could see the cargo ships of the north Atlantic wallowing through impossible weather and fighting through the heavy waves washing over the decks of the ships. I would sometimes see the sailors on ice-caked ships. They would be on the decks washed by the waves. The sailors were chipping away. The ice was solid up to the top of the superstructure. Icicles drooped from the numerous antennas and rigging.

The whole thing was under a heavy blanket of ice and it looked forbidding. One was very careful. He did not just walk out on the deck without grasping an anchor point. Tons of icy water washed across the bow and flew as high as the bridge, itself dipped under the breaking dam.

I asked the aircraft crew why the sailors in the shipping lanes were chipping the ice. They said it was obvious. The ice is enormously heavy. When the ice load became too heavy, the ships sometimes capsized or just rolled over. Death was then inevitable.

"As we flew, cake ice appeared everywhere in this corner of the world. There were Nova Scotia, the Baffins, Newfoundland, Greenland and Labrador, to mention a few. It was sometimes hard to get a perspective on how large the ice cakes sometimes are. Nevertheless, I estimated that some of the flat cakes were the size of a city block or larger.

It could be said that the sailors on the decks were chipping the ice for dear life. That would be correct. I knew there were military people down there on a tiny sliver of an island or on board an anchored ship for months at a time. The movies depicting the north Atlantic in winter actually have a large amount of reality in them."

"The sea simply froze solid, many miles out from land."

Viking settlers steered far to the south of Cape Farewell, the most southerly point on Greenland, until they assumed they had reached the more benign weather of the west coast."

Eric the Red was a colorful Viking character. He had killed a man and had been exiled from Norway. He became active in the arctic activity. But he did 'some killings' in Iceland and was driven from that settlement. He became a leader of a movement to settle further in Greenland. He organized a settlement expedition. In the spring of 986, he with 500 to 1,000 settlers sailed with 25 ships toward Greenland. The central ice cap dominates the island. It covers Greenland, leaving only an iceless strip of 50 miles or so around the whole periphery of the island.

When the immigrants reached this land they thought was Greenland, they found a territory with soil and grass that was purported to be untouched by human hands. They called this Vinland.

Here, they found a paradise. There was plentiful game. This included rain deer, polar bears and other wild animals so meat was available to them and also valuable skins and furs. The sea also presented fish, seals, walruses and whales. Soon there was a steady trade between them and Iceland. They traded exotic furs, and other luxuries in exchange for grain, metal tools and timber (that Greenland lacked).

The trade included surprising goods. These included hunting falcons and Norwhal whales that were the most valuable. The only place in the world to find these whales with the long tusks was between Canada and Greenland. A large specimen is perhaps 16 feet long and 3,500 pounds. He might have a tusk that is 10 feet long and weigh 20 pounds.

Europe in the Middle Ages found the legend of the unicorns was at its height. Unicorns were symbols of purity. It was believed that only virgins could tame them and they had an immunity to poisons. And, it had a miraculous ability to cure any ailment. Does this sound like the propensity of Chinese even today to ascribe similar beliefs to elephant tusks or to cape buffalo horns?

During this time, most captains tried to keep land in sight. However, Leif Erickson, son of Erik the Red, formed a crew and pioneered a direct route from Norway to Greenland. By sailing due east along the 60th or so parallel or latitude, he completed the journey of about 2,000 miles without sighting any land at all. They then sailed to the Baffin Islands.

They had made a crossing to the new world. However, a new phenomenon occurred. They sighted North American Indians, or Intuits. The Inuit are a group of culturally similar indigenous peoples inhabiting the Arctic regions of Canada's Northwest Territories, This included Denmark's Greenland, Russia's Siberia and America's Alaska. Inuit means "the people" in the Inuktitut language.

The Indians made it plain that the Europeans were not welcome and fights broke out. Leif, their leader, was killed by an arrow. Another expedition left Greenland a few years afterwards. It consisted of three ships with 600 men, women and children. After settling, there were internal tensions between Pagans and Christians and bad weather. The "ever present hostile natives" in addition to the other provocations proved too much. After three years in Vinland, they abandoned everything and returned home.

For a long time, it was thought that there was no evidence of Vikings in Newfoundland. Then an archaeologist, Anne Ingstad, found artifacts in 1961 at Canadian L'Anse aux Meadows that proved the Vikings had been there for some time. Most archaeologists today doubt that Newfoundland was the "Vinland" the Greenlanders thought it was and reported by Leif Erikson. Instead, L'Anse aux Meadows is usually thought to be a kind of Viking way station, a staging post. They most recently have found another site, Point Rosee on the south of Newfoundland.

At the end of the Middle Ages, Greenland was abandoned by the settlers. It appears that the southward movement of Inuit peoples originating from Canada caused this. There seems to have been a thriving community throughout the Viking period. One must await further research and findings to continue the story of Vinland. Meanwhile, the romantic notion of Vinland is kept in mind although it may be apocryphal.

Lars Brownworth in his book, *The Sea Wolves*, said the first Vikings to reach Vineland did so purely by accident. He says they reckoned navigation through careful observation, and trial and error, not sophisticated navigational tools. Land was found by noting changes in the color of the water, differences in the flight pattern of birds, and the presence of driftwood.

Vikings calculated latitude by the midday sun during the day, and by the stars at night. If neither of these were available because of fogs, storms, or otherwise, they relied on instinct or a water wheel on the bottom of their boats or similarly with air currents. This was converted to dead reckoning change in position.

He cites another trip where the captain got hopelessly lost in a fog and drifted for days. When the fog lifted, the crew voted for a particular course to their destination. The captain told the most experienced navigator to decide. "*I want the shrewdest one to decide because the council of fools is all the more dangerous the more of them there are.*"

In the middle of the ninth century, a Norwegian named Daddodd got lost on his way to the Faroes, lost by 400 miles. The captain looked for land by scaling a high mountain, but it was fruitless. He reported this back to Scandinavia on return.

All these stories support the notion that the discovery of Iceland was haphazard. A footnote says that the earliest sources claim that there were some Irish monks on Iceland when the Vikings got there so one could not claim to be the first. There are usually all kinds of reports claiming discovery followed by counterclaims that other people were there first.

This description of the discovery is prototypical of the story.

The Vikings explored Greenland for settlements. However, signs of trouble to come soon faced them as they hiked around the potential sites. They discovered a hut that looked like it had been used to store grain. It was clearly not a Viking hut.

When they returned to the beach, they saw three mounds. These turned out to be canoes, each with three strange looking men. The Vikings reported these Indians were ugly and made a strange noise. They named them as "Skraelings" since they sounded like that. Or, the names were an onomatopoeia matching both name and sound. These natives were found and reported to Norway by Lief Erickson in about the year 1,000. These Indians put up a short struggle where eight of these were captured. However, one of these escaped in a canoe. After the Vikings had killed the captives, they noticed what looked like the huts of a small village in the distance. Meanwhile, the escaped man returned with a countless fleet of canoes. The two sides attacked each other, but the Indians soon fled. The area had a native population for certain.

This begins my flash-forward or trip to Greenland and the north.

I was to take a trip through Iceland and Greenland on an American military airplane. Our landing on Iceland was uneventful. We then drove from the Keflivik airfield to Reykjavik, the capitol. The area from

Keflavik to Reykjavik was strewn with large rocks or boulders. These were lying flat on the ground. The rocks were such that the tops looked like a flat field where all the rocks looked similar. They looked hand-placed to be a flat field. These occur in fields as far as the eye can see. Similar fields probably grow much further away than that.

These rocks or boulders are from two to four feet in length and three to four feet thick. Likens smooth out the rocks. These are very dark, almost black. They were very unusual and gave the impression that the field is dark green and covered with moss or likens. They are scattered randomly so the sizes are rather random and difficult to describe with any accuracy. The end-result was a two-dimensioned field completely covered in rocks. The 25 or more miles observed was like this. The liken completely covers the boulders. Further, there are no trees or bushes or shrubbery around so this emphasizes the uniformity of the fields. There are 'forests' in Reyflovik where clumps of dwarf trees hold sway but there are none as we drive along.

This prompts the saying that the tallest things that grow in Iceland are likens.

These fields of rounded boulders take their toll. It is said that even the sheep and goats sometimes get confused and break their legs on the irregular placements of the rocks.

The population of Iceland hovers somewhere around 250,000 people. They are all well dressed, knowledgeable and well-traveled. After all, Iceland is wealthy and is only a thousand miles or so from Europe. There were several hotels in Reykjavik. There was a tradition that Friday and Saturday were dance nights. A large percentage of the population gathers in these hotels where the lobby and other rooms were in the mode of ballrooms with open spaces between them. Each had a band.

One wanders from room to room having drinks and cocktails and looking for companionship. With such a small population, it is not unusual to meet ambassadors, ministers, government representatives as well as common fishermen and workers. It seems to be a melting pot where all are equal. At least, this is the way it was in 1970 or so. It may be different now, I don't know.

The Icelanders worry about the loss of the population identity. After all, with an American military base in Keflavik, only 30 miles away or so, the population mix cold become undesirable. There was not an outright ban but there was an agreement that soldiers would not visit the towns, the dances, or socialize in their uniforms. The Americans have been there since 1941. Otherwise, they seem to get along splendidly. Their population seems to remain constant. The Americans have their dances on their base also. Further, their dances and drinking parties occur seven days a week. This certainly beats every Friday and Saturday night.

CHAPTER 33

Greenland

After a trip to Greenland, I was home and received an unhappy letter on a lawyer's letterhead. I don't know exactly how it happened but it certainly was no surprise to me. Julia and I were deep into the yelling and screaming stage. Our marriage had been slowly slipping away. We yelled a lot and I was concerned that it had come to a hitting stage.

It was all I could do sometimes to contain myself, to hold back. Her claims were so outrageous and she knew just where to dig to get me. Further, Julia had slipped in her work each time I saw her. I was getting deeper and deeper into my work and I was accepting more responsibility. I was traveling a lot. She no longer had any desire to travel with me or to smooth things over.

Her mother was always in the background. She always had a slicing comment to add. Really, I hardly saw Jane any more. She cuts too deep.

I received a registered letter in the post office. I could tell it was serious since it had a lawyer's letterhead. "Dear Sir", it said. The writing was so mechanically perfect. I can't say it was a surprise. I expected it. What else could it be? I just knew it was. The letter was announcing that Julia had filed for a divorce. Why had it taken so long?

At this time, I had just returned from a trip. I was experiencing the joy of a successful dig in Europe. I guess it balanced out…a successful dig versus a divorce notification. She was not asking for much: just a smooth backing out of a bad relationship. She just wanted to be rid of me. What was it she called me in college? A bug. Well, I had not changed my standing, at least not by much.

Bluie West One airfield is the military name given to the airport in 1941. Its purpose was to service aircraft being ferried to Europe. This was later known as Narsarsuaq Air Base and the civilian Narsarsuaq Airport. This was built on a glacial moraine at what is now the village of Narsarsuaq, near the southern tip of Greenland. A moraine is a pile of debris, often extending for miles, deposited by a glacier. It is composed of rock fragments transported by the ice, which are left behind when the ice melts. Most of Greenland is composed of glaciers.

Construction by the U.S. Army began in June 1941 with materials landed by the USS Munargo in July 1941. The first aircraft landed there in January 1942, as a link in the North Atlantic air ferry route in World War II. The base had a peak population of about 4,000 American servicemen, and it is estimated that some 10,000 aircraft landed there en route to the war in Europe and North Africa. This seems to be quite a success and it was a critical function for moving war planes across the Atlantic.

The initial ferry was with P-38 and P-39 fighters, piloted by combat crews who had been given special training in long-distance flying. They were escorted by the longer-range B-17 bombers

Aircraft could fly from the new Presque Isle Army Airfield in northern Maine to Prestwick Airport in Scotland with no leg of the journey longer than 850 statute miles.

Stops were made at the Canadian-built base at Goose Bay in Labrador, Bluie West 1 (or BW-1) in southern Greenland, and Reykjavik or Keflavik in Iceland

Bad weather is frequent in southern Greenland. The airfield at Narsarsuaq is virtually surrounded by high mountains, making the approach to the steel-mat runway exceedingly difficult. The usual approach was a low-level flight up a fjord. Because the runway slopes up west to east, landings were made to the east, with take-offs to the west, regardless of the wind direction.

Narsarsuaq is the site of Erik the Red's longhouse at Brattahlid. He is attributed to discovering Greenland or at least to leading its settlement there that later reached about 10,000 people.

I've read dozens of stories by American airmen who passed through Greenland during World War II. A few mention the "Eskimo" settlement across the Eriksfjord from Narsarsuaq, practically under the final approach to Runway 07. But not one seemed aware that this was the site of Brattahlid, where Erik the Red built a longhouse toward the end of the 10th century, and where his descendants lived for longer than any European family has been in the U.S. They disappeared toward the end of the 15th century, the victims most likely of climate change or global cooling.

If you lay a string on a globe, in search of the shortest route between the U.S. and Britain, it runs the Great Circle Route from northern Maine to the western isles of Scotland. This skims the shores of Baffin Islands, Labrador, Greenland, and Iceland. If planes were to fly from American factories to British airfields, this was the route they must take; and for them to refuel, there must be airfields and fuel in all these places.

In addition to its potential as an Arctic aircraft carrier, Greenland had two other attractions for countries at war. Ivigtut, not far from Narsarsuaq, boasted a cryolite mine, and cryolite, this sandy, exotic rock of yellow and pink strata, was needed to make aluminum. Finally, Greenland was a weather breeder for Europe. Weather observers there would be of immense value to the combatants that got there first.

So it was that British marines seized control of Iceland in May 1940, and that a month later the U.S. Coast Guard began a survey of Greenland. While they charted Greenland, Lacey and Shields took turns flying their biplane with its big central float and 600 hp Wasp engine, a combination that gave the Seagull a cruising speed of 133 mph and a range of 675 miles. Scouting from Disko Bay above the Arctic Circle to Cape Farewell in the south, they found eight sites for military bases on the comparatively hospitable west coast. Navy code masters would designate them Bluie West One through Eight. Meanwhile, the cutter *USS Northland* did similar duty along the eastern shore, finding three sites worth exploiting.

Of them all, BW-1 at Narsarsuaq was the standout. In the Inuit language, the name means "Great Plain," which by Greenlandic standards it is. The area is a glacial moraine two miles long and half a mile wide, conveniently surfaced with gravel.

Diplomatic cover for an American intervention was provided by Henrik Kauffman, the Danish minister to Washington. On April 9, 1941, he signed an agreement making Greenland a U.S. protectorate. Less than three months later, the freighter Siboney landed construction materials and a few army airways specialists at Narsarsuaq. The troopships Munargo and Chateau Thierry brought in an engineer battalion, and service troops, to a total of 469 officers and men.

Not long afterwards, President Roosevelt put the world on notice that American interests did not stop at the continental shelf: "The USA will hold itself responsible for the defense of the Western Hemisphere, and the transfer of any territory from one European state to another will not be tolerated." In other words, Germany's occupation of Denmark gave it no rights to a weather station in Greenland, regardless of what Copenhagen or the government removed to Britain might agree to.

By September 1941--three months before the United States was catapulted into World War II—Narsarsuaq was a town of 85 buildings, mostly of wood and tarpaper construction. A runway was roughed out, and a pier built a short distance down Eriksfjord, with water deep enough for ocean-going ships. A three-mile road ran from the harbor on the west, past the future airfield, to the high ground on the east. Very likely this was the longest road in Greenland, which even today has almost no land links from town to town.

Nor was the US military the only one to come ashore. On Sept. 12, on the east coast of Greenland, the cutter Northland intercepted a Norwegian trawler. The fishermen explained that they'd just dropped off a 12-man German weather party with a radio transmitter. (Norway too was under German occupation.) Several Americans went ashore, and captured three Germans and a codebook, which they sent back for examination. For the next four years, a low-grade and frigid war would be fought on the east coast of Greenland. American sled dog patrols, helped by providing long-time Danish hunters and fishermen.

At the end of that first summer of 1941, civilians in the employ of McKinley Dredging Co. arrived to finish the runway at Bluie West One. It would be 5,000 feet long and 145 feet wide, with a base of pea-sized gravel and a surface of 'pierced-steel planking'--perhaps the first use of PSP by the U.S. military. The compass magnetic deviation in south Greenland is 30 degrees, so the direction actually runs from southwest to northeast. At the fjord end, the altitude is 12 feet above sea level; it rises 100 feet in about half a mile, then levels off as it nears the glacier.

"If you haven't landed at BW-1," writes Army pilot George James of his ferry flight in a twin-engined B-26, "you have missed one of life's biggest thrills. We were briefed for hours with talks, movies taken from the nose of an airplane, and a topographical model. The reason for what might seem like overkill is that BW-1 is 52 miles up a fjord with sheer cliffs and walls several thousand feet high. There are numerous dead-end offshoots, no room to turn around, and usually overcast below the tops of the walls. You had to get it right the first time."

Pity those engineers and civilians, marooned on a glacial moraine through Greenland's awful winter! On Dec. 11, when their work was legitimized by Germany's declaration of war on the United States, the sun rose at 9 a.m. and was gone six hours later. There were back-to-back days when the thermometer stuck at that magic figure where Fahrenheit and Celsius agree: 40 degrees below zero. And the wind! In one report, someone wrote that the wind funneling down the glacier reached 141 mph, though the military that day recorded gusts of merely 75 mph. I'm willing to believe either figure.

On a summer day in Narsarsuaq, I was buffeted by 50-knot gusts, obliging me to take shelter in the lee of the old headquarters building, now a museum. There I found the port landing gear and a Twin Wasp engine from a DC-3 or C-47, which the museum's founder had salvaged from the dump. The Gooney Bird had been picked up by a gust of wind and slammed down so hard that it shattered. This was not the only plane destroyed by the wind at Bluie West One.

Housed in tarpaper shacks, with no movies or radio programs to divert them, they had the job done soon after the New Year. On Jan. 24, 1942, a Grumman Duck amphibian off the USS Bear made the first landing on Runway 07. On March 3, a Lockheed Lodestar of the Canadian Royal Air Force made a test flight from Goose Bay to Bluei West 1. Goose Bay was still being carved out of the Labrador wilderness by US and Canadian engineers. The Lodestar returned to Goose the same day, having proved that Bluie West One was open for business.

CHAPTER 34

Cold War

BW-1's importance declined after World War II, but the US Air Force maintained it as Narsarsuaq Air Base during the early Cold War years, when it served as a refueling station for jet fighters and for helicopters crossing the North Atlantic. The runway by this time had been paved with concrete. Jets require a longer takeoff run than do propeller-driven aircraft, and the air base used a small tugboat to move icebergs out of the way of planes taking off over the basin west of the runway. There is a detailed account of a visit to BW-1 in the early days of World War II by Ernest K. Gann, in the book *Fate Is The Hunter*. Some of Gann's observations are used here.

The advent of aerial refueling, and the opening of the larger Thule Air Base in northern Greenland, made the base redundant, and it was turned over to the Danish government of Greenland in 1958.

In 1950, I was in the air National Guard and flew with the crew of another flight that originated in Newfoundland. Needless to say, it was cold, dark and bleak as we left Newfoundland. From there, we flew to Labrador. When we arrived, there was snow everywhere. It was about three feet deep everywhere on the airbase except the runways. This was winter or very early spring, so we were not surprised that snow covered the whole area.

Since that time, Labrador has joined with Canada to form a province of Canada. I notice that little has changed since then except the name of 'Goose Bay', Labrador to 'Happy Valley', Labrador. This smacks of the naming of Greenland. Our purpose was to fly from Goose Bay to Bluei West One in Greenland.

The crew had been well briefed about the hazards of Greenland. First, it is a long way and weather closes in at a moments notice. When Bluei shuts down because of weather, there is no place to go except returning to Goose Bay. This was a very iffy thing considering the distances and the quickness of weather changes. Furthermore, there is a 50-mile canyon to negotiate from the coast of Greenland to the airfield.

We were provided quarters by the staff stationed there. There were numerous buildings bunched up toward the runway. Everything suggested impermanence such as multiple Quonset huts. One was particularly large that was meant to house small planes.

We parked our planes on the tarmac aprons. When we tried to leave the next morning, our engines would not start regardless of how we tried. The mechanical parts of the four Pratt-Whitney engines were just too cold and the oil too sluggish to operate normally. Further, the aircraft we were on was a Navy version of the B-24, or a PB4Y2, which had substituted a single very high tail and lengthened the nose about 20 feet. The very high tail of our plane certainly was too tall to go into the hangar.

Someone suggested rolling our aircraft nose-first into the hangar just far enough to warm the engines. Once these were warm, we rolled the plane out and went through the normal engine starting procedure. It worked fine.

Remember the comment about the overcast over the fjord walls. Well, the sides of the fjord were sheer, going straight up as he said to more than 2,000 feet. The fjord was narrow. It looked like maybe 400 to 500 feet across. One could not descend like a corkscrew down to the landing runway. So, you took your chances and came in from the ocean, descending from the start of the fjord while banking left and then right continuously to match the pattern of the fjord turns.

After about 50 miles of this, one broke out at the last turn. One must have wheels down and be ready to land since multiple peaks formed a bowl where you had little chance of changing the flight pattern. Boom! The wheels scratched the runway and everyone breathed a sigh of relief. The 5,000-foot runway left little room to correct errors or to change one's mind. The flat length of the runway was the only flat space in the area. In fact, even the runway was not really flat but meandered up and down as we rolled out.

When we were ready to leave Greenland, the pilot decided he could wind upward like a corkscrew and ascend out of the bowl. We kept a heavy bank until the aircraft cleared the deadly fjord peaks. Denmark, the owner of Greenland, would have been proud of us. This was one more niche in the modernization of Greenland.

CHAPTER 35

Baffin Islands

We were then clear to do what we set out to do. A civilian on an outpost on the Baffin Islands had fallen into the water and quickly drowned or froze. Our mission was to fly his body back to Placentia, Newfoundland. There was a huge airbase next to Placentia Bay so plenty of facilities were available. We later flew the body to Newfoundland completing our assigned task.

In fact, Placentia became famous at the start of the war. Roosevelt and Churchill met in Placentia Bay in 1941 and proclaimed the Four Freedoms that encapsulated the aspirations of the Allies in WWII. Each delegation arrived in the Bay rendezvous by a warship from their own country. This meeting made the bay famous.

Our aircraft crew had stuffed current magazines and other reading material into 50-gallon steel drums. These were to be dropped for the staff at Baffin Islands. Our plane flew 10 to 15 feet above and along the runway to get ready for the drop. For some unexplained reason, three locals had a jeep and they drove at break-neck speed almost directly underneath us. When the drop occurred, the barrels burst and strew everything along the runway. They assured us that no one was hurt so it was O.K. It had been a successful drop.

After the drop, we landed on Baffin Island for weather reports and to see what it was like. The one thing that struck me was the number of mosquitoes.

They swarmed around our heads and no amount of swatting by hand seemed to make any difference. They were horrible. How do the weathermen on Baffin stand it? That is one thing that I notice. The mosquitoes in the tropics are bad but they are smaller and bearable. As one goes north, however, somewhere above the border with Canada, they become far more numerous and bigger. They seem to reach the size of bumblebees or larger. As one walks, a swarm of bugs can be seen surrounding one's head and face. Yikes!

Yet, the historical parade marches on. At the end of the WWII, America just abandoned many of these posts leaving huge piles of debris. Greenland, even in this 21st century, features perhaps thousands of steel drums that at one time stored oil. Even old truck bodies and collapsed buildings can be seen across the abandoned airfield.

It looks like everyone got an order to abandon the facility so everyone just dropped what they were doing and headed for the airport. Steel drums are lying and rusting all over the place. Wooden frames and the ribs of small buildings could be seen. Only the framework of the buildings was standing. The sideboards lay in confusion on the ground. Denmark, who owns the Island of Greenland, protests but ineffectively. One can see photos of this on Google search under Blue West One.

CHAPTER 36

Viking Age Limits

The period from the earliest recorded raids in about 790 until the Norman conquest of England in 1066 is commonly known as the Viking Age of Scandinavian history. Vikings used the Norwegian Sea and Baltic Sea for routes to the south. The Normans were descended from Vikings who were given feudal overlordship of areas in northern France—the Duchy of Normandy—in the 10th century.

In that respect, descendants of the Vikings continued to have an influence in northern Europe. Likewise, King Harold Godwinson, the last Anglo-Saxon king of England, had Danish ancestors. Two Vikings even ascended to the throne of England, with Sweyn Forkbeard claiming the English throne from 1013-1014 and his son Cnut the Great becoming king of England from 1016-1035.

Geographically, a Viking Age may be assigned not only to Scandinavian lands (modern Denmark, Norway and Sweden), but also to territories under Scandinavian dominance, mainly in Britain, and Danelaw including Scandinavian York, the administrative center of the remains of the Kingdom of Northumbria, parts of Mercia, and East Anglia.

Viking navigators opened the way to new lands to the north, west and east, resulting in the foundation of independent settlements in the Shetland, Orkney, and Faroe Islands; Iceland; Greenland; and L'Anse aux Meadows, a short-lived settlement in Newfoundland, circa 1000. They may have been deliberately sought out, perhaps on the basis of the accounts of sailors who had seen land in the distance.

The Greenland settlement of Vikings eventually died out, possibly due to climate change. The Viking Rurik dynasty took control of territories in Slavic and Finno-Ugric-dominated areas of Eastern Europe; they annexed Kiev in southern Russia in 882 to serve as the capital of the Kievan Rus state.

This ends my flashback from a trip to Greenland and the north.

CHAPTER 37

Olga of Kiev

Attila was the legendary king of the Huns — a Mongoloid people who began invading the Roman Empire in the 300s. The Huns were originally from a tribe of Mongolians from Central Asia, who settled in the area known later as Hungary. Attila was born in 406. Soon, the Huns ruled a large empire. Attila conquered, pillaged and attacked his way through eastern and central Europe. He attacked Greece and threatened Constantinople, which was the center of the Roman Empire in the East.

Attila then moved onto the East Roman Empire and in 450, he demanded that Honoria, sister of the Western Emperor, Valentinian III, marry him and also receive half of the east Roman Empire as her dowry. Valentinian refused. To enforce his demand, Attila then attacked Gaul, France, but the Romans and barbarians stopped his attacks in 451.

In 452, Attila and his horsemen crossed the Alps to invade Italy, which caused Pope Leo I to pay money to Attila to save Rome from total attack. Attila devastated the eastern half of the Roman Empire between 451 and 452 and controlled a region from the Danube River to the Baltic Sea and from the Rhine River to the Caspian Sea. Before long, all raiders out of the north became known as Huns.

Attila died in 453 at the age of 47, on his wedding night.

Olga of Kiev was the third ruler of Kievan Rus'. She was the descendant of the Vikings. She married Prince Igor, the son of Rurik. Olga is remembered as the first Russian ruler to convert to Christianity. But most of all she is remembered as the woman who gave revenge a whole new meaning. Her life was full of great deeds described in numerous historical records. Legendary facts are usually believed but these are still disputed by many historians.

According to the traditional theory in the Primary Chronicle, Olga was born in Pskov to a family of Vikings or Norsemen.

"Hold it," Cried Julia. "Did you make that up? The family immigrated to the territory of current Russia, and their forebears were Vikings? That seems strange."

"I know. Another fact was that Olga was famous for the revenge she inflicted on Rus, Ukraine and Belarus during the 8th and 9th centuries. Olga married Prince Igor, who was the son of the Novgorod Prince Rurik, a founder of the Rurik Dynasty of Russian Czars. After the death of Oleg in 912, Igor became the ruler of Kievan Rus. In 945 Prince Igor went to the Slavic tribe of the Drevlyans to gather tributes. After he demanded a much higher payment, the Drevlyans killed him."

The death of the Kievan Prince raised a question about the next ruler of the country. Igor's son, Svyatoslav, was only three years old and hence Olga took the power into her hands as the regent. Interestingly, she had the full support of the Rus army, which attests to the great respect she held among the people.

After killing Igor, the Drevlyans sent their matchmaker ambassadors to propose that Olga marry their Prince Mal, their favorite. However, the Princess sought revenge for her husband's death.

Olga was not content to simply stand by after her husband was killed. Not only was the death of her husband a deep personal loss, the concurrent open rebellion against the royal family threatened to shake their power. On top of that, shortly after killing and burying her husband, Prince Mal of the Derevlians sent an envoy of matchmakers to Olga with a proposition of marriage. Olga's revenge, outlined in the Russian text *The Tale of Bygone Years*, was wreaked in four steps.

1. **Buried Alive.** Olga first met with the envoy of matchmakers outside Kiev's city walls. She pretended to be intrigued by the offer of marriage, and told them that, before answering, she would like to honor the envoy with a public ceremony the next day where they would be carried in their boats into the city. After the flattered Derevlians returned to camp, Olga ordered a long, deep trench dug in town. In the morning, she had her people carry the richly-dressed Derevlians in their boats into town, then had them cast into the pit and buried alive.

2. **Burned bathhouses.** But Olga was not done. She sent a message to Prince Mal asking for a company of his best men to escort her to Dereva. Not knowing what happened to his previous envoy, Prince Mal agreed and sent a company of his best warriors to Kiev. On their arrival, Olga suggested that they bathe themselves before seeing her. Once the warriors had all gone into the bathhouse, Olga had them locked in and burned the baths to the ground, burning alive all the men inside.

3. **Killing the revelers.** With a company of the Derevlian's best men now dead, Olga set her sights on the rest of their warriors in Dereva. So, this time she went to Dereva's capitol Iskorosten, with the official reason of holding a funeral for her late husband. The Derevlians threw a grand feast with much, much alcohol. Olga waited until the Derevlians were quite drunk, then ordered them all killed. Around 5,000 Derevlians were killed in the ensuing slaughter.

4. **Firebirds.** What followed the next year was full-on war. Olga marched into Dereva with her armies, eventually laying siege to Iskorosten itself. The starving and weak Derevlians offered to surrender, but they had none of the usual tribute to appease the attacking army. So Olga demanded three sparrows and three pigeons from each household. The aggrieved townspeople complied and delivered the birds, thinking their ordeal over. Olga's armies tied burning rags dipped in sulphur and lit on fire to the feet of each bird and released them. The birds returned to their

> nests in the city and burned it. The Derevlians perished in their homes. Let's face it. Olga was not a Viking for nothing.

Many people in WWII recalled the US had a project to connect incendiaries to bats with the same objective as Olga. By this time she was responsible for well over 5,000 deaths. We don't profess an equality of these versus death in some other area. It is worthwhile, however, to make such a comparison.

History records several tricks like this with Bats: 1. The Olga bird ruse, 2. The US Navy WWII Bat incendiary trick, 3. The WWII US Navy Bat radar glide bomb project on Privateer air craft, and 4. The Taiwan high-flyer and low-flyer project. These all can be found on Google.

The modern world often looks at the cruelty and deaths of the middle ages, but this is seldom compared to our own activity.

"OK," said Julia. " Let us do an example to get an idea of what you are talking about."

"I would be glad to," I volunteered. The four incidences of revenge caused over 5,000 deaths. But, Americans look beyond that to the manner of killings themselves. Look at the Syrian operations of Isis. Isis often beheads their victims. We view that as particularly bloodthirsty and barbaric.

"For instance, we are particularly incensed by beheadings."

"Let's compare Olga's revenge against the Americans', 'Trail of Tears.'"

CHAPTER 38

American Removals

"At the beginning of the 1830s, nearly 125,000 Indians lived on millions of acres of land in Georgia, Tennessee, Alabama, North Carolina and Florida — land their ancestors had occupied and cultivated for generations. By the end of the decade, very few natives remained anywhere in the southeastern United States. Working on behalf of white settlers who wanted to grow cotton on the Indians' land, the federal government forced them to leave their homelands and walk thousands of miles to a specially designated "Indian territory" beyond the Mississippi River. This difficult and sometimes deadly journey is known as the Trail of Tears.

"To Americans, Indians seemed to be an unfamiliar, alien people who occupied land that white settlers wanted. Some officials in the early years of the American republic, such as President George Washington, believed that the best way to solve this "Indian problem" was simply to "civilize" the Native Americans. The goal of this civilization campaign was to make Native Americans as much like white Americans as possible by encouraging them to convert to Christianity, learn to speak and read English, and adopt European-style economic practices such as the individual ownership of land and other property (including, in some instances in the South, African slaves). In the southeastern United States, many Choctaw, Chickasaw, Seminole, Creek and Cherokee people embraced these customs and became known as the "Five Civilized Tribes."

"Indian removal took place in the Northern states as well. In Illinois and Wisconsin, for example, the bloody Black Hawk War in 1832 opened to white settlement millions of acres of land that had belonged to the Sauk, Fox and other native nations.

"But their land, located in parts of Georgia, Alabama, North Carolina, Florida and Tennessee, was valuable, and it grew to be more coveted as white settlers flooded the region. Many of these whites yearned to make their fortunes by growing cotton, and they did not care how "civilized" their native neighbors were: They wanted that land and they would do almost anything to get it. They stole livestock; burned and looted houses and towns; and squatted on land that did not belong to them.

"Andrew Jackson had long been an advocate of what he called "Indian removal." As an Army general, he had spent years leading brutal campaigns against the Creeks in Georgia and Alabama and the Seminoles in Florida–campaigns that resulted in the transfer of hundreds of thousands of acres of land from Indian nations to white farmers.

"The law required the government to negotiate removal treaties fairly, voluntarily and peacefully: It did not permit the president or anyone else to coerce Native nations into giving up their land. However, President Jackson and his government frequently ignored the letter of the law and forced Native Americans to vacate lands they had lived on for generations. In the winter of 1831, under threat of invasion by the U.S. Army, the Choctaw became the first nation to be expelled from its land altogether. They made the journey to Indian territory on foot (some "bound in chains and marched double file," one historian writes) and without any food, supplies or other help from the government.

"The Indian-removal process continued. In 1836, the federal government drove the Creeks from their land for the last time: 3,500 of the 15,000 Creeks who set out for Oklahoma did not survive the trip.

"By 1838, only about 2,000 Cherokees had left their Georgia homeland for Indian territory. President Martin Van Buren sent General Winfield Scott and 7,000 soldiers to expedite the removal process. Scott and his troops forced the Cherokees into stockades at bayonet point while whites looted their homes and belongings. Then, they marched the Indians more than 1,200 miles to Indian territory. Whooping cough, typhus, dysentery, cholera and starvation were epidemic along the way, and historians estimate that more than 5,000 Cherokees died as a result of the journey.

"It is recognized that 4,000 Cherrokees, 3,000 Seminoles, 3,500 Chickasaws and 5,000 Choctaws died along the trails to the new Indian lands, for a total of over 15,500 souls. Many of these estimates did not include Black slaves so the numbers are probably largely understated. Thus, Olga's 5,000 victims are compared to 15,500 victims. Humm…

"I rest my case. By 1840, tens of thousands of Native Americans had been driven off their land in the southeastern states and forced to move beyond the Mississippi to Indian Territory. The federal government promised that their new land would remain unmolested forever, but as the line of white settlement pushed westward, Indian country shrank and shrank. In 1907, Oklahoma became a state and the state was sovereign. The Indian Territory was gone for good.

"As seen, all areas can be bloodthirsty, cruel and barbaric."

Olga converted to Christianity, leading most of the country to becoming Christian. In the 950's Olga went to Constantinople. While there, she converted to Christianity, being baptized by the Patriarch (the highest figure in the Eastern Church). The Roman Emperor Constantine VII himself was her godfather. This was a huge risk on her part, as Christianity was as yet a minority religion in her home country.

Despite her urgings, her son refused to convert, although he did not oppose the new religion. She apparently had a huge influence, however, on her grandson Vladimir the Great. In 988 he made Christianity the official religion of the Kievan Rus (modern day Russia). She became a Saint and was officially equated to the Apostles.

In 1547, the Orthodox Church named Olga of Kiev as a Saint, equal to the apostles, one of only five women ever honored in this way.

Olga's rule over Kievan Rus officially lasted until her son reached his full age. Having grown up, Svyatoslav preferred to spend most of his time abroad, organizing military campaigns in order to widen and strengthen the borders of his state.

Olga, left in charge of the internal policies of Kievan Rus, became known for establishing the system of tribute gathering, which is sometimes considered to be the first legal tax system in Eastern Europe. She ordered the creation of centers of trade and taxation. The lands subjugated to Kiev were divided into administrative units, which were controlled by the Prince's representatives. Olga set fixed amounts of tributes, with a detailed schedule for their gathering.

Princess Olga is also thought to have been the initiator of the first stone city building in Kievan Rus, especially in the cities of Kiev, Novgorod and Pskov.

One of the most well-known among Olga's actions was her conversion to Christianity. She was one of the first to bring this religion to the pagan society of Kievan Rus. According to the Primary Chronicles, Olga was baptized in Constantinople either in 955 or 957. Her son Svyatoslav was a Viking who didn't support his mother's decision and was worried about losing the respect of the army because of Olga's new faith. Apparently, she had a big influence on her grandson, Vladimir the Great, who in 988 made Christianity the official religion of Kievan Rus.

In 957 Olga paid an official visit to the Byzantine emperor, Constantine VII, in Constantinople. Presumably, the negotiations didn't bring the expected results, since the historical records describe a cold greeting for the Byzantine ambassadors during their return visit to Kiev.

Western European sources mention that in 959 Olga sent her ambassadors to Otto I, the Emperor of the Roman Empire, asking them to appoint an archbishop and priests to serve in her country. The chronicle accuses the Princess's envoys of lying, but details in conflicting historical records make it difficult to say whether Olga was sincere in her request or not. The Emperor's bishop, Adalbert of Magdeburg, having spent some time in Kievan Rus, decided that all his efforts to develop Christianity in the country were in vain. On his way back to Italy all his companions were killed by Svyatoslav's allies, and Adalbert himself barely survived.

At the time the Christian church was not yet divided into Roman and Greek branches. The separation officially took place in 1054, though in fact it had began a long time before that. Olga's attempts to build connections with both the Byzantine and Roman Emperors, the highest church authorities, are assessed differently. She either hesitated about which to choose, or conducted a forward-looking policy of bringing pressure on Constantinople, in order to gain the most beneficial positions in the Eastern Christian Church.

It is difficult to say when Svyatoslav began his full reign; though up to 959 both Byzantine and Western European records name Olga as the main ruler of Kievan Rus. Apparently, Svyatoslav shared power with his mother, Olga, until her death

CHAPTER 39

Vladimir the Great

Vladimir I, Grand Prince of Kiev and of all Russia, was an outstanding political figure. During his rule, Christianity was adopted in Russia. He ruled through 1028 and died that year.

Vladimir I, called Vladimir the Great, was born around 956. His father died in 972. Vladimir was the youngest of three sons. According to legend, his mother Malusha was a housekeeper for Vladimir's grandmother, Olga. Despite the family's relatively high status in the court, Malusha was a slave. Vladimir spent his childhood with his grandmother, Olga; by the time he was born, she was one of the first in Kievan Rus to have been baptized into the Orthodox Christianity. This proved to be of great importance later, when Vladimir had to choose a new religion for Russia.

Following Svyatoslav's death, an internecine war broke out between his potential successors. At that time, Vladimir was Prince of Novgorod (a city in the northern part of ancient Russia). The eldest son, Yaropolk, was Prince of Kiev. He was a very overbearing man who wanted to rule all of Russia. He expelled Vladimir from Novgorod, but he was forced to flee to Scandinavia and the Vikings. There, he began to muster an army to retake the throne from Yaropolk.

In 980, Vladimir besieged Kiev. He lured Yaropolk out, supposedly for negotiations, and then killed him. Yaropolk's wife became a concubine in Vladimir's harem. After Yaropolk's death, Vladimir had no other rivals for the throne — middle brother Oleg had died in 977. He became the independent sovereign of the entire Kievan Rus.

The new Prince of Kiev took steps to move the country back towards paganism. He erected a temple in the capital displaying idols of six major Slavic pagan gods. He also introduced the practice of human sacrifice. The shift towards paganism is assumed to have been a response to his rival brother, Yaropolk, who was known to favor Christianity. At the time, Vladimir was a zealous pagan. He was infamous as a vindictive and bloodthirsty warrior. He was also known as a libertine, for having five wives and some 800 concubines.

Vladimir was an expert commander. During his reign, Russia's borders were well-protected. The Prince of Kiev managed to subdue hostile neighboring tribes. He also undertook a successful campaign against the Poles, Latvians and Bulgars. As a result of these campaigns, the Kievan Rus made significant territorial gains.

But Russia's main struggle in the second half of the 10th century was the adoption of a single, monotheistic religion. The move was intended to unite the people of the country, and strengthen the international renown of the Kievan Rus as no longer a wild, barbaric country.

According to legend, Vladimir 1 had to choose between three religions: Christianity, Islam and Judaism. It was also important to decide what kind of Christianity was better for Russia: The so-called Latin Orthodox — Catholicism — or the Eastern Orthodox.

When neighboring nations heard about Prince Vladimir's intention to adopt a national religion, they sent ambassadors to persuade the Prince to adopt their faith. Vladimir listened carefully to them all.

The very first messengers came from the Volga Bulgars, who had already accepted Islam. But Vladimir saw their prohibition laws as a strain on the Russian soul. The ambassadors of the Western Catholic Christians also failed, because their faith had been rejected once already by Vladimir's ancestors. Judaism was rejected as "the religion that did not even help the Jews to keep their own land." Vladimir finally chose Eastern Byzantine Christianity. For many decades, Russia and Byzantium had close political and commercial relations.

The Prince demanded to marry Anna, a sister of the Byzantine Emperors, Basil II and Constantine VIII; or else he would attack Constantinople. The Emperors agreed, but demanded the baptism of the Prince in return, because their sister was only to marry a man of the same religion. Vladimir agreed to the conditions. The Byzantines sent Anna to Korsun with priests. There, Vladimir and his warriors were baptized by the Bishop of Korsun. Vladimir and Anna then married according to Christian tradition.

At that time, the major power centers of the Rus were Kiev in south central Russia, Saint Petersberg, Lake Ladoga (near Saint Petersburg), Novgorod (about 100 miles south of Saint Petersburg) and Moscow.

CHAPTER 40

Anna Porphyrogenita (Vladimir's Anna)

Anna Porphyrogenita (Vladimir's Anna) had a profound effect on the Eastern Orthodox religion. She was descended from a Viking family that gave her pedigree in both Scandanavia and Rus. She effectively converted the Rus to Christianity but also changed their tastes in the humanities, the arts and many other aspects of their lives. Anna had lived under the Italian influence and understood it well.

When she was shipped off to Constantinople, she carried a retinue of priests and nobles and these had princes and personal attendants that were also believers of the Italian renaissance. She had to make a choice of either Catholicism or Eastern Orthodoxy. Constantine and eastern Rus power centers had more or less made up their minds which path the Rus should take. Constantinople I, her husband, announced that his empire would be Eastern Orthodox. Some have been contesting that for a millennium but it is obvious that the decision continues.

Of course, this ignores 1453, the year that Mamet razed Constantinople and assumed power there for the Ottomans. The disintegrating Eastern Roman Empire supplanted the rites and attachments in trade as all the institutions became eastern Orthodox. The various Rus enclaves and power centers became combined to constitute the state of Russia and incorporated all the culture of that religion.

From this we conclude that a large number of Rus nobility were well versed in and were believers in the Catholic Italian way. Eastern Orthodoxy soon reached from Constantinople across European Russia to the Volga in the east. East of that, there lay Siberia, an enormous territory. Orthodoxy counted not only the number of adherents but also the number of square miles. Beyond the Volga, Islam fought to be the dominant religion. The fight still continues into modern times.

It is often said that 'Colonization is the Essence of Russian History'.

When Vladimir returned to Kiev, he ordered the destruction of the temple's pagan idols. On September 1, 988, Vladimir gathered the citizens of Kiev on the banks of the Dnieper River. They were all solemnly baptized. This year is considered to be the official date of the baptism of Russia. This baptism was accompanied by the establishment of the church hierarchy. Russia became a metropolis of the Patriarchate of Constantinople.

In Kiev, the baptisms passed peacefully. But in Novgorod, about 150 miles south of St. Petersburg, the second greatest city in Russia after Kiev, the people rebelled. This uprising was suppressed with troops, but the old pagan cult would continue to be practiced in Russia for centuries.

Vladimir made great contributions to the development of Russian cultural and social life. During his reign, literacy began to spread across the Kievan Rus, with Byzantines and Bulgarians as teachers. Under Vladimir I, large-scale stone construction projects began, and the foundations of church art and architecture were laid.

In the last years of his life, Vladimir likely intended to name his beloved son Boris as successor. His two oldest sons, revolted against their father in 1014. Vladimir imprisoned his elder son and was readying for war with Yaroslav.

Unfortunately, Vladimir I suddenly fell ill and died on July 15, 1015.

Historians estimate that Vladimir had around 800 concubines, and a number of wives. In 995, Vladimir divided the Kievan Rus for inheritance, to be ruled among all his sons. Historians believe that this was a fatal mistake on Vladimir's part, which led to civil war and the fragmentation of the Kievan Rus into three separate kingdoms.

Vladimir stands as a central figure in Russian history. The Orthodox Church named him "Holy" for introducing Christianity to the country. Among his people, he earned the name "Great" for his rulership. He became Vladimir the Great.

CHAPTER 41

Pre-Russian Rus

Vladimir apparently wanted to unite the people under one religion, so around 988 he sent envoys to examine the major religions. His options for consideration were Islam, Judaism, the Catholic Christianity of Western Europe and the Orthodox Christianity of Eastern Europe.

The story of Vladimir's choosing Orthodox Christianity is part legend, part fact. According to the tradition, Vladimir didn't like the dietary restrictions of Islam and Judaism. Catholic Christianity was all right, but what impressed the grand prince was the dazzling worship his ambassadors described, seeing the great Cathedral of Hagia Sophia in Constantinople: "We knew not whether we were in heaven or on earth, for surely there is no such splendor or beauty anywhere."

This unlikely marriage lead to great changes for Kievan Rus. The kingdom was allied with the Byzantine Empire and, with Anna as his religious adviser, Vladimir rejected paganism and began to Christianize the people. This was the beginning of the Russian Orthodox Church, a religion that now has an estimated 150 million adherents worldwide. This is why Vladimir's Anna became "the Godmother of Orthodoxy."

Rus areas in those days were mainly independent. They are sometimes referred to as Variagians. They traded mostly up and down the Volga region. The Vikings thereby established links among the tribes. The growth of Rus tribes in about 300 and the Byzantine or Eastern Roman Empire was breaking up.

The Vikings were a weak glue holding them together somewhat. The results cemented these tribes into a nation, Russia. Before this date, the Rus tribes were looked upon as separate tribes, but afterward, they began to look at themselves as Russians. Their culture was similar to that of the Vikings. The Rus and Vikings often collaborated in establishing trade routes and both frequently established joint armies for their marauding attacks. History eventually evolved into this nation state of Russia.

These Ukrainians and Russians had been Vikings, or Norsemen who went eastwards and southwards through what is now Russia, Belarus and Ukraine, mainly in the ninth and tenth centuries.

Initially, they engaged in piracy and trade, navigating through the waterways. These Varangians first settled in on Lake Ladoga, then moved southward to Novgorod and eventually reaching Kiev. The Primary Chronicle claims that a Varangian, or Viking, named Rurik first established himself in Novgorod, located in modern Russia in about 860 before moving south.

The chronicle names him as the progenitor of the Rurik Dynasty. The Rus tribes or power centers had a profound effect on the formation of Russia by the Vikings. This was politically true, it was militarily true, it was culturally true and it was economically true. The eastern trading territory for the Vikings moved ahead and expanded.

The Vikings have generally been credited with the founding of Kievan Rus. According to the *Russian Primary Chronicle*, Kiev was founded by prince Oleg of Kiev, a Varangian prince, about 880 moving the capital from Novgorod to Kiev.

The Varangian Guard in Istanbul was composed primarily of Vikings and Scandinavians for the first 100 years. The guard began to see increased inclusion of Anglo-Saxons after the successful invasion of England by the Normans. In 1088 a large number of Anglo-Saxons and Danes emigrated to the Byzantine Empire by way of the Mediterranean.

One source has more than 5000 of them arriving in 235 ships. Those who did not enter imperial service settled on the Black Sea coast, but those who did became so vital to the Varangians that the Guard was commonly called the Anglo-Varangians from that point. In this capacity they fought in Sicily against the Normans.

The Varangians relied on a long axe as their main weapon, although they were often skilled swordsmen, were adept with knives, and expert archers as well. In some sources they are described as mounted. The guard kept close to Constantinople. It probably found barracks in the palace complex.

Furthermore, they were the only element of the army to successfully defend part of Constantinople during the Fourth Crusade. Of the role of the guard, then composed of the English and Danes, it is said, "the fighting was very violent and there was hand to hand fight with axes and swords, the assailants mounted the walls and prisoners were taken on both sides."

Although the Guard was apparently disbanded after the city's capture in 1204, there are some indications that it was revived either by the Empire of Nicaea or by the Palaeologid emperors themselves, though it is not likely that they lasted too long. In Russia, Varangian remained a synonym for Swedes and Vikings until the late sixteenth century.

The duties and purpose of the Varangian Guard were similar—if not identical to—the services provided by the Kievans. The Varangians served as the personal bodyguard of the emperor, swearing an oath of loyalty to him; they had ceremonial duties as retainers and acclaimers and performed some police duties, especially in cases of treason and conspiracy.

The Varangian Guard was only used in battle during critical moments, or where the battle was most fierce. Contemporary Byzantine chroniclers note with a mix of terror and fascination that the "Scandinavians were frightening both in appearance and in equipment, they attacked with reckless rage and neither cared about losing blood nor their wounds." The description probably refers to berserker gang since this state of trance is said to have given them superhuman strength and no sense of pain from their wounds.

These mighty men with super strength lead to speculation of whether drugs were involved in the Warriers' spirit. I, myself have witnessed a man on drugs that kept about 6 police officers held at bay while he jumped on their police car, flattened the roof. He continued jumping up and down on the flattened roof while tackling the officers. They tussled on the ground and had a terrible problem subduing him while they tried to arrest him. He exhibited a drug "super strength."

When the Byzantine Emperor died, the Varangians had the unique right of running to the imperial treasury and taking as much gold and as many gems as they could carry, a procedure known in Old Norse as polutasvarf ("palace pillaging"). This privilege enabled many Varangians to return home as wealthy men, which encouraged even more Scandinavians to enlist in the Guard.

Unlike the native Byzantine guards so mistrusted by Basil II, the Varangian Guards' loyalties lay with the position of Emperor, not the man that sat on the throne. This was made clear in 969 when the guards failed to avenge the death by assassination of Emperor Nicephorus II. A servant had managed to call for the guards while the Emperor was being attacked, but when they arrived he was dead. They immediately knelt before the murderer and hailed him as the new Emperor. "Alive they would have defended him to the death."

Anna Porphyrogenita was the daughter of Byzantine Emperor Romanos II and the Empress Theophano. She was also the sister of Emperors Basil II Bulgaroktonos (The Bulgur Slayer) and Constantine VIII. Anna was a Porphyrogenita, a legitimate daughter born in the special purple chamber of the Byzantine Emperor's Palace. Anna's hand was considered such a prize that some theorize that Vladimir the Great became Christian just to marry her.

Anna did not wish to marry Vladimir and expressed deep distress on her way to her wedding. Grand Prince Vladimir was impressed by Byzantine religious practices; this factor, along with his marriage to Anna, led to his decision to convert to Eastern Christianity. Due to these two factors, Grand Prince Vladimir also began Christianizing his kingdom. By marriage to Grand Prince Vladimir, Anna became Grand Princess of Kiev, but in practice, she was referred to as Queen or Czarina, probably as a sign of her membership in the Imperial Byzantine House. Anna participated actively in the Christianization of Rus: she acted as the religious adviser of Vladimir and founded a few convents and churches herself.

Anna was a figure in preparing the Rus people for statehood. She died in 1011. To anchor a historical point in our past, Peter the Great died in 1725. This put about 714 years between their deaths. Her influence was great in bringing the Rus to statehood.

When a man named Temüjin was given the title of Genghis Khan in 1206, the Mongols were a recently united people, living in the northeast corner of Asia. By the time Genghis Khan died in 1227, they were sunning themselves on the shores of both the Black Sea and the Caspian Sea. By 1241 they were knocking at Vienna's door, and they remained the terror of Eastern Europe for the rest of the century. The Mongols claimed the largest consolidated land empire in history. Seemingly the only way to keep them out was to put the Himalayas between you and them. Many historians believe their power stemmed from an incredibly simple innovation: the saddle and the stirrup.

The saddle and stirrup are believed by central Asians to have been invented and developed by Genghis Kahn and his hordes. Museums in central Asia and Mongola usually display these items to substantiate these claims.

No one knows when the saddle and stirrup were first invented, but it was a boon to any military that used it. Even the simplest of stirrups, a leather loop, let mounted soldiers ride longer distances and stay mounted on their horses during battle. The military success of the forebears of the Cossacks is often attributed to two loops of leather. It was the same with the Goths and the Huns where the Vikings were considered the Goths and the Huns preceded the Vikings. Some believe the stirrup even shifted the balance of power in Europe from foot soldiers to mounted knights

In 2016, archaeologists at the Center of Cultural Heritage of Mongolia unearthed the remains of a Mongolian woman dating back to the 10th century AD. Along with sturdy leather boots and some changes of clothes, she was buried with a saddle and metal stirrups described as in such good condition that they could still be used today. The stirrups are one continuous thick piece of metal with an open loop for a saddle strap on the top and a wide, flattened, and slightly rounded footrest. The stirrups had to be comfortable and tough, because Mongols used them to ride in a way no one else rode. This would have allowed the rider unprecedented mobility.

A general of the Song Dynasty (960-1279) described the Mongols riding long distances standing up in the saddle, with "the main weight of the body upon the calves or lower part of the leg with some weight on the feet and ankles." The stirrups were meant to keep the rider centered and upright in even the most tumultuous situations. They hung from a saddle that was made of wood and had a high back and front. These, supplemented with endless hours of practice, gave a Mongol rider unprecedented stability. The rider could maintain hands-free balance on the horse while the horse twisted and turned and while the rider himself turned in the saddle. A fluidly mobile rider could then use his hands to shoot arrows in any direction as he rode. It also kept the rider stable while undergoing violent maneuvers in the heat of battle.

The new state of Russia transcends the name Rus. Although we make changes in the political names, it remains the same physical state.

Russia consists of plains from their western borders. These are nominally flat until the Urals are reached. Then, fertile farm land continues beyond the Urals. These are little more than rolling hills onward toward the Pacific. Mountains of the past had military significance; but in these modern days with aircraft and satellites and with nuclear weapons, the mountains as defense barriers have probably lost their protective value.

Other means of protection must be developed. In the south of these regions lies the steppes and the black earth strips of two to three hundred miles width. In ancient times, this stretch ran from the Atlantic to the Pacific Ocean but farms now restrict a large part of this. In any event, nomads riding horses falling from the great plains of Eurasia can no longer surprise their enemies. This exposure to invasions across the west has attracted invaders from the Teutonic Knights to the armies of Hitler.

The peasants included a vast majority of the people. The role of these was essentially that of slaves in the west. The task of peasants was to produce food, labor, pay taxes and serve in the military. The serfs were bound to his little patch of ground and they had to live there for all their lives. The gentry lived far superior lives but they had no real power.

The Czar could change that at any moment, there was no constriction in law. In fact, for the serfs, there was precious little law. Alexander II gave an emancipation law in 1855 but that was essentially ignored, naturally. It was treated somewhat as did bootleg and the prohibition laws in the US. Did I say, Alexander was assassinated for his efforts?

Not much has changed since Russia is now ruled by a strong-man, through Russian oligarchs.

CHAPTER 42

Where do Archaeologists work?

Archaeologists work in a wide variety of settings as employed by federal and state agencies, museums, historic sites, universities, engineering companies and as consultants. Many work in cultural resource management, they direct field and lab work and generate reports describing surveys and excavations. Many are engaged in education. They share their work through sites, tours, publications and exhibits.

Archaeologists do more than dig. They also work in governmental agencies and are responsible for managing, protecting and interpreting the use of public lands. Working in museums, there are archaeological parks or historical cites. They often manage artifacts and collections. Some are in education and work as administrators. They teach undergraduate and graduate courses. They are active researchers and encourage funding of projects. They oversee the analysis and interpretation of projects and publish their results in books, journals, and scholarly papers as well as popular publications to make their research available to the public.

It must have been obvious by this time that there were a lot of problems I had with the interpretations we were making. We have a tendency of following the leader or the project manager and assigning success to them alone. An example of this was after the NASA 'man on the moon' project. I was consulting for an aerospace company that had tasking by a prime contractor. The management made a celebration for those who worked on the project. I really felt good about myself.

Afterwards, I thought about it and I realized the company had about 5,000 people that worked on the project and their part was not a major one. The total number of workers on the project must have been from 20 to 100 thousands. How could I feel so good? It was probably like the pyramid builders. The little Egyptian must have stood back, looked at the crowds celebrating and felt the same thing. Both were monumental accomplishments in any event.

I believe a man does not do these things because he is promised riches and glory, nor is he motivated by having a job and eating. He does this because our wiring demands it. Our nervous system demands no less. The same thing can be said about our patent and copyright laws. I believe we do not invent because someone waves rewards toward us. The intellectual property rights in any event is usually rewards to the manager class. It is seldom sent to the technically responsible individual. In fact, it is an inhibitor to spreading such property. These are hung up in the courts so long that an argument is made that it is a net loss to the economy.

CHAPTER 43

Russia

I once had an opportunity to motor from Minsk to Saint Petersburg (or the former Leningrad before it was renamed after the Soviet fall).

I went alone on this trip to Russia. I was happy in my work and the archaeological education and the opportunity that provided. I was extremely lucky in getting the trip while announcing a dig to an archaeological society meeting. The society had reviewed a paper I wrote and wanted it presented at this particular meeting.

The trip traced the historical invasion route between Russia and the West. Napoleon followed it to Moscow and back; The Vikings followed it in their trade routes and their later marauding trips. In addition, Hitler thrust into Russia by followed it before the Germans were decisively driven back from Moscow.

The drive confirmed the land to be flat all the way with hardly a hill more than a hundred feet high across the whole of Europe, even to Saint Petersburg on the shores of the Baltic Sea. This remained true up to the Urals (but those mountains are in Asian Siberia). The map showed the road system of Europe and the west to be filled with primary roads. The number of good roads then drops significantly across East Germany and even more so across Poland. The map of Russian Europe; however, only shows a handful of good roads, in marked contrast to even eastern Europe's development.

After passing through northern Europe and part of East Germany, our transportation arrived in East Berlin and we checked into the hotel.

The bus was to carry us into West Berlin the next morning, then back to East Berlin for another day. We strolled through East Berlin that night. It was a forbidding, dark place. Vopo's (East German Police) or the local police were often apparent. They were very formal and suspicious in their attitudes. There was unease in strolling here.

As our transport neared the border into West Berlin the next morning, there were a large number of Vopo's. Everyone was warned not to take a picture or the police would take the camera. The guides warned them not to look directly at the police nor take their picture. Do everything exactly as they say.

After a considerable wait in a busy bus courtyard, a Vopo came aboard with dark uniform and a machine gun across his chest. He starred menacingly at each passenger. Then there was a discussion with the guide. Satisfied, he waved us on. After a wait, we were waved through the famous Checkpoint Charley into the American Zone of West Berlin. The West Berlin police looked at the papers of the guide, and then waved us on with a sour smile.

The contrast between East and West Berlin was palpable as we saw West Berlin flooded with people busily shopping on Saturday. The traffic rushed this way and that; people crowded into the stores and across the streets in their summer's delight. Children scurried around and played with each other. They laughed, played, scurried around, and acted as the West has come to expect on a pleasant day of sunshine.

East Berlin, on the other hand was in sharp contrast as the group and I returned and strolled through the city. East Berlin was behind the Wall where a hundred yards of no-man's land had been cleared and watchtowers constructed to hold police with machine guns.

When they returned to East Berlin, the mood of the few people on the streets was somber. The traffic was sparse with a few busses and trucks and even fewer private automobiles. The heart of pre-war Berlin was the wide boulevard, Unter den Linden, named for the stately Linden trees marching along the street and sidewalk. This street remains the heart of East Berlin, but it was especially forlorn and even foreboding. This was more evidence at the street ending, stopping abruptly as it did in the no-man's land in front of the Brandenburg Gate where tank-traps, barbed wire, guard towers, and other military paraphernalia appeared.

Many police boxes dotted the sidewalks along the street. The people were few and they were taciturn, sullen. Clearly, the better part of them had fled and then swelled the streets as West Berliners on the other side of the Wall. The Easterners even continued to rush the wall from time to time. They are summarily shot in their flight.

These sullen, unsmiling, unhappy faces were the rule across the whole Eastern Bloc. They were so foreign to those in the West! It was hard to believe it could be so.

The roads across the East were all paved. They were reasonably good in East Berlin and Poland. They looked good in Russia but were like a washboard giving a malaise like seasickness to the traveler. The traffic ranged from very little to none. Trucks were on the road occasionally but there were very few cars. The cars across the East looked the same. These were very small, four person vehicles. The body appeared to be from a plastic mold. They looked so very cheap. A high percentage of them appeared beside the road with the drivers' legs extending from the hood. In fact, that would make an appropriate logo for their producers.

The borders in the East Bloc were tedious, each requiring about an hour to clear customs. Otherwise, the borders were not difficult. During this time, only a bus or two, a few trucks and several automobiles arrived. The border traffic was very sparse.

The group had passed Calais, Arnhiem, Hannover, and Berlin; it then crossed into Poland at the Ober River, and continued to Posnan and Warsaw. The Poles appear distinctly different peoples from the Germans in their attitudes, language, and the way they react to one another and even in appearance. These Roman Catholic people filled the village churches on Sunday morning as I and the group passed. They rebuilt Warsaw with 10-12 story apartments stretched to the horizon. These seem better built than those we saw in Russia.

The front of the hotel where we stayed in Warsaw revealed a strange sight. About 20 Gypsies in bright costume were on the street harassing Poles and tourists alike. They were dirty; cigarettes dangled from their lips; they were hostile to the passersby; and they had unlikable ways as they begged and crowded around people.

Violent arguments erupted between them and the Poles as they pandered for anything they could get. They were ugly, crass, and ill mannered and most likely were breaking the law, but they remained for hours and a number were in the same place when our group left the next day. I even saw some in Russia. The police state appeared to have no better solution for these renegades than the West.

Warsaw evoked visions of Chopin and the wartime ghetto, representing perhaps man's apogee and perigee. The razed ghetto was a grassy park with a monument; the holocaust and Warsaw's role was but a concept existing in memory and within dusty blue-jacketed books. Our group was later taken to a music conservatory for a private Chopin piano recital we had arranged. Each person was lost within the self; Chopin's music is also but a private thing. Perhaps this, like the ghetto, was real and those rising apartments were only ephemeral images with no solidity. Who will know of them a hundred years from now? But, Chopin will survive.

Beyond Warsaw, the woods became deep and this deep forestation with occasional fields continued right across Russia and across much of Scandinavia. Horses appeared as work animals in Eastern Poland with the rubber-tired carts characteristic of that area; these are anachronisms and gave the appearance of another time.

We crossed into Russia at Brest, of Brest-Litovsk Treaty fame, on the Vistula River. The road stretched on to Minsk and later Smolensk on the way to Moscow. The Nazis completely overran these cities in the great Patriotic War as the Russians called it. Of 40,000 people in Smolensk before the invasion, 37 remained after the war, the tourists were assured, although I doubted this. The Soviets have built a new city on the ruins of the old. Ten-to-twenty story apartment buildings were in all directions in this city, now of 200,000. Many restorations had been made of parks, monuments and museums.

The most majestic of all the restorations was the Assumption Cathedral on a high cliff near central Smolensk. A service was underway when the group visited it. The interior was one of the most magnificent in the world with elaborate golden filigree housing icons and religious artifacts behind the altar.

A chanting chorus of the Russian Orthodox Church was a characteristic part of the service. In this instance, it consisted of four female and three male voices. The choir continued the chant throughout the service. This is one of the most beautiful, haunting and stirring rituals in religion. The participants, like most the group saw in Russia, were old women with head-covers making the curious Orthodox genuflection of the cross; in the Orthodox religion, one makes a cross from the right horizontal side.

The priests were young men in their thirties with a lesser number of older men. No one had a real explanation for the anomaly of these young priests. However, someone pointed out these had probably been appointed by the secret police to manage the religion. This sounded plausible.

The burdens of history weigh heavily on this whole region. During the war, the German Army occupied it from the Baltic in the North almost to the Black Sea in the South. The army's siege of the suburbs of Saint Petersburg lasted for three years, bringing the city to starvation.

Meanwhile, the German military line stretched south; it reached the outskirts of Moscow, and continued down through much of the Ukraine toward the Black Sea. The fighting was furious reaching its crescendo in 1943 south of Smolensk in Orel and Belgorod near Kharkov where it is said two million Soviets and two million Germans fought a massive battle with tanks arrayed with only several feet separation along the massive front. The battle determined the fate of the German invasion, and ultimately, that of East Europe.

The misery and hardships along this occupation line were incredible. This was especially true in the depths of winter where, as the guide said, the winter is as cold to Russians as it is to Germans. The Scythe of Death swung along the mighty arc of the Nazi's eastern thrust; then, the grim work was repeated as the Red Army swept west along the same historical route. This route is often red with the blood of marching armies and their victims. The enormity of the events reduced the last few years to a moment that was palpable to those in the region.

The tourists at this time trailed the Intourist guides through the parks and past the memorials. Surprisingly, German speakers were more vocal than anyone else in announcing they were in the battle or their brothers, uncles or fathers were part of the Wehrmacht in the region. Someone asked the Intourist guide whether this was offensive. She confided. "We respect all our visitors, but we believe the Germans should have the courtesy to remain silent." This native of Orel, however, remained even-handed to all.

Byelorussia is the province containing Minsk. Smolensk is in Russia between Minsk and Morcow. Since byelo means white in Russian, the province was once called White Russia. The province known as the Russian Federation, abutted it and then continued from the Byelorussian border north through Moscow and further north through Saint Petersburg, south down to the Ukraine and east to the Urals, 800 miles east of Moscow.

The Ural Mountains run north and south above the Caspian Sea and form the demarcating boundary between Europe and Asia. This is at the longitude of Eastern Iran. The European boundary then follows along the Ural River south until it empties into the Caspian Sea. Then, it runs back to the oil city of Baku on the western shore of the Caspian. It continues west over the Caucasus Mountains from Baku to the Black Sea, and then across this sea until it reaches its western-most limit at Istanbul, Turkey. Thus, Europe reaches well over a thousand miles east beyond Istanbul. When considering the whole of Europe, it is surprising what a low percentage of the land mass Western Europe really is.

Europe had become illusory as a continent; after the end of the war, the familiar Free Europe contracted toward the Atlantic while the rest of the continent receded behind the Eastern curtain. One easily forgets that a major part, although out of mind, was within the Soviet Union. A full 60 percent of the European land mass was behind the Iron Curtain, although only 10 percent was within the East European Satellites.

Thus, European Russia made up over half of the European land mass. When measured in terms of population, 44 percent of the Europeans lived behind the Iron Curtain and 18 percent lived in the Satellites. The Soviets accounted for 26 percent of the Europeans. The openness of news and travel, the commercial and cultural interchange in the West, and general interest led Westerners to think of the area as including only Western Europe. However, that was not the case. Europe is the whole continent with one social continuum and historical centrality, and this Europe extended to the Urals. Our concepts of Europe, however, do not usually extend nearly this far.

The Russian Federation or the Russian SSR held the Muscovy principalities of the early times. Ivan and Peter brought the Boyars and Metropolitans of those regions into their dominion leading Peter to proclaim it his empire. The empire expanded into Byelorussia.

Later, the Ukraine was absorbed. Traditional Slavic Russia consisted of these three provinces, having a similarity of history and peoples. This seemed to be true although many Ukrainians considered themselves unique from the Russians and a subjugated people; it seems it is the nature of man to grasp for a sovereignty of his own.

The people of the three are Slav so have a common lineage, appearance, and language. They had preference in the government, from the heart of the officer corps in the Army and Navy and generally constituted the elite of the empire. The people appeared very fair, perhaps as fair and blonde as any in Europe.

The young women were often quite beautiful. Their older age often brought overweight and sloth but this surely reflected their greasy meat-and-potato fare and the harshness of their lives. Many were quite handsome, even with old age. Their appearance must have given Hitler pause because they appeared as blonde and Aryan as his German models and certainly, they were far more so than he and many other Germans.

The group then continued beyond Smolensk and the famous Russian battlefield at Borodino toward Moscow. Russia then had enormous fields surrounded by light forests where heavy farm machinery appeared. Mostly, the fields grew grain and occasionally corn and potatoes. No such truck farms with vegetables evidenced themselves.

We entered Moscow in late afternoon. Moscow was a very large city with eight or nine million people, we were told. Public monuments to the last war were everywhere as they were in all Soviet cities. The outskirts had broad avenues with most of the buildings being 10-15 story apartments or offices. Traffic was far more prevalent in Moscow than the other cities. It consisted of numerous black government limousines, buses, electric trams, trucks and more of the cheap Soviet passenger cars. Traffic did not reach the level of that in the West with jams and delays. Neither Moscow nor Saint Petersburg seemed abandoned or eerie, as did the lesser cities of the East.

As we neared the center of Moscow, the streets became more twisting and turning. The ancient buildings were in restored condition and those used by high government officials were seen to be of high Western quality. These were concentric, spreading outward from the Kremlin. They sat along the Moscow River. The city had a surprising Near East Oriental look to it, like Istanbul; but one cannot quite put a finger on why. This historic city seemed strange, remote and exotic although Russia, in a sense, had been close to the center of European culture, literature, the arts, and history for centuries, yet it had been extremely remote at the same time.

CHAPTER 44

Red Square

It was late evening when we entered Red Square for the first time. Only a few scores of people were shuffling through the huge cobblestone plaza at such a late hour. The Square was an enormous open space on the opposite side of the walled Kremlin from the Moskva River. From the Square that is adjacent to the Kremlin, one could see the golden spires and domes of the Czarist Cathedrals rising above the walls, as well as the classical yellow and white Palaces.

The Kremlin had been the site of the Czars' crownings, their home, their seats of power, their place of worship, and the site of their entombment for centuries. The red brick Kremlin wall defined one side of Red Square. The word Kremlin means fortress in Russian and this, the most famous of all, clearly had been a fortress in the dim recesses of the past.

The main side of the rectangular Square ran along this twenty-foot wall; just behind it appeared the palaces inside the Kremlin. The subdued lighting from the side of the wall facing the Square played with the shadows high on the palace facades and columns, eaves and roofs. There was subtle lighting from behind the stately fir trees standing in a line along the red wall with neatly uniformed soldiers marching along the Kremlin wall. These walls and fir trees outlined the silhouettes on the wall or they suggested the Czar's silent soldiers guarding the shadows of history.

The Communists had placed large ruby-red lights on several spires in the Kremlin. Rather than remove these remarkable markers, they continued to shine as beacons that belong. One could rationalize these as markers for the 75 years of Communism and more recent history of Russian life.

The other side of the Square was GUMS, the block-long, state-owned department store, of sorts, which had developed from the marketplace on this site since ancient times. It was a single building housing hundreds of individual stores as it did in the past, a kind of glass-roofed, oriental market. At the far end of the Square was a dreary brick building with a spired clock tower.

The medieval St. Basil's Cathedral provided the drama of Red Square. It sat at the near end, at the entry to the Square. It was crowned with a spray of brightly colored, spiraling onion-shaped domes that were associated with the traditional Russian Orthodox Church. These were not exactly on top of the cathedral but seemed to reach almost to the ground; the cathedral itself was composed of these variegated domes, each with spiral stripes of different colors. The multicolored spirals were awash in the light of many electric beams placed high on the structure. This gorgeous, resplendent, exotic cathedral was a fantasy and set the fairyland tone of the entire Square.

I know this sounds like a travel odyssey as my group and I ogled at the exotic Russian seat of government. Well, that is what it is, a travel odyssey. This is describing something totally foreign to me. The architecture seems somewhere between an ancient fortress and golden cathedrals. The sight is through a lens never seen by me and it was so out of focus that it was baffling. At any rate, I will do the best I can to describe it.

Things have changed now but this was about 1970. Squatting next to the Kremlin wall was Lenin's Mausoleum of polished red granite. The smooth surfaces of this recent structure looked out of place in this Czarist setting. A sequence of fir trees stood guard all along the backlighted Kremlin wall and their silhouette softened the scene.

Young men in blue toy-soldier uniforms goose-stepped along the wall to relieve the other young guards at Lenin's tomb while the crowd silently watched. Above it all, many spires inside the Kremlin were crowned with internally lighted, ruby-red stars to represent the Communist regime and to complete the fantasy.

How Tolstoyan and classically Russian it seemed to us! Red Square and the Kremlin were a magical place at this hour. Only at night do the shadows of history haunt the Square and provide this magic.

The next day we returned to the Square. There was then a very different reality in the morning. The Square was a hard place then, with thousands of people eager and aggressive in their search for sights, wonders, and historical marvels. Now the great Square was stark. It coincided with mental images of dictators and commissars atop reviewing stands in bitter Mayday cold as the Red Army marched past; heavy tanks and vehicles that carried nuclear missiles punctuated their ranks. However, on this day, there were no marching armies.

The crowds were always multicolored, multinational, multiracial and polyglot; they represented a crossroads of the world's people. There were Russians who looked the same as those in the Moscow subway, schoolchildren, tourists from the soviet provinces; They were from Europe, Africa, Asia, America, the West in general; there were Mongolians in odd dress, Turkmen and Kazakhs from Kazakhstan, China, Japan, Ukraine, Byelorussian, East European, African, some in tribal dress, and on and on it went. There was no end to the fabulously varied dress of the visitors. Their tongues were strange and as exotic as their dress.

Parents with children ogled and scurried to see the changing of the guard. Criss-crossing these crowds, there was a line of people, several-abreast, stretching into Lenin's Tomb from a mile or two beyond the Square. Oddly, dozens of brides in white gowns with their grooms dotted the line and the square. They had a curious tradition of a civil wedding followed by a trooping through the tomb to review the body; they then drove to a viewpoint above the city by Moscow University.

A curious thing happened as crowds milled here and there. I had a little personal camera. All of a sudden some woman screamed at me. This person was obviously a Mongol. Many people visiting Red Square wear their national dress. This makes a very colorful crowd wandering through the Square.

The wall protecting the Kremlin was still the backdrop for posturing soldiers in neatly pressed uniforms and rifles with shiny bayonets. The Mongol Woman (if that is what she was) was becoming more and more aggressive. She had a strange tongue that I did not recognize at all. She yelled. She tried to yank my camera from me but I yanked back. I tried to ignore her but that was a chore.

Finally, I walked on and left her. She just meandered away and so did I. The guide that had been some distance away when this happened came up to me later. She did not want her image in a box, the guide explained. She thinks you are capturing her soul. You did the best thing, just walk away she said. I suspect that is not always easy to do.

It was times such as this that I always missed Julia the most. She would have loved the costumes and the fanciful outfits they wore. She would have loved the toy soldiers standing guard as they marched meaningfully along the wall. However, she was gone. She lived in New York and sometimes Los Angeles. I missed her but that phase of my life is over.

However, I still think of her. I loved her jaunty personality. I loved her humor. She even indicates that I thrill her sometimes. I still hear of her sometimes in trade magazines or through friends. I still call her occasionally and she appears to enjoy our long conversations. These are almost always about her business and what she had done recently.

I still love her. God, help me but I still get a thrill even when her name is mentioned. What can I do? I love her. We were meant for each other.

Red Square by night was a Czarist place where the only anomaly was Lenin's Tomb. However, by day, it was a Communist place, a beacon to the empire, much of which the Czarists captured and Saint Petersburg now ruled it. The might and size of that day's empire were beyond the dreams of the acquisitive Czars, even of Peter with his worldview.

The Russian Empire stood testimony to the dreams, political acumen and military adroitness of talented Russians who labored for more than three centuries to bring it about; and it remained a dynamic, expansionary world force even to that day. The Square, to the communists, symbolized this continuity of purpose, a bond that united the seemingly ephemeral and intangible Russian past with the ironclad reality of that day.

In truth, the symbol was even more faithful. It provided a bridge connecting the cruelty of Czarist expansionism with the starkness and Gulag misery of the Soviet system. The bridge connected the feudal serfdom, the near-slavery of the Russian peasant brought into this century with the subservience of that day's silent automatons, the citizens who bore the despotic weight. One could not escape the awful weight of history in Russia or the awesome responsibility of rationalizing the present with the future.

CHAPTER 45

Kremlin

Our group went on a tour of the Kremlin. Such tours combined walks past ancient palaces used for the present working government. Walks through Cathedral Square revealed the palaces and cathedrals used by the Czar through the times of Ivan, Peter, Catherine and into this century. The footsteps of history continue to ring through these seventy-two acres of land, sacred to the Russians.

Czarist power was centered here and now the Kremlin was the center of Communist power. Czarist palaces are now used for high government offices and diplomatic reception halls. The Kremlin also held the modern Palace of Congresses that hosts the sessions of the Supreme Soviet, the Communist Party Congresses, and even cultural events such as opera and ballet. As they walked, golden sunlight squinted off the many gold gilded domes of the cathedrals that gave them an unparalleled exotic beauty.

The Kremlin and Red Square epitomized and symbolized Communist Russia; they reflected the enormous power in the hands of a few while they simultaneously conjured up literary and cultural Russia that the Party wanted to exploit. This symbolism was orchestrated by the Party to imbue the perception in all people of the Russian historical continuum. It promoted the people to see as one the military dominance and rich history from the time of the early Czars through the current might of the Red Army and its recent history, from the glories of Russia's actual cultural history to those the Soviets would have liked people to believe. Red Square and the Kremlin were the focus of the Russian land empire that stretched from Lubek, West Germany, near the Atlantic Ocean, to the Pacific through eleven time zones. It ran from the North Arctic to the Iranian border in the South. This formed a contiguous whole unequaled in size through the history of acquisitive man's urge to build empires. The Kremlin and Red Square were symbols of the whole, the focus.

As we were to see, the magic was symbolic only. In reality, the empire was a throwback toward feudal times for its people. The reality began on the edge of Red Square, at GUMS, There, thousands of stalls were filled with such inferior products that they could not have been sold in any Western nation; probably, most of its wares could not even have been given away. Moreover, this was the Soviet Union's best for those without privilege.

Russia appeared to be a segmented society into those with privilege and those without. The Communist Party represented about seven percent of the population in the USSR. The privileged included many of these but certainly it was a small percentage. Many of the privileged were high government officials, cultural leaders, military leaders, those wearing the hero's mantle because it suited the Party, the family of many of these, and so forth. And, best of all for a few of the others, it included many who knew these people, were friends, or were friends of friends.

As with any severely rationed product, corruption and 'under-the-table-transactions' became imbedded in the system. The basics of life were the severely rationed products in the USSR. These included food, meat, housing, clothing, transportation, jobs, and a thousand more. This diverse and amorphous privileged social class inherited privilege from the Czar's aristocracy and nobility, while most of the remaining people were a vast unprivileged class.

If there were people between these two classes, they were not in evidence. The economic middle classes of Western Capitalism and the standard of living enjoyed by most Westerners of all classes appeared to be totally missing during all the travels in both the Soviet and East Bloc countries.

Many Russians did not see any relationship between the works and rhetoric of Communism and the harsh reality of the Soviet Union. The

Soviet Union totally conformed to this: it conformed to a reasonable man's expectations of collectivization, lack of incentives, economic mythology, and state sponsored lying and propaganda and more lying until no one including the state knew what the truth was nor recognized its importance. The Union conformed to the reasonable man's expectations from conspiring terrorists and saboteurs preaching Utopia, from contempt for law and impersonal justice, from generations of rapacious state actions, and from people supporting a Murder Machine.

The sins on the perpetrators of lies and deceit are magnified a thousand fold on those who believe without question, when a reasonable person can or should know. Gullibility in serious social matters carries the guilt of all the obscene crimes committed in its name. 'I didn't know' ceases to be a defense, but an allegation. The gods who gave us brains charged us with knowing.

Monuments of concrete and steel are important but what do they matter if a people loses its soul? Almost four generations had forsworn their souls, voluntarily and involuntarily, to the Soviet aberrations. How many hundreds of millions of people bought into or sacrificed their souls in this intellectual aberration and physical blood bath?

Why was this? All this was for an economic myth that could put spacecraft into orbit but could not house or feed its people. It could send armies, missiles, ships and submarines to terrorize the world but it could not feed its people. It told them they were proud but it robbed them of their souls. The Soviet Union was one vast prison house. They could harness prisoners to mighty projects, but a convict society is no credit to humanity or to itself.

The cities had only apartments and no houses. The apartments were inferior and crumbling from the time they were built. The housing accommodations placed grandparents, parents, and children in tiny 900-1000 square foot shabby apartments. When the city with its 10-15 story apartments ended, the countryside abruptly began with little to no transition as is found in the West.

The countryside had houses, these being similar-sized unpainted units. It is difficult not to call them hovels. These had outhouses and no running water. In fact, outhouses were in great abundance on the edge of Moscow, no more than ten miles from the Kremlin. Drinking water was more often than not provided by buckets drawn from public wells, often appearing every ten houses or so along a row of houses. Electricity was a welcome concession to modern times and appeared in all the houses between Brest on the Polish border and Saint Petersburg on the Baltic.

Television antennas were also prominent around the cities. Television seemed to be for propaganda only and bore little resemblance to that medium in the West. However, even colorful propaganda must have been a godsend in the stark realities of Soviet life.

About five to ten percent of the houses appeared to be log structures. They all appeared more than a hundred years old but that did not seem likely. The countryside had only these houses in the small villages with a mixture of apartments in larger villages.

Moscow dwellers had to stand for hours in line to attain the basic foodstuffs. Long lines were always in evidence at the doors to grocery stalls and at the kiosks and stalls outside on the sidewalk selling a single item such as potatoes, cabbages, melons, tomatoes, or other necessities. Russia was a basic meat-and-potatoes country with few of the food attractions of most of the world. This inconvenience in the thousand details of daily life permeated the existence and defined the routine of living. In a thousand ways, life in the Soviet Union was inferior, humiliating, and worthy of only a backward, remote, stagnant country that was hardly aware of life after the early- to mid-industrial revolution.

Buildings in the Soviet Union appeared modern from a distance. They were similar, with horizontal lines; balconies contributed to the horizontal parallel-lines aspect. This 'Soviet Apartment Architecture' was characteristic of most buildings in the USSR constructed in the last several decades. When examined even loosely, the materials were crumbling; the workmanship was unbelievably bad. One could hardly believe such poor quality was possible since one had never seen this in the West.

Buildings constructed in the last few years appeared ancient already. A rapid building program must have spawned this situation, one assumed. The concrete was precast and hauled to the construction site.

One could see but could hardly imagine the concrete beams that were flaking and had chunks falling out. Even the backyard work of amateurs in the West showed a quality far above this. The inferior workmanship and quality generally applied to most buildings in the Soviet Union.

Even most secondary monuments found in the countryside and out-of-the-way places were chipping and crumbling in a similar manner. It was difficult to believe these rickety complexes could survive even a nominal wind without squatting; and the mind refused to entertain even the thought of an earthquake.

In fact, when earthquakes did occur in the Caucasus and those were routine events, the buildings collapsed by the thousands. It was hard to avoid a conclusion that the extremely high death rates were caused by inferior construction.

One could not travel in Russia without experiencing the vastness and pervasiveness of the uniquely Russian Intourist organization. Tourists inevitably stayed in their hotels, ate in their restaurants, shopped in their facilities and saw the country under the tutelage of their guides. In the cities, many of these hotels were vast with 3000 rooms or more. Guards were at the entrances and often on each floor to prevent ordinary Russians from entering, so the tourists were close to being isolated to themselves. Foreign companies had built the major hotels under contract to the Soviets.

These were first-class buildings, totally at odds with the other buildings. These magnified the enormous discrepancy between Soviet and Western construction. A question jumped out to the visitors: how can foreign managers use the same native materials and workers to achieve a superior product?

During the travel, meals were served in major dining rooms, usually buffet style. A large number of traveling strangers on tight schedules jostled for position so a barracks and siege mentality quickly developed. The drinking water had to be avoided throughout Russia; even bottled mineral water had visible contaminants and was suspect. The dishes were wet, greasy or dirty more often than not. No one was satisfied with the food. It was greasy; it consisted mostly of lots of pork and potatoes; there were very few fancy or interesting dishes beyond the basics. The finicky travelers often chose to eat only bread with coffee or tea. Even those who are not so finicky often chose the same.

The Russian service personnel sometimes were nice, even extraordinarily nice. In most cases, however, they were sullen, taciturn. They had a chip on their shoulder and scowled or barked at the travelers. They appeared to dislike travelers as a class but then seemed no better to one another.

Such a mass of people in a hurry does not bring out the best in one, however; this can easily be observed by asking directions in a place like Grand Central Station in New York. Considering this, perhaps their attitudes were partially understandable. Intourist, Russia, was one enormous Grand Central Station!

Gorbachev's glasnost was delivering a vast river of Westerners to Russia. Those that were in English-speaking groups, in the high majority, were 60-80 years old. They were a horde of same-class people. Most have been everywhere, seemed to travel many times a year, have been to most corners of the world and were reasonably well-off, or they went out of their way to convince one another of this whether it was true or not. Many were retired workers, traveling in groups; some were part of social clubs or groups; they often were loud, pushy, unseeing, unknowing. Sinclair Lewis's Main Street must have still been alive somewhere out there to send so many of his people.

Many of our group were anxious to travel on the famous Moscow subway so the guides took them for such an outing. They made their way to a number of stations and used several trains. The Metro was efficient. It was well constructed, modern. The escalators were long, of high quality and served their purpose well.

The trains were fast, clean; they run often, every two or three minutes on some routes. They were similar to the metros in many modern cities around the world. The stations were spacious, well designed. These accommodated the movement of great crowds.

The famous artworks could be seen everywhere. Some stations had backlighted colored glass windows or panels; these were apparently temples for the Communist Atheists, their place of worship. Up above, chandeliers hung from the ceiling. Murals were on the walls and paintings on the overhead depicted scenes and heroes of the Soviet Union. Truly, the

Metro was an impressive place, somewhere between an art gallery and a very efficient and modern transportation network.

One could not escape the irony of this place where the Soviet system gave unnecessary and irrelevant art under the ground to the masses while it hardly provided bread to its people above the ground. The Paris Metro likewise provided art in some of its stations, but France is a country of means where art is universally expressed so there is no irony.

The Soviet people were moved efficiently to the factories but they were moved slowly through inevitable lines to eat. The priorities of the Party were strange things, implying exclusivity or one instead of the other. A ranking is preferable to most Western minds where all things are important. One is just more so than the other. Surely, these Soviet ironies resulted from priorities; some things mattered and would be done, others do not and will not.

Many of the things that supposedly mattered to the Party were not visible to our group. They saw hardly any evidence of the military except for a lone truck here or there, a few soldiers, entry to a naval station and a naval cruiser in the distance at Saint Petersburg. A number of military officers were seen in Moscow and Petersburg; they walked purposely with military mien and almost always carried attaché cases. They appeared identical in size and in every way to the officers in the Army and Navy in Washington or Norfolk going about their business with attaché cases. It appeared to be the Pentagon East.

The caricature of the overweight Russian general swaggering along the street or swilling vodka was certainly not seen in these professional young men who included an occasional general and admiral. Little evidence of space flight was seen except for a space museum in Moscow although this was clearly a high priority for the Party. They saw no monstrous factories nor steel mills. They had no doubt they existed however and that they were of the highest quality.

Like the modern Metro, the Soviets, no doubt, produced modern armies, spacecraft, factories, ships and fleets, transportation, aircraft and so forth. They, at the same time, appeared to produce shoddy structures; insufficient, almost medieval housing; only a few automobiles and these are of very low quality; poor unproductive farms and only foods for a simple diet; insufficient food for its people; inadequate and substandard distribution of goods and services; poor consumer goods; a poor cultural variety. The list of critical deficiencies went on and on; it was almost unending when listing things or services produced for the average people.

As Marx and the Party proclaimed, the notion of the State, the whole, was important and the person was not; this was in the sense of exclusive priority. The population was not ranked as to degree of importance, but prioritized: so the privileged mattered and the unprivileged did not.

As the group saw, those bugaboos put up by Marx, Trotsky, Arthur Koestler, George Orwell in 1984, and the others were real after all. They were not just haunts and specters to scare us in our intellectual night. They were not fictions from Russia's black soul as revealed by Doestevskii, Tolstoy and the others, but real medieval horrors kept alive somewhere in the Lock Nesses of the East. We ignored that dark forest but somehow we knew not to get too near nor try to see it too well.

While we went our way, however, about tens of millions people were in the forest; some were born there but many had been dragged in. It was easy to hear their murmurs and occasionally their bumps in the night but they never returned. The Americans still wander if the Russians are like us. On the other hand, do they have some dark Doestevskiian recess in their soul that separates us?

The group finally left Moscow and drove northwest towards Saint Petersburg. The Russian farmhouses were fenced into perhaps three-quarter acre plots. The fenced yards were always full of vegetables, fruit trees and every inch was planted, forming mini-farms. These, assumedly, were the State's concession to these workers.

Saint Petersburg was a tourists delight. The buildings are old but substantial. The Baltic provides numerous photographic opportunities including the Summer Palace. We were saddened when it was time to go.

We continued on with our trip. There were many anomalies in the Soviet Union. One was played out to us long after we left the Soviet Union. I only know of it because of an e-mail sent everywhere.

It started off as a small dance group and grew. There were hundreds of people of university age milling around on a concrete square overlooking a great view of Moscow. As we watched, a single man walked through the crowd carrying a "boom box" tape recorder. At some point, he sat the box down. He then started a few dance steps.

Another man walked up to him and he fell into step with the first. This was repeated. After some time, the dance crowd had consumed the whole plaza of people. All were synchronized in dance and only a few remained observers. The street dance was well synchronized and made everyone anxious to join the dancers. Large speakers on poles then joined the dance music, synchronized with the boom box.

As the music played with huge loud speakers, more dancers joined the group. They were street dancing or were all in correlated and synchronized steps. The dancers had obviously chosen their place. It appeared to be in the vicinity of Moscow University so they may have been students. Soon there were hundreds of synchronized dancers sweeping across the large concrete plaza. The numbers of dancers must have reached hundreds or more. It could have been a professional dance group with the ballet.

The pièce-de-résistance then appeared. It was a bride in full bridal dress. She and her entourage got out of their cars. She was a beautiful, young bride. She then joined the dancers. No, she took the lead in front of the dancers that grouped around her. It was a thrilling sight. It was enough to rid me of all negative thoughts about Russia. Hail to the street dancers!

Finally, the trip was over for us. We drove north-east into Finland that is less than a hundred miles from Saint Petersburg. The Finnish trip was uneventful. We then caught a ferry from Helsinki to Stockholm, Sweden.

Sweden is a beautiful country. We visited green grocer markets and many outdoor flower gardens and florist shops. Everything is just in its place in Sweden. Even the forests and the trees of the forests have their proper place. We visited the Old Town of Stockholm that makes one proud to be a human being. Can we really do such things now? Again, everything seems to be in its rightful place. I had visited Sweden before.

I then visited Copenhagen in Denmark. I then took a ferry from Copenhagen to Malmo, Sweden. The distance between these two is about 1.7 miles, although it is one of the busiest shipping straits in the world. We were able to get a good sense of how the Norsemen lived and how their villages looked. Malmo is a remarkable Museum.

CHAPTER 46

Skagerrak and Kattegat Straits

The Skagerrak Strait comes from the north Atlantic down to the Kattegat Strait that empties into the hectic shipping activity of the Baltic Sea. The Skagerrak comes past Norway down past Sweden on their north bank and then the Kattegat with the Denmark peninsula on the south bank. The Kattagat is a strait of tiny width, less than 2 miles that lies between Copenhagen and Malmo, Sweden. This waterway is the center of the past Vikings or nominally their seats of power. The Scandenavian countries are pinched together here so that their capitols of Oslo, Stockholm and Copenhagen are only a few miles apart.

The Skagerrak contains some of the busiest shipping routes in the world, with vessels from every corner of the globe. It also supports an intensive fishing industry. The ecosystem is strained and negatively affected by direct human activities. Oslo is the only large city in the Skagerrak region, if one excludes Copenhagen and Stockholm.

One of the grand castles of Europe is the Inverness Castle. This is the castle in Shakespeare's play, Macbeth. This castle guards the Kattegat. The castle is still kept alive, flying the colorful flags and pennants from the great hall's ceiling. The castle is a beautiful setting with green gardens and pools. There are black swans swimming and white swans. Both are regally sailing, appearing to those given to imaginative forms, as ballet. It is recognized that our visits have been to Scandinavia, those countries being Norway, Sweden and Denmark.

Modern Norway maintains a combination of market economy and a Nordic welfare model with universal health care and a comprehensive social security system. Norway has extensive reserves of petroleum, natural gas, minerals, lumber, seafood, fresh water, and hydropower. The petroleum industry accounts for around a quarter of the country's gross domestic product. On a per-capita basis, Norway is the world's largest producer of oil and natural gas outside the Middle East.

Norway has the fourth-highest per capita income in the world. Norway has the highest Human Development Index ranking in the world.

If one travels, many sights present themselves that are new and unique. The world is manifested by unbelievable things that are happening every minute. There are so many wanders that one cannot find nor digest even a tiny fraction of them. One then tries to tell a friend about this phenomena, but words fail us. We tuck it away in our enormous capacity of memory. We know what we saw but only transfer a tiny sliver of it. We are reminded of Liza Minnelli in 'Cabaret'. A guerilla-costumed Joel Grey sang, "If you could see through my eyes." It was a smash, to use another onomatopoeia.

To illustrate this, on one of my many trips, I flew to Europe. On my return trip, the pilot who was very talkative made an interesting comment. We had taken off from Copenhagen non-stop to Los Angeles. He said that he had chosen a great circle path that minimized the great circle route. This put the sunrise at a particular angle on our left side. The sunrise was determined as the reference spot.

We were then to hold the spot generally in that direction until sunset. That is, we would observe sunrise and sunset and all the points in between. This took us over Jan Mayan Island and north of Thule, Greenland, which is near the northern end of Greenland. He said that we were not far from the North Pole as we crossed. I did not confirm this beyond believing the pilot. He indicated that this was a unique flight and day of the year.

I have traveled considerably in Norway and to a much lesser degree in Sweden and Denmark. Two especially remarkable towns are Bergen, nominally on the south sea coast and Tromso, probably the northernmost city in the world. Russia and Norway have a common border in the far north where Tromso and Murmansk in Russia cap off the northern extent of Europe.

Tromso, at one time early on, had a monopoly on cod fishing products and got its economic power from there. In modern times, she still depends on Codfish products but must compete. Tromso is a beautiful little town on an island. A sweeping bridge near the town adds a touch of archaeological magic to the area.

In the winter, the twilight never reaches the light one sees in the summer. The shops are open in this twilight and the townspeople go about their business as in the light of summer. There is a muffled sound that is far different from the city noises one expects. Many baby carriages have sled runners that slide through the soft snow and ice. This still adds a Santa Clause and Christmas feel to the town during the winter.

The Aurora Borealis or northern lights often waiver in this sky when the clouds allow it. There are then green silk lacing, like silk cloth. No. The waiving is too fast for that description. It is more like dancing silk. I have seen these lights in reds and greens as far south as North Carolina when I was a boy. It is a sight not to be forgotten.

I have also been shopping in other Norwegian towns in the same circumstances. The car tires and sleds slush through the snow and ice making their onomatopoeia sounds similarly. The "slush" onomatopoeia would recognize a single car or sled but this is greatly amplified for lots of tires or sleds. Again, one expects Santa Clause to appear in from a side street with his rain deer and overfilled sleigh of Christmas packages.

This book is primarily about Scandinavia and the northern regions. It would be remiss to ignore latitudes above 60 degrees or so. For this, one might look at the navigational discoveries in the north. The top of the Atlantic Ocean is capped by Norway and Russia, firmly attached to Europe. Greenland extends the cap that belongs to Ellsmere Island. The western side of Greenland going north from Labrador sees Baffin Island and then Ellesmere Island. Ellesmere is the northern cap. Two islands, Novaya Zemlya and Spitzbergen, are rather isolated forming only a dot on the map.

Most geographical explorers had a compulsion to be the first to reach the North Pole. Aside from the enormous hardships of traversing the distance across Ellesmere and part of the Arctic Ocean, There is the Navigational problem of getting there and then pinpointing exactly where the North Pole is in geographic coordinates. One can see that the Arctic Ocean, being all water and ice is a real navigational problem. The depth is over 13,000 feet so sensing a position through thick ice and snow is not always feasible. Since it is ice and water, the pole is but a point on a map, or the result of a geographic observation and calculation. Further, we try to pin-point a moving geographic position, and it is moving with unknown kinematics.

Modern navigation is now used where submarines and surface ships find no problem using GPS to pinpoint the North Pole, even in drifting waters.

CHAPTER 47

North Pole

Rear Admiral Peary (1856–1920) was an American explorer who made several expeditions to the Arctic in the late 19th and early 20th centuries. He is best known for claiming to have reached the geographic North Pole with his expedition on April 6, 1909.

Peary was born in Cresson, Pennsylvania, but raised in Portland, Maine, following his father's death at a young age. He attended Bowdoin College, then joined the National Geodetic Survey as a draftsman. Peary enlisted in the navy in 1881, as a civil engineer. In 1885, he was made chief of surveying for the Nicaragua Canal (which was never built but was replaced by the Panama Canal plans).

In 1886, Peary visited the Arctic for the first time. He made an unsuccessful attempt to cross Greenland by dogsled, which was thwarted by a lack of supplies. He returned in 1891 much better prepared, and by reaching Independence Fjord (in what is now known as Peary Land) conclusively proved that Greenland was an island. Peary was one of the first Arctic explorers to study Inuit (or Eskimo) survival techniques, which he used to his great benefit.

On his 1898–1902 expedition, Peary set a new "Farthest North" record by reaching Greenland's northernmost point, Cape Morris Jesup. He also reached the northernmost point of the Western Hemisphere, at the top of Canada's Ellesmere Island. Peary made two further expeditions to the Arctic, in 1905–06 and in 1908–09. During the latter, he claimed to have reached the North Pole. Peary received a number of awards from geographical societies during his lifetime, and in 1911 received the thanks of Congress and was promoted to rear admiral.

Peary's claim to have reached the North Pole was widely debated in contemporary newspapers and often contrasted with a competing claim made by Frederick Cook. This eventually won widespread acceptance. However, in a 1989 book British explorer Wally Herbert concluded that Peary did not reach the pole, although he may have been as close as 60 miles off. His conclusions have been widely accepted, although disputed by some authorities.

One hundred years ago today, April 6, 1909, a team of explorers led by Admiral Robert Edwin Peary became the first people to document a visit to the geographic North Pole.

Their claim to be the first to stand on top of the world has become controversial over the ensuing century.

Peary may have miscalculated and been a great distance off the mark, according to one theory. The honor of being first at the pole might more properly belong to the American explorer and physician Frederick A. Cook, who claimed to have reached the pole on April 21, 1908, the year before Peary's claim.

Peary had made a number of attempts to reach the Pole prior to his 1908-1909 expedition. On May 8, 1900, he passed the farthest point north ever reached by previous explorers.

Drifting pack ice repeatedly blocked his way on subsequent expeditions. A new record for farthest north was achieved in 1906, for which U.S. President Theodore Roosevelt awarded Peary the National Geographic Society's Hubbard Medal.

Then in August, 1908, on an expedition sponsored by the National Geographic Society, Peary boarded his three-masted steamship schooner, the *Roosevelt*, with 22 Inuit men, 17 Inuit women (a total of 49 native people), 10 children, 246 dogs, 70 tons of whale meat from Labrador, the meat and blubber of 50 walruses, hunting equipment, and tons of coal. This was exploration in grand style. On April 6, 1909, after a month of trekking with the dogs, Peary wrote in his journal: "The Pole at last!!! The prize of three centuries, my dream and ambition for 23 years. Mine at last."

In 2003, there was a news story about an African-American, Matthew A. Henson, who accompanied Peary on a number of expeditions, and stood with Peary and four Inuits at the North Pole on April 6, 1909. In 2000, the National Geographic Society posthumously awarded Matthew Henson its highest honor — the Hubbard Medal.

The experts doubted Peary's claim almost from the outset. In an effort to end the controversy, Wally Herbert, a British polar explorer was commissioned to make a detailed investigation of all the claims. In September 1988, Herbert published an article that argued that through a combination of navigational mistakes, Peary probably missed the pole by as much as 30 to 60 miles.

Whatever the truth is, there can be no doubting that the expedition a century ago was an extraordinary test of courage and determination. Since then people have trekked to the pole in almost every conceivable way to make it more of a challenge. A submarine has sailed to it under the ice.

A century from now, if global warming scenarios play out as predicted and all the polar ice disappears, getting to the North Pole might involve no more than a luxury cruise, a sleigh ride or other comfortable pursuits.

CHAPTER 48

Jackson-Rhodes Ventures, Digs in Montauk and Quebec

The last time I saw Julia, she was the epitome of a fashion plate. Everything was just right. I had kept in touch by phone but only she can tell her story, or a part of it.

"Julia," what are you doing with yourself? I read about you in the papers and magazines and on your website. What are you doing now?"

She responded, "Well, I am now a buyer for the fashion house that I've been with for years. As the head buyer, I get to control our future and our success. Basically, I run the show for our house. And I get well paid for doing what I do."

"What happened to Dr. Ahmed?"

"That's a long story," she said. "Actually, he and I were a number in the tabloids for a while. I still get mentioned quite a bit. The paparazzi still follows me around once in a while. Enough to satisfy my ego.

Actually, I was putting him on the fashion map. Our profits were astonishing. I will say this for him. He treated me fairly. In fact I kept getting a larger and larger part of the house. It was a little like a hedge fund. We were not regulated, thus profits were a question between you and God. In the hedge fund, the star has a contract in which his share of the profits are a written agreement. The star might get 50 percent of the profits. The rest of the house gets the remainder, that is, the star gets 50 percent of the profits in his pocket. That is being a bit greedy so the average is about 20 percent. That's into one's pocket!"

"Wow. That is unbelievable," I said.

"She continued." Ahmed had made me a partner after the second year. He then got carried away and tried to control what I was getting. I knew my worth and I made them pay. The Doctor read the signs and knew he was about to lose it all. In the end, He settled with me for about 20 percent of the house. I controlled 51 percent. It is mine to win or to lose."

"Julia, I knew you could make it. You moved to Manhattan and are now in a different world. Good luck." I was gasping as she said this. I could not imagine these numbers. After all, She owned a highly successful fashion house in New York and I was an average archaeologist digging dirt in remote areas of the world.

"Thanks," said Julia. "I know this sounds foolish, but I'm not happy. I was trained as an archaeologist and I miss the work. I wanted an academic environment. I know I can never have that but I can have some of the things I was promised."

"What! I have never been so astonished." She wanted to join me in a dig. Or was she asking for more than that?

You see, she said. I am asking to form a joint venture with you in which I would make charity contributions for funding digs we would work on

"What would you do about your company?"

"Well, I have thought about that. I have a second in command now. She is very talented and an excellent manager. She would make a great CEO. Why can't I go with you on your next gig, or your present one."

"C'm on. You are probably making 7 or 8 figures now. You are willing to give that up for maybe five figures. It does not make any sense."

"Aw, Shaun. Most of my income is not from salary. It is from profit. That will remain. After all. I still get 51% of the profits. I always cover myself from that angle. Further, in moments of deep crisis, I can always take a couple of days off, go to NY and cast my vote with the board. I don't expect that to happen.

"Shaun, think about it, we could be the Lord Carnavon-Howard Carter of today."

"Wow," I exclaimed. "The Carnavon-Carter team! "You do think big, don't you? And you have thought about this, I see.

"Shaun, I've never been so serious."

"As you remember," said Julia. "They discovered Tutankhamun's nearly intact tomb. It was funded by Lord Carnarvon with Carter providing rchaeology and Egyptology expertise. It sparked a renewed public interest in ancient Egypt. The Nefertiti Bust (or sometimes called Mask) remains the most popular artifact of antiquity. It was shown in several museums in Germany. The Nefertiti Bust is a painted stucco-coated limestone bust of Nefertiti, the Great Royal Wife of the Egyptian Pharaoh Akhenaten. The work is believed to have been crafted in 1345 B.C. by the sculptor Thutmose, because it was found in his workshop in Amarna, Egypt. It is one of the most copied works of ancient Egypt. Owing to the work, Nefertiti has become one of the most famous women of the ancient world, and an icon of feminine beauty."

Nefertiti was an Egyptian queen and the Great Royal Wife of Akhenaten, an Egyptian Pharaoh. Nefertiti and her husband were known for a religious revolution, in which they worshiped one god only, Aten, or the sun disc.

"Wow! The Carnavon-Carter team!" That is something.

"You know," Julia. I've always thought of you in a special way. That has never changed."

"I know. I know," she said. "Let's give it a go and anything is possible. Who knows what may come of it."

"What I really believe in and want to prove is the evidence of Vikings migrating to America south of Newfoundland," I said.

"I know, but that has been looked over and over again and we really have no clues to start digging."

"Wait a minute. How about the use of satellites. They see things that look different far out. But if we put a team together to write software to look at special clues from space, that would be different. Further, if we partially fund the project ourselves, that would be a new thing."

"No, no," I said. They are doing some of that now. They are using satellite images in Newfoundland. What we don't have are imaging algorithms that can see differences from the surroundings, remove the surrounding false images and detect enhanced images by the algorithms.

"It is a question of examining enormous amounts of information and reducing that to something that can be finally looked at in great detail by human beings. They will have markers pointing them to enhanced probabilities. I believe we can do this and search huge areas by underground radar, by aircraft searches and by satellites. Think of what that would mean for humanity."

"I confess." I have been working on things I consider important. One is category placement. As a historian, it drives me to distraction to see things miss-categorized. Once something is miss-categorized, it is difficult to change it. I know how difficult it is to define a category, such as a historical event, and get it right.

"This is typically a problem addressed by library science. We approach this problem through the descriptions of the Hun Age before the Viking Age and the Hansiatic League in the age after that of the Vikings. All three became traders, some using terror.

That is, there was a pre-Hun age at about 100 CE until about 200, the Hun age from about 200 until 750, The Viking age from about 750 until 1050, and the Hanseatic age from 1050 until 1450. All of these had trade characteristics as well as militarists, technologists and political organizers.

Another way of looking at the question is that a hostile culture cannot remain. The opposing Indians in America caused the necessity to sweep the Americas clean. This was done mostly through unintentional rampant diseases. We look at a few of these major weaknesses. We look at the consequences of lack of horses. What is the effect of the hostility of the Indians, the modern weapons of the Europeans versus Stone Age equipment and finally we should examine the diseases that decimated the Indian populations. These are a few of the problems undertaken by Iron Age men against stone aged enemies. Both the American continents had to be swept clean.

I have made numerous notes supporting these conclusions. I address the Vikings as they followed trade routes on the territories of Europe and even further into Asia. First it was through Europe, then Russia using the Dnieper and Volga Rivers and finally across the north America pathways of the Arctic. About 100 years after trading defined their activity in the Viking Age, they found it easier to attack monks, priests and church officials because that is where the rich implements of religion were.

Fundamental to travel on land or sea is the problem of navigation. "Where are we?" is an ancient cry. It is right up there with, "Doctor, Doctor. Save me." Yet, men have set out to the far corners of the earth, confident that they can find their way to their objective and back again. This is described here with a few examples of how man has navigated. Even the GPS satellites in their book on *Theory and Applications,* state that man has been cleverly addressing this problem for 6,000 years. Somehow, they prevail. This addresses the exploitation of latitude, the Pythagoras Method for Beijing to Perth, Iceland and latitude, the Lewis and Clark Method, Roman Water Clock method and the GPS method.

Then, new lands are addressed such as Faroes, Iceland, Greenland, Baffin, Kiev Rus, Huns, the Rus and Russia, the Kremlin and the North Pole.

"Think of this," she said. "We could help remarkably in moving us forward."

"You go and think of this for a couple of days." She said to me. "Don't get into anything you will be sorry about. I will think of it as I have been for a year or so. Right now I am unhappy and I have been for some time. I need to get dirt under my fingernails and sweat on my brow. I am not getting the thrill in fashions that I used to. I want a change."

"Okay. But it sounds wonderful," I said. She did not know what I would decide but she could read me better than I could read himself. Everything I said was an open book to her. How could I not know that she was continuing to play me? With some, one might hear a violin in the background. But with her, I was a complete orchestra. The muscles in my face twitched and rearranged themselves. Each time I spoke, she could read these hidden meanings."

I tried to do the same thing. But I could not do it. She was, after all, in the jungle on a hunt. She could read me. "Stop it, she said to herself." She had been doing this for so long she was not even conscious that it was happening. She would have to work on that.

Meanwhile, I was logically considering the proposition she offered. Is it likely to happen? Where is this going to go. During this time, I felt a revolution within myself. "My God," I said to myself. "I still love her! After all this time and all the nasty scenes, I still love her." I react uncontrollably every time she looks at me or talks to me.

I had better stop this and get out of here. I have no idea what else she has up her pretty little sleeve.

A major dig site for the University of Alabama was L'Anse Aux Meadows, on the north point of Newfoundland. While this was going on with Julia and I, the archaeological team in Newfoundland continued to dig. Near the end of the 2017 dig, This team of experts spent three weeks digging into the dirt of Point Rosee, in Codroy Valley, taking samples and searching for evidence of Vikings. Point Rosee is on the southern end of Newfoundland.

Sarah Parcak of National Geographic and the University of Alabama was the team leader for this dig. On a meadowy spit of oceanfront land in southwestern Newfoundland, a team of scientists spent part of the summer of 2016 working to both uncover history and make it, modern explorers trying to track down ancient findings.

"This is not a bad place to spend a couple weeks outside, playing in the dirt. It's special here," said Parcak. It's a spot that could easily vie for the title of most beautiful workplace in the world, but with cliffs that tumble into the sea, the only way in is a long hike or an ATV ride that is not meant for the faint of heart, or stomach.

The archeologists have uncovered evidence that Point Rosee was once a wooded peninsula, and are working to determine when it was deforested. This is Parcak's second season at Point Rosee. Last June's dig, a cold and rainy affair, turned up enough tempting clues, such as 20 pounds of bog iron that looked to have been roasted in a slag, the waste product from smelting iron, is the holy grail of Norse archeology in Newfoundland and Labrador. Only the Vikings in North America had the knowledge base to transform bog iron into nails and other items.

A good chunk of their days was spent hunched over, sifting though the dirt in an attempt to confirm a long-held theory that the Viking settlement at L'Anse Aux Meadows, more than360 miles north of Point Rosee, isn't the southern-most landing of Norse in North America.

Uncovered in the 1960s, L'Anse Aux Meadows — on the northern-most tip of Newfoundland — took years of digging to become the only proven Viking site on the North American continent, and remains so to the present day.

But material uncovered there points to explorations further south, most convincingly in the form of butternuts, a species not found anywhere north of New Brunswick which is south of Newfoundland.

Material from the Viking Sagas —tales that blend myth and history — also contain descriptions that align with a route down Newfoundland's west coast.

"For sure, there are other Norse sites out there. L'Anse Aux Meadows was not it. I'm confident that, as we continue to refine our methods and our approaches within the next couple years with new images, new satellites, I think we've got a much better shot of finding it," said Parcak.

Archeologists widely believe Vikings sailed down Newfoundland's west coast from L'Anse aux Meadows, eventually making it to northern New Brunswick and the Gulf of St. Lawrence.

New images and new technology is exactly how Parcak and her team were lured to the Codroy Valley in the first place.

Parcak is a leader and pioneer in the field of space archeology — the use of satellite imagery and remote sensing to glimpse what lies beneath seemingly undisturbed soil, a technique she has put to use with much success at other archeological sites.

"With the human eye, there's a lot we can see, but we're restricted to the visible part of the light spectrum, and the great thing about satellites is they record information in the part of the light spectrum we can't see," said Parcak.

Sarah Parcak's main research up to now has been in Egyptology, where she's used space technology to map finds. That spectrum includes thermal infrared and radar, which Parcak can capture from orbiting satellites and examine in her university laboratory to reveal human impact upon the earth.

"All of a sudden you see these vibrant colours and signatures showing individual plant species, or particular kinds of rocks, that all look the same to us. And that's really the magic of remote sensing: It allows us to manipulate the data, and see things differently."

Norse expert Karen Milek says Vikings usually chose settlements that had good landing sites for ships. Point Rosee's beaches are filled with large, unnavigable rocks and steep cliffs. And Parcak's team needs all the technological help it can get.

"Looking for the Norse in North America is like looking for a needle in a haystack," said Karen Milek.

We are surveying the site with a resistance meter, sending electronic pulses into the earth and measuring how easily those currents pass through the ground, potentially signaling objects or features underneath.

But with the help of the remote images that haystack has become a lot smaller, and that needle a lot bigger. Parcak used such images to scour the Labrador coastline and then Newfoundland's western edge, and at Point Rosee. That, along with a 2014 site survey that pointed to signs of burning, were enough hints of man-made meddling with the landscape to lead to the 2015 dig, which expanded considerably in 2016 with equal parts hope and disappointment.

Greg Mumford, the dig's co-director and Parcak's husband, takes careful notes of rock placement as layers of the earth are uncovered.

"This is a difficult site," he says.

While the bog iron collected in 2015 was radiocarbon-dated to 1200 — well within the 1000 to 1400 A.D. timeline the archeologists have sketched out for Newfoundland Norse sites — the 22-metre strip that was thought to be a wall hasn't turned out to be as definitive as the archeologists hoped.

Despite interesting strips of sediment not found elsewhere at Point Rosee, suggesting a human hand, it appears too wide to be a wall, and each layer of soil is being carefully sampled to be tested later in a lab.

"I keep flipping my hats. I'm a skeptical scientist, but you have to be an optimist to be an archeologist. I mean, it's scraping bits of soil for hours at a time under the hot sun. If you're not an optimist, you're in the wrong field."

Renowned archeologist Birgitta Wallace worked on some of the initial digs at L'Anse Aux Meadows and has written a book about the site, which took years of excavation before it could be verified as the westernmost Norse site in the world.

Each time the evidence uncovered this summer sways towards more definitive Norse territory, it then appears to swing right back into vagueness — the archeological equivalent of being lost in the fog, a conundrum no doubt faced by the seafaring Vikings.

"You can't say slam dunk. This is definitively a Norse site." But I think it looks like there was human activity here, and it's going to require a lot more lab testing," said Parcak.

The Norse tendency towards tidiness has proved difficult for the excavators. They rarely left behind large volumes of artifacts, using sod instead of stone to build shelters and re-purposing each valuable scrap of iron and carting it along their journeys. The sparseness of what was found at L'Anse Aux Meadows — a spindle whorl, a bronze pin — shows that.

No such cultural artifact, not even a nail head, has been found during the 2016 dig.

Compared to some other cultural groups, Vikings left few artifacts in their wake, so the archeological team isn't fazed by the lack of objects at Point Rosee.

"If they had stopped for just a very brief while, say a few days, we'd never be able to prove that," said Birgitta Wallace, a renowned Norse archeologist who has done extensive work at L'Anse Aux Meadows, participating in some of the original digs in the '60s.

Wallace made the trip from her home in Halifax just to examine what Parcak's team uncovered, and saw another stumbling block upon her arrival: the landscape of Point Rosee itself.

"That's one thing that bothers me most," said Wallace, pointing to the lack of a nearby freshwater source and sharp cliffs ending in rocky beaches, an opinion shared by other members of the team.

The team is careful to document the original placement of stones as they unearth sections of turf, checking to see whether they were naturally strewn across the peninsula by glacial activity or if a human hand played a role.

"It does not look like a logical place for the Norse to settle, because there isn't a good landing site. That was really key. All their settlements had very good landing sites, beaches usually," said Karen Millek.

"No doubt of Vikings ... somewhere".

Despite the odds, no one at Point Rosee is shutting the door on its possible Viking connections, or of the chance of a settlement nearby.

"There's absolutely no doubt that the Norse sailed around this coast, and probably stopped in many places," said Wallace.

The archeologists don't camp overnight on the site, instead hiking out 40 minutes to boarding houses, but use the tents during the day for shade, as the peninsula has no tree cover.

"If you're going to undertake this journey, as it were, you have to do it and be a skeptic. That's good science. When we first undertook this project, my hypothesis was that we wouldn't find anything."

In one way, Parcak has already found something: Through Point Rosee, she has created a new way to look for Vikings via a combination of space archeology and hands-on excavation.

"Ultimately, I'm most pleased that we've created what I think is a sound methodology to search for Norse sites."

CHAPTER 49

Point Rosee, Third Dig Candidate?

A man from the Codroy Valley is coming forward with what he says is evidence of a third Norse site in Newfoundland, in the wake of the buzz about an archeological find suggesting Viking activity on the island's southwest coast.

A team of researchers made international headlines in early April when they revealed the presence of a hearth, along with bog iron at Point Rosee, signs that point to a Norse settlement, although that find is far from definitive.

Wayne MacIsaac of St. Andrew's welcomed that news, as it backs up his own research in the area, as well as a story his grandfather told him, about a massive storm years ago that changed the shape of the sandbar at the mouth of the Little Codroy River.

"When the people went out there after the storm, they found it had unearthed a boat — a plank-built boat," He adding the wood was unlike any the locals had ever seen.

"And under that boat were three skeletons of tall men, and one stone arrowhead. MacIsaac doesn't know what happened to the boat, skeletons or arrowhead, but believes they were Norse remains.

The site of the skeleton find is almost within eyesight from Point Rosee, according to MacIsaac.

In the same area, he said there is a long, straight earthen mound, and also "a collection of other mounds, including one that's completely, perfectly square."

It was like pieces of a puzzle, falling into place over the years, he said.

MacIsaac has studied the Viking sagas, ancient tales that blend fact and fiction as they detail Norse voyages, and believes the area around Little Codroy River lines up with those descriptions.

"It was like pieces of a puzzle, falling into place over the years. Everything fit. And there was not one thing that was contradicted by what I read in the sagas," said MacIsaac.

MacIsaac said despite years of trying to bring the site to archaeologists' attention — a fruitless ordeal he compared to "reporting a UFO" — it wasn't until the Point Rosee researchers arrived to dig last summer that his idea gained traction.

One of those team members on the Point Rosee dig is looking forward to investigating MacIsaac's claims, calling them "possible."

Point Rosee is about 360 miles away from L'Anse aux Meadows, fitting with a description from the sagas that Vikings sailed south.

"The entire area in the region is a good place for farming. It's a good place for settlement," he said.

"I wouldn't be surprised if future work shows that it's not just Point Rosee where there was Norse activity, but that the area around it may have additional Norse ruins or remains."

"The material that we have at Point Rosee is suggestive of Norse activity in the area. At this point, it's not clear if this really is a settlement. Where are the houses, or the domestic residences, Douglas Bolender asks?" He is a research assistant professor of anthropology at the University of Massachusetts and a Norse expert.

Overall, Bolender cautioned that even the discovery at Point Rosee is far too ambiguous to be confirmed as Viking at this point.

"We do want to be very cautious about it, because it's an important claim that actually has to be validated," he said.

"There's very little work that's been done, and so definitely more work needs to be done to open up new areas, to really take a detailed look at it."

Bolender said the Point Rosee find does have two major points of credibility — the bog iron, which is known to only have been produced by the Norse, as well as a lack of other human activity, by Inuit for example.

Researchers plan to return in the summer for further excavation, and MacIsaac is looking forward to that visit.

In the meantime, he won't reveal the location of the mounds he has found, worried about possible damage from amateur archaeologists.

One thing is certain. It will take a lot more digging, evidence and research to fully validate any Norse activity in the area.

"Archaeologists really want evidence from the ground," said Bolender.

CHAPTER 50

Archaeology Institute

Things moved very fast after I agreed to join Julia in our endeavor. We needed to make arrangements with a Museum or University. "It was a pleasure dealing with the Museums," said Julia. "This was greatly different than the hard-nosed companies. We had made a good choice to go with the museums."

They both agreed that joining a Museum was the most practical. It was obvious that they would be called amateurs in any event. They could not accept that. They interviewed several museums but it still required a good deal of time to reach a conclusion.

In the end we made arrangements with a museum in Los Angeles. That hardly mattered since the museum was very rich with a well thought-out plan for major contributions. Besides, it had a first class exhibition hall that showed everything in its best light. We were fortunate in that respect since Julia had acquired a PhD degree. This is most fortunate when dealing with the academic world and we had to do that. It would in time be critical if we were successful.

Both Julia and I had PhDs in archaeology. This made a considerable impact as we presented our plans to our candidates. These were not straight degrees in either case. She was very aggressive. She earned her degree in a couple of stints. That was really difficult to earn an advanced degree while she was working in the fashion trade.

With me, it was even more difficult. I kept plugging away and did it a little at a time. That is what I mean that these were not straight degrees as with full time applications. At any rate, there were a couple of hungry PhDs out there. How could we not succeed? Of course, there are numerous ways dictating against us succeeding.

Julia had done most of her advanced degree at night and off-campus. Everyone knew who she was but they did not know how hard she was working to succeed. She dressed in dungarees and off-the-rack clothes when going to school. She did her best to keep her private life private.

I did my work but it was a struggle, nevertheless. I worked full time and went to school by allotting my time the best I could. I finally got the degree. I had excelled in my work and had established a national reputation in Archaeology.

It was clear that we had to approach this thing sequentially and not jump off willy-nilly. There are several things that must be addressed. The first is the algorithm development. Our whole approach is to expand our automatic search area. For this, we would fly planes and earth satellites for the search. This phase of the program had to be done before anything else. In fact, we can determine the effect we will have right there in the development of algorithms.

We could therefore see an organization reflecting this. The first department would be Algorithm Development. Then Photographic Analysis Group would be defined. A Detailed Investigation Department would be implemented. We would then organize a Microanalysis Investigation Department on site and in the field. Of course, one must have a support organization so a Services Department will be formed to manage the operation, to keep the lights on, and generally have a well functioning team that administers the management function.

"You can stop right there," she said. "We will organize the departments named above. Those are critical to operationally generate areas for technical analysis and detailed analysis. Once we have these operating, we can generate candidate sites on a small scale, probably using aircraft to fly the sensors."

"We can set up the organization with about 50-100 technologists. This will look like a small software company to start with. Meanwhile, we will keep the money burn rate low until we have something approaching a product. We can keep things in control by writing a business plan like a functioning software company."

"Well then," I interjected. "What can we do to develop the algorithms? Starting hints may be as follows: man-made edges are hard and reflective. Man-made edges tend to be straight or orderly. Amplitudes in a patch may be offset. These are amplified after heavy rains or floods. Differences probably change at each amplitude level in depth. When a detection is made, several passes at different depths should be part of the analysis. Analysis should search for each spectral coefficient."

Julia then proclaimed with some emotion. "Any algorithms that are developed or methods of doing things will be held as an ultra-secret. This rule will be held inviolate and probably justifies discharge. This will be one of the cardinal rules of this organization. Everyone will be apprised of this and a confidentiality agreement in perpetuity signed by each employee."

"Good." said Julia. "It will be perfectly obvious from the start that I will be in charge. This only makes sense since I have been running a large company. I had a large department of programmers to manage in Manhattan so I figure I know something about a programming organization."

"Meanwhile, Shaun will be running the main technical effort of developing algorithms. But he will report to me."

"How are we doing, Shaun?" She already knew the answer because she could see the parking spaces. Further, she checked it every morning. She also checked it during the day so she could identify those with long lunches even if she could not count the number of drinks they had for lunch.

"Don't worry," I said. But she did worry. "I said she should not worry because nothing like a critical mass of the programmers were available, yet that would soon happen." Then, something like a mass occurred and even a certain kind of élan developed. However, furniture, desks, computers, telephones and the support infrastructure was not even in place.

Our whole office building was in disarray. As the office supplies and equipment arrived, the programmers must have inspired them and soon you could hardly pull them away from their machines. This was a challenge. Programmers and engineers loved challenges. Soon the place was humming.

Julia kept an open eye on me. She had her own ideas of how to set up and run an organization. Yet, she realized that her experience was far from her past. She liked me but she wanted to make sure I was not developing 'pie in the sky.' However, things were relatively slow considering what must be accomplished. We could throw money at them, exhort them to move faster, do any number of things to move things along. Yet, none of them seemed to work to our satisfaction. We depended more and more on the published literature.

A parable is a story with a message. One is given here.

Computers were brought into our everyday activity but it took 30 years for this to happen, about 1950 to 1980 for the personal computers. The tasks of computers are hard and difficult. The personnel that brought this about had to have a great knowledge and technical background. After all, the early computers were mathematical wizards and most people thought that was where this new technology was going.

Most people knew that this new technology was going to cause many daffy outcomes. Little did we all know that the highest calling for decades of computer development was accounting for bills in grocery stores and was now its use in smart telephones.

When computers were first introduced, there was an adaptation period where companies sought methods to replace humans with machines. The target in this example was an oil refinery company. The oil refinery company made arrangements between them and the computer company to work out the problems so they could remove the human factor at the refinery as much as possible.

The humans acted as cooks in this process. Refineries are an infinitely complex process. They would go around and measure temperature and other relevant parameters at various points in the pipelines. The theory was to automatically reset all the valves and components continually so the process could run on its own. One such effort was a start-up computer company and an established refinery.

The two entities interviewed each other at some length. Naturally, the computer role represented the start-up, a few young programmers. A gnarled, old hand represented the refinery. He was skeptical from the start but he played the game. The oil man described the process the best he could while the computer man took notes. They were on the verge of quitting when the old man, as an afterthought mentioned that the innards of the refinery had to have a clean-out time.

"Whoa," the computer man was completely nonplussed. "What is that all about?"

"Well, the internal walls get gummed up so we have to have a maintenance period. We close down the refinery for the whole month of February every year and do the cleanup."

"What? That must be terribly expensive. What if you don't finish the process on schedule? Isn't that a very expensive and unexpected outgo?"

"It certainly is," answered the oil man.

"Then, what do you do," asked the computer man. "How do you manage that?"

"Well," The oil man answered. "I run down onto the floor and yell to everyone: "Hurry up, hurry up."

"You mean that is your management technique?"

"That's it," said the old man.

We often see this daffy management technique in our enterprises.

Basically, this parable teaches us that even a weak response is preferable to none at all. It is an exasperation parable.

A lot of things can happen in the 7 years we had allotted for our time horizon. It seems they all have happened to Julia and me. We were expecting big things from our algorithm group. This was all held in secrecy, of course.

Meanwhile, we had developed a business area, designing and manufacturing smart phones that we put on a limited market. This was in a small way since we could not compete in a world of 75 million units at launch. We were happy to confine most of our activity to APS that rode on several platform types.

Although we were concentrating on archaeology, we were soon developing products that could also be profitable in the commercial market. We did not try to enter the systems market but produced major components for the end product. We were a high-end supplier to the Original Equipment Manufacturers (OEM). We exploited that and soon developed products to serve that market. This held the loss somewhat and we tried to hold the burn rate or expended dollars in check.

The algorithms had been winnowed down to Pattern Recognition APS that did a decent job. However, our signature line was a huge program implementing algorithms and advanced computers. These required special high-speed programs to match the enormous amount of data being received. By this time, we had presented a number of papers and were being recognized. We were operating with about 400 staff members, still mostly technical people.

A major problem that we encountered first of all was when we restricted the search patch to a very small area the search was unacceptably poor. We were searching a large number of dimensions using an aircraft. This looked promising. The probability of detection was high but so was the false alarm rate. This was not ready for prime time.

Further, it was not nearly robust enough to be implemented. We then concentrated on a dozen patches and continued to change the algorithm. This was disappointing and must be fixed. Julia forced this into our brains every day. Move faster. Think better. She was always there.

There was a further cliff challenging us. We were making a lot of changes and from this, we had some feel of how fast the data search had to be to achieve our goal. We had to increase the search pattern by a factor of several hundreds or thousands. The numbers were frightening.

We need to do a lot more digging and a lot more algorithm development. We expected that. There is no change so far. During this phase, we gathered patch samples. We could then free the image holding the patch for observation. We could now examine each dimension or characteristic one by one.

Each patch chosen might have a 100 x 100 pixels area or hold 10,000 pixels. This could be turned this way and that in degrees, hold these for every searched aspect and depth. Again, the search could be on any conceived area of correlation. There are a multitude of mathematical transforms, each a candidate for search. We must search not only straight-line dispositions but also some objects that are circular or other shapes.

Needless to say, this description only addresses the general concept. The techniques suggested are only for understanding the underlying concept. They don't work and we have tried them for thousands of ways. We have a monumental pattern recognition job ahead of us.

Further, we know a lot more about the process and how to succeed than discussed here. Remember, everyone is sworn to secrecy.

Julia was Jewish. She was sometimes very aggressive about religion. At other times she seemed unconcerned. She sometimes had bouts of conscience that she did not support Israel enough. She was too busy.

As her fashion company had greater success, she had formulated how she might address her form of charity. By this time, her wealth was in the billions. Her 10-figure fortune would make a mark regardless of where she put it. She always thought of a charity institute centered around Julia as an archaeological institute.

Now that we had this American Institute going, the path became more obvious. The Institute had developed this relationship with a similar institute in Israel and with the Israeli government. This had not been made public yet, but it would be at an opportune time. Julia had committed several million dollars to the Israeli Institute so they had a continuing relationship between the two institutions.

They planned to identify a dig and implement it in the near future. She and I had many conversations about this over the years. We knew we wanted to work in the area of Masada above the Dead Sea but we did not have a real plan.

CHAPTER 51

End Viking Age

Historically, the Viking Age began with the Viking attack on Lindisfarne Monastery in 793, and ended with the Battle of Stamford Bridge in England in 1066, when an English army successfully repelled the Viking invaders. These end-points were identified earlier. The Age was over.

There was a close kinship between Norway Vikings or Scandinavians and the Rus. In the early part of the pre-Vikings Age, or 200 to 800 CE, Europe was tribal and there were mass migrations of whole group populations. Thus, we find the Rus in the north around Lake Ladoga in the east and a great mixture of tribes. Finally, after the period of Byzantines losing power, the Rus converged into the single state of Russia. Many Scandinavians held royalty or premier positions in the new Russian government or there was a mixture of the people.

The Caspian expeditions of the Rus were military in what are nowadays Iran, Dagestan, and Azerbaijan. The Vikings-Rus undertook the first large-scale expedition in 913; having arrived on 500 ships, they pillaged present-day Iran, taking slaves and goods.

Raids continued with the last Scandinavian attempt to reestablish the route to the Caspian Sea taking place in 1041 by Ingvar the Far-Travelled.

The Rus and Vikings first penetrated to the Muslim areas adjacent to the Caspian Sea as traders rather than warriors. By the early 9th century, the Norsemen settled in northwestern Russia, where they established a settlement called Lake Ladoga about 6 miles south of the entry into the Lake.

From there, they began trading with the Byzantine Empire (Constantinople) along the Dnieper and Volga trade routes and with the Muslim lands. They even went as far as Baghdad in Iraq to sell their goods. In territory segmentation, this would be the eastern Viking territory, ranging from Western Europe to the Volga.

The Vikings became so interspersed with the Rus west of the Volga Valley that the Rus accepted the Vikings as the elite traders and warriors of the East. When the Rus finally merged to form Russia after the loss of power by the Byzentine, the new state was accepted by the Rus as their leaders and the new Vikings-Rus royalty. In those days, every polity promoted itself as being a kingdom with aspirations of forming larger and larger groups.

The Vikings-Rus launched the first large-scale raid in 913. A fleet of 500 ships reached the southern shores of the Caspian Sea, the Dnieper to the Black Sea, then by a portage to the Volga and the Caspian Sea.

Across the sea, the Rus raided Baku, penetrating inland a distance of three day's journey, and plundering the region. Everywhere they looted as much as they could, taking women and children as slaves.

Baku city in Azerbaijan province initiated the oil business in about the year 300 CE based on hand digging while it was too early for a real business. Serious promotions were not to be until the 18th century when Russia let licenses based on rotary drilling bits. This made the Noble family including Alfred enormously rich. The Russian government let licenses to groups and companies. The Nobles had these monopolies on mines, lumber, oil wells, oil refineries and other profitable enterprises.

There is evidence of petroleum being used in trade as early as the 3rd and 4th centuries. The following paragraph are from the accounts of Marco Polo in 1324:

"Near the Georgian border, there is a spring from which gushes a stream of oil, in such abundance that a hundred ships may load there at once. This oil is not good to eat; but it is good for burning and as a salve for men and camels affected with itch or scab. Men come from a long distance to fetch this oil, and in all the neighborhood no other oil is burnt but this."

A Turkish scientist in the second part of the 17th century reported that "the Baku fortress was surrounded by 500 wells, from which white and black acid-refined oil was produced"

Now, we will summarize this the best we can.

Baku city in Azerbaijan province initiated the oil business in about the year 300 based on hand-digging. Marco Polo says by 1324 Baku could load a hundred ships simultaneously indicating a significant market had developed. In this neighborhood, no other oil was burnt than this. Prior to this, whale oil was a mainstay for lighting and heating. Meanwhile, demand was now being met by Baku oil.

We also know that 'Greek Fire' was sought for warfare based on naphtha oil. This counter to castle and fortress warfare was increasing the market explosively. Naphtha is a flammable liquid made from distilling petroleum. It looks like gasoline. Naphtha is used to dilute heavy oil to help move it through pipelines or nozzles. This was introduced and was revolutionizing castle warfare and other forms of fixed or static defenses.

The first detailed description of the Baku oil industry was in 1683. The notes confirm the existence of places where natural gas discharges to the surface. It is said that two kinds of fire were produced: one a billowing flame and the other, a jelly-like stream that sticks to anything and ignites on contact.

This expanded the oil market. By this time in the mid 19th century, the oil well pumps were impact-type but that was being abandoned for rotary drill bits.

In 1859, "Colonel" Edwin L. Drake struck oil on American soil for the first time, at Titusville Pennsylvania. He threw parts and pieces together and innovated a make-shift rig. He struck oil at 69 feet depth in Pennsylvania. Although only peripherally associated with the Vikings, oil became crucial to any technical enterprise. Again, digging in the dirt has a long and rewarding history. In recent times, oil has been found in great quantities in the North Sea. The Vikings had oil riches beneath their feet but they could not know it.

When the Vikings entered America, the land was rich in natural resources. This favored the newcomers for those that could adapt. Here we see, the land was rich and growing richer with new resources. These resources were in the trees of the forests if you could invent lumber-working tools to use them, the waters of the Grand Banks with brimming sea life if you knew how to harvest them, with coal and agriculture if you could adapt to them, and even new resources available like oil if you were sufficiently adaptable.

The Grand Banks of Newfoundland are a group of underwater plateaus southeast of Newfoundland on the North American continental shelf. These areas are relatively shallow, ranging from 50 to 300 feet in depth. The cold Labrador Current mixes with the warm waters of the Gulf Stream here.

It is generally accepted that the Portuguese fished here in the 1,400's (or before Columbus. The mixing of these waters and the shape of the ocean bottom lifts nutrients to the surface. These conditions helped to create rich fishing grounds. Fish species included cod, swordfish, haddock and shellfish include scallop and lobster. The area also supports large colonies of seabirds such as northern gannets, shearwaters and sea ducks and various sea mammals such as seals, dolphins and whales. In addition to the effects on nutrients, the mixing of the cold and warm currents often causes hazardous fog in the area.

Newfoundland hosts the Grand Banks on their southeast. We know that fish were eaten since we find bones in their digs. Whales and seals were also in their diet. We don't know their fishing methods. They could have used the Portuguese method of fishing but that was hazardous. The Portuguese build flat rafts that can be stacked aboard so that many rafts can be accommodated at once.

When they reach the fishing grounds, they offload the rafts after putting a single fisherman on each raft. These float away until they meet their quota of fish. The fishermen try to keep in touch with the mother ship the best they can. When the fog rolls in, and fog is ever present, their search for the mother ship is a roll of the dice.

For this reason, the wife of each fisherman on each departing ship for the Grand Banks says goodbye to husbands as if it is forever and it may be. It is a hazardous business, even today by government statistics. The Chinese do the same thing as the Grand Banks fishermen. They build flat rafts of bamboo so they can put 30-40 rafts on the fantail of a single 'junk'.

Again, navigation is crucial to each of the fishermen just as we have reasoned above. Each fisherman has to determine how to find the mother ship, or the consequences are severe. It used to be a common sight in Hong Kong harbor to see junks on their way to their fishing grounds with these bamboo rafts stacked high on the fantail.

Back to the Vikings, the second large-scale campaign is dated to 943, when Igor was the supreme leader of the Rus, according to the Primary Chronicle.

The city was saved only by an outbreak of dysentery among the Rus'. Ibn Miskawaih writes that the Rus "indulged excessively in the fruit of which there are numerous sorts there. This produced an epidemic among them . . . and their numbers began thereby to be reduced." In 965, Sviatoslav I of Kiev, the son of Vlademar I, and Anna, finally went to war against Khazaria. Anna was now free to push Vladimar to war.

In 1042, Ingvar the Far-Travelled led an unsuccessful large Viking attack against Persia with a fleet of 200 ships (around 15-20 thousand men). Afterwards, no attempts were made by the Rus and Vikings to reopen the route between the Baltic and Caspian seas.

I immediately began my studies of the situation and how I was going to put together an organization that could accomplish what was being promised. As usual, she and I threw our selves into whatever enterprise we undertook.

We did it in different ways, of course. She was a people person and succeeded in anything relating to technology and artistic works that can be combined. She had expressed herself beautifully in the fashion business. I concentrated with even greater concentration than she but in a much narrower field.

As the investigative part of our modern American Institute, we looked at the cost per hour of jet aircraft. Not surprisingly, this was exorbitant. We then looked at the price of satellites and that rocked us back a good deal. It appeared that the cost of flight time would end up controlling a lot of our activity.

We could not just start flying and hope something good would happen. We had to pick our spots and prioritize them. We chose the Long Island site because it looked the most promising. We would expect it most likely that any Viking activity in that area would be permanent and leave artifacts. The priorities for the candidates were as follows: Newfoundland, Long Island, Quebec on the Saint Lawrence River, Labrador, Patuxent River in Chesapeake Bay and Norfolk. Those samples, if successful, would be expected to point the way for further prioritizations.

Many of these ancient sites have resulted in modern cities, probably for the same reasons as the candidates were chosen.

CHAPTER 52

Our First Find

Then it happened!

We had confirmed that we had discovered a Long Island settlement at Montauk NY.

There was no rejoicing or beating on tin pans. Archaeologists were far too disciplined for that. First, one of the analysts bent over the table and said something to another analyst in a very low voice, almost a whisper. He then approached another table and repeated the process. Julia was the first to notice. Her antennas are tuned for sensing the environment around her.

"What is it." she asked.

"Julia." We have done it. We have hit the jackpot.

The analysts did a couple of 'high fives' but that was it. Julia and I and a few analysts had been watching this with real anticipation. They had watched the data come in. The 'find' was at the east end of Long Island in New York. This was not the final conclusion; however, the 'quick analysis' confirmed that it looked very good.

It looked like it was sure to be confirmed with continued analysis. It had to meet the standards, in any event. It had to appear conclusive. It had to provide evidence through various weather systems including heavy storms and floods. It had to satisfy the diggers. On and on, it went. It was a long and painful process. But, the analysts had faith that this 'quick look' method would prevail.

"And why not," we asked. It has convenient landing for the longships. There was protection from the wind and storms. There were forest trees suitable for ship repair. There was a profusion of sea life. It looked like crops would grow. The Indians appeared relatively benign. Maybe we can live with them.

We were not the first to recognize these. Now it is some of the richest real estate in the world. But in the days of a thousand years ago, this was just barren land with little attraction. The real problem there for the Vikings was the Indians. There had been several encounters between the Indians and Greenlanders that resulted in fighting and killings. This did not bode well.

Try as they may, they could not stop word leaking out about the Long Island find. Even the magazines that report archaeology findings got a whiff of this. Nevertheless, these were only whiffs. Nobody at the institute knew anything. It was all a big secret. After a while, the excitement drifted away as did the interest in the story. We were safe now, at least for a while.

They had to share some of the knowledge with their museum partners. That was alright. They too had been sworn to secrecy. Furthermore, no one outside a few analysts with Julia and I knew much about the secretive algorithms.

We had discovered our first new Viking settlement at Montauk on Long Island in New York.

America had always had to live with neighboring Indians and their tribes. After Columbus, the Indians diminished because of warfare and disease.

We had been working this dig for over two years. We had pulled up a number of artifacts that indicated that there had been Indian villages there off and on for a thousand years. We finally have found the strata for the Viking years. From there, we had excavated evidence of occupation representing their stay there.

We had extracted several artifacts. These included several iron nails consistent with boat building and repair. We also found many pieces of wood. We found many stone arrowheads. The findings also yielded several items that we could not identify. One in particular was a leather garment of some kind. We thought it may be stirrups but we could never verify the identity. There were also several items that appeared handmade iron implements but we could not identify these either. These had all been sent to the lab for testing of identity and age but the final versions of some of them had not been made.

There was also a battle-axe. This was a very significant find; perhaps the most significant of all since the wooden handle could be aged very accurately. Further, the Indians had no iron so this was also a very important find.

There was considerable disagreement as to whether the find was legitimate. One has to expect that sort of thing in this business.

After this miraculous Long Island find, we struck out due westward on the Saint Lawrence River looking for a likely dig site. We then made another fabulous strike. We discovered what appeared to be evidence of another Viking village. This was in the environs of Quebec, on the river.

I would remain as the chief investigator of both the Long Island digs and the Quebec digs. I spent a lot of time commuting between Long Island and Quebec.

The Saint Lawrence River begins at the outflow of Quebec City before draining into the Gulf of Saint Lawrence, the largest estuary in the world. The river becomes tidal around Quebec City.

The Saint Lawrence River runs 1,900 miles from the farthest headwater to the mouth and 740 miles from the outflow of Lake Ontario. Its drainage area includes the Great Lakes, the world's largest system of freshwater lakes. This is 68,000 square miles or 261 miles on the side of a square.

I have been to Canada several times and can attest to the ravages of wind, sleet, snow and blizzards during winter. Summers can be quite pleasant. One can't have everything. Today the whole city has 8 million people. Clearly, they find the snow, cold, and blizzards pleasant experiences. If not pleasant, then it must at least be tolerable.

The Norse explored the Gulf of Saint Lawrence in the 11th century and were followed in the 15th and early 16th century by European mariners, such as John Cabot. The first European explorer known to have sailed up the Saint Lawrence River itself, was Jacques Cartier. He sailed up the Saint Lawrence on 19 May 1535.

At that time, the land along the river was inhabited by the St. Lawrence Iroquoians. The earliest regular Europeans in the area were the Basques, who came to the St. Lawrence Gulf and River in pursuit of whales from the early 16th century. The Basque whalers and fishermen traded with indigenous Americans and set up settlements, leaving vestiges all over the coast of eastern Canada and far into the Saint Lawrence River.

Basque commercial and fishing activity reached its peak before the Armada disaster in 1588. Then the Spanish Basque whaling fleet was confiscated by King Philip II of Spain and largely destroyed. Initially, the whaling galleons from Labrador were not affected by the Spanish defeat.

Until the early 17th century, the French used the name Rivière du Canada to designate the Saint Lawrence upstream to Montreal and the Ottawa River after Montreal. The Saint Lawrence River served as the main route for European exploration in Canada of the North American interior, first pioneered by French explorer Samuel de Champlain.

Because of the virtually impassable Lachine Rapids, the Saint Lawrence was once continuously navigable only as far as Montreal. Opened in 1825, the Lachine Canal was the first to allow ships to pass the rapids. An extensive system of canals and locks above Quebec, known as the

Saint Lawrence Seaway, was officially opened in 1959 by Queen Elizabeth II representing Canada and President Dwight D. Eisenhower representing the United States. The Seaway now permits ocean-going vessels to pass all the way to Lake Superior.

As to the finds here, we had reconnoitered the most obvious sites near Quebec. We then starting digging. After a couple of years, we found unassailable artifacts that could be aged and identified. We were lucky in this since the site had been used by the Vikings but no one else. This purity of finds in the stock market would be called a "pure play" for the same reasons. Apparently, the Vikings saw things differently from others.

It was a pleasure to see strata that was almost pure and clear of other settlements. After the first find and recognition of the pure strata, the remainder was quick and a pleasure.

After a couple of years, we celebrated finds in Quebec. Our reconnoitering had led us to the site. The quick look capability did a fantastic job in their sensing and analysis. It was a thrill beyond mention when we made the first recognition that we had found a Viking settlement, almost half a millennium before Columbus.

I was thrilled with this find beyond all reason. 'I reasoned that this was my find.' Again, the find consisted of nails, lumber, logs, stone arrowheads and other items associated with Vikings or Intuits. There was also a battle-ax with stone cutting edge, said to be the Viking's favorite weapon.

In this case, we had found buildings so there was much more analysis to be done. Some of the buildings were built partially underground with thatched roofs. In some instances, the sidings were thatched. The underground portion of some dwellings must have improved the habitability greatly when considering the harsh winds and snow of deep winter.

We had bottles of champagne for celebrating just this type of find. It was one sweet experience but the bottles expired too soon.

We finally reached the day for a joint news release of our Long Island first dig.

We and the Museum wanted to make a big deal about this, so we had it catered. We had plenty of bunting and balloons. The press had been invited and there were canapés. Pretty good wine was served. This was an invitation-only affair with tuxedo optional. We were sure that all the employees did not want to go out and rent tuxedos.

We considered several venues for this occasion that was so important to us. It could be at the actual site on Long Island but that was a long ride to get there. Julia had the good sense to invite all the employees. We had made up our minds to have the release in mid-town. That was a class thing to do.

We estimated that about 250 of them would show up. We were surprised. It was more like all 500. We also had far more of the public than we anticipated. Clearly, the public, the news people and the many of the Museum crowd surprised us. They considered it a happening. We had rented a swanky hall in mid-town Manhattan.

We had organized things well. For the formal part of the proceedings, we had a dais for the speaker. Julia used it to make the introductions and welcome everyone. She then gave a very short synopsis of our Institute history. This also was our first announcement that we had probably discovered a second Viking settlement in Quebec, Canada. This was a sensation. The buzz almost derailed our presentations.

She was followed by me, as I described our thoughts about algorithm development. This was using a few words to give little to no information.

We had brought a few artifacts from the Long Island digs that were put on display in a lighted showcase.

The head of the Museum made a few remarks, thanking our Institute for all that had been done for science.

Now it could be celebrated. Even so, the joy was deep although barely shown.

CHAPTER 53

Julia Digs Montauk

The party seemed to be over. We had made the announcements. Everyone seemed to be happy.

In the aftermath of the press releases, we all relaxed and told stories.

"Shaun, you keep promising to let me dig for a few days. I still don't have the feeling of being on the technical team. I want to go to the Long Island dig and participate for a short time in a dig," Jilie pushed. For this time, she seemed more aggressive than her earlier initiatives."

"Julia, you would have no way of knowing what you are getting into. How are you going to sleep in sub-zero weather? The only shield from the weather is a tent and a sleeping bag. There is electricity only if someone fills the diesel tanks. There are no amenities. How about a shower? There is probably no hot water. We dig or work from sun-up to sundown.

"I know," said Julie.

"Okay," I surrendered. "We will take you next week. You can then remember how much you hated it when you were in school."

The arrangements had thereby been made. Julie would get her refreshment course dig.

On the way to the Long Island dig before sunrise on Monday morning, Julie was full of questions. Since she already had an advanced degree, she was prepared for most of the answers. She certainly did not embarrass herself in the questions she asked.

"Shaun," she inquired. "How do you determine the age of an artifact?"

I answered, "We send samples to our museum Lab in New Jersey and they determine the age. I thought you were going to ask the prevalent question, that is, how do you determine if it is a dog bone being sent? You get the same answer. The lab figures that out. We work very closely with them. They have a couple of professors there that are really knowledgeable. Actually, our employees on site are very knowledgeable so we would not expect too many false identifications.

"How does the Lab date things ---- I mean, in general?" she asked.

"As you know," I said. "The field that specializes in that is called dendrochronology." Basically, this describes radio carbon dating as calibrated with Tree Ring technology and other esoteric corrections. In fact, Leonardo Di Vinci was the first to note this tree ring phenomenon so it has a good pedigree.

Dendrochronology, or tree-ring dating, is the scientific method of dating tree rings to the exact year they were formed in order to analyze atmospheric conditions during different periods in history. Dendrochronology is useful for determining the timing of events and rates of change in the environment and also in works of art and architecture, such as old panel paintings on wood, buildings, etc. It is also used in radiocarbon dating to calibrate radiocarbon ages.

New growth in trees occurs in a layer of cells near the bark. A tree's growth rate changes in a predictable pattern throughout the year in response to seasonal climate changes, resulting in visible growth rings. Each ring marks a complete cycle of seasons, or one year, in the tree's life. The oldest tree-ring measurements in the Northern Hemisphere are a floating sequence extending from about 12,580 to 13,900 years.

The Greek botanist Theophrastus in 371 BCE first mentioned that the wood of trees has annual rings. In his *Trattato della Pittura*, Leonardo di Vinci was the first person to document this, that trees form rings and that their thickness is determined by the conditions under which they grow.

A number of techniques are used to date an artifact. First is the date on tombstones to determine a time line the best we can. That is the best and most reliable data since people do not usually make errors or fun in birth and death dates in stone.

"That's good." She allowed. "The victim is hardly in a position to complain."

DNA is also often of great help, especially in identifying who a person is. Is he who he says he is?

Scientists have long known that soil in caves is filled with valuable DNA. But ancient DNA is very fragmented, and until recently, the technology didn't really allow us to analyze this damaged genetic material and get very accurate results.

The technique described in the study was able to identify genetic material that belonged to hominins as well as a variety of animals such as the woolly mammoth and woolly rhino, both of which are extinct. That's how the researchers were able to identify the DNA of several animals, as well as DNA belonging to Neanderthals. The Neanderthal DNA was found in four caves, including one in Belgium and one in Russia. This work extends the applicability of DNA in aging bones or from other DNA.

"Okay," I said. "The next part of the answer is about Tree Rings. I know that is dear to your heart. So you have something to look forward to. It is essential to our methods of aging, so listen."

Dendrochronology, or tree-ring dating, is the scientific method of dating tree rings to the exact year they were formed in order to analyze atmospheric conditions during different periods in history. Dendrochronology is useful for determining the timing of events and rates of change in the environment (most prominently climate) and also in works of art and architecture, such as old panel paintings on wood, buildings, etc. It is also used in radiocarbon dating to calibrate radiocarbon ages.

New growth in trees occurs in a layer of cells near the bark. A tree's growth rate changes in a predictable pattern throughout the year in response to seasonal climate changes, resulting in visible growth rings. Each ring marks a complete cycle of seasons, or one year, in the tree's life. As of 2013, the oldest tree-ring measurements in the Northern Hemisphere are a floating sequence extending from about 12,580 to 13,900 years.

In his *Trattato della Pittura* (Treatise on Painting), Leonardo da Vinci was the first person to mention that trees form rings annually and that their thickness is determined by the conditions under which they grew.

Radiocarbon dating has become one of the most essential tools in archaeology. The 'Radiocarbon Revolution' transformed how archaeologists could interpret the past and track cultural changes through a period in human history where we see among other things the massive migration of peoples settling virtually every major region of the world, the transition from hunting and gathering to more intensive forms of food production, and the rise of city-states.

In brief, radiocarbon dating measures the amount of radioactive carbon 14 isotopes in a sample compared to normal Carbon 12. When a biological organism dies, the radioactive carbon in its body begins to break down or decay. Before death, the isotope is constantly replenished. This process of decay occurs at a regular rate and can be measured. By comparing the amount of carbon 14 remaining in a sample with a modern standard, we can determine when the organism died. However, there are a number of other factors that can affect the amount of carbon present in a sample and how that information is interpreted by archaeologists.

The radio carbon technique is poor without a calibration method. The normal way for calibration is 'tree ring dating'. We can therefore measure the number of rings in a tree that is chopped down

Several species of trees live almost indefinitely. The giant sequoia trees of California are known to live over 3,000 years, discerned through tree ring dating. Under normal circumstances, woody trees add one ring per year. A ring typically consists of a light-colored growth portion and a dark-colored portion produced in a stabilization season. However, some trees do not produce annual rings at all, especially those in temperate or tropical regions.

Tree rings are more than a record of years. Year-to-year variation in the width of rings records information about the growth conditions in the particular year. Insect infestation clearly manifests itself, as does disease or fire damage. Each of these interrupts the normal growth cycle. The day length, amount of sunshine, water potential, nutrients, age of tree, temperature, rainfall, height above ground, and proximity to a branch all impact tree growth and tree ring production. By assuming the outer ring records the most recent year and that each ring signals one year, a researcher can determine the date of a particular ring simply by counting rings.

But how valid is the assumption of one ring per year in a climate where tree-growing conditions are variable? That very assumption is regularly put to the test by research foresters. They investigate how a tree grows, how and when it adds a new ring, effect of nutrients, rainfall, etc., over a range of related conditions.

Hundreds of individual trees have been observed over multi-year periods. Researchers monitor tree growth by attaching sensitive probes onto and into actively growing trees. Measurements are sometimes taken every fifteen minutes throughout the years of study! These are not mere ring-counting efforts on living and dead trees, but an observation of living trees and how they react to ambient conditions—how and when they make a ring.

Thus, we know a lot about trees and we can use all our techniques to calibrate one another with a great deal of confidence.

"There, Julia. I have answered your question about how archaeologists age a specimen. Was that Okay?"

"Okay," she said. "I could not stand another word of it. Next time I will go to a search engine. I think your explanation was longer than any they dreamed up. But never mind! That was an excellent dissertation. I loved it."

When we arrived at the site after an hour or so, most of the diggers knew her, at least by sight or reputation. She was introduced all around. Everyone was eager to go to work. "What shall I do," she asked. "Well, come along with me. I will spend part of the morning getting you knowledgeable and by that time you should be ready to go to work. I will give you an assignment for that so you can be a real participant.

I then, took her around and familiarized her to our methods, the tools and how to use them and gave her whatever she needed. We were not going to soften her bed, however. She can pull her weight. She seemed eager to get to work.

At the end of the day, she was beginning to feel the pain. She was getting blisters on her hands and they hurt. Her knees were also beginning to hurt even more.

After the second day, she was beginning to suffer. She was getting mosquito bites. The blisters were rising and bursting and the covering skin stopped protecting the underside. Her knees were now really hurting but she did not complain. "Is this Julia?" I asked.

She looked like a homeless person or much worse. She was dirty. Her hair was stringy. Her clothes were beyond description. The real badge of a digger are the fingernails. And yes, they were dirty, dirt ledged beneath every one. We all laughed at this but we could not laugh too hard. She was sensitive to her condition but was making the best of it.

One of the diggers whispered to me, "What are you going to do when she finds nothing? She is really into this thing and she will be terribly disappointed."

"I don't know, I said, and that was the truth." After all, we had been digging for some time and had hardly found anything.

"But don't worry. Some of us were born under a lucky star. Something might even show up."

Sure enough. On her last day, she was beginning to like the camaraderie, the give and take of hard work. Then she started screaming. "My God," I said. "What is happening?" We all rushed over. She was on her knees with her head and upper body down in the hole. In her hand was the unmistakable form of an iron nail. It was all encrusted with dirt but one could see the outline. To all of us, it looked like a fine piece of diamond jewelry. She was now part of the team.

Her finding had been a single iron nail. But even this after only 2 weeks of digging was a miracle. After Julia's dig on Long Island, she returned to Manhattan, a happy woman. We all basked in her sunlight. She was absolutely radiant knowing she had done something for mankind and for her.

Everyone went back to work. The dig must go on.

We had not provided an archaeological profile of the Long Island dig. This was now a good time for that.

CHAPTER 54

Indians on Long Island

This chapter is a shortened and re-written version of the Garvies Point Museum book, *Indian Archaeology of Long Island*, in Google. It identifies some of the activity that could have been by Vikings on Long Island. This identifies the first people on Long Island as American Indians. They may have arrived as early as twelve thousand years ago. The prehistoric Indians of Long Island left no written records. We do not know the names of the Indian tribes or the languages they spoke. The information here is based mostly on archaeological studies. Changes were brought about by the periodic migration of new peoples and the introduction of new ideas to the Island.

The movement of Indians into the Northeast followed the glacial ice melt. The newly freed land was gradually populated with plant and animal life. Dense coniferous forests covered much of the Northeast. By 10,500 BCE, man could have occupied southern New York.

Studies of the Paleo-Indian sites on the High Plains of Western United States has shown that these people lived by hunting big game animals such as the mammoth and archaic forms of bison. In this, they lived and hunted much the same way as the other animals. It is probable that a similar elephant-like animal, the mastodon, was present in the Northeast when the Indians first entered the area.

Many archaeologists suspect that the first Indians in the Northeast were hunters who lived in small bands and followed the movements of such animals as the mastodon, mammoth, caribou, elk, and deer. The presence of fluted points, knives and hide scrapers, tools essential to a hunting economy. Through a piece of caribou bone, radiocarbon dated at 10,580 BCE was recently discovered in the same soil layer as the fluted point in a cave in Orange County, New York, just north of the New Jersey border in Bergan County.

The Paleo-Indian way of life gradually disappeared, perhaps about 7,000 BCE. The mammoth, mastodon, and many other late Pleistocene animals became extinct. The Paleo-Indians may have hunted these animals to extinction. A changing environment that featured a warmer, more arid climate, and the gradual disappearance of the great coniferous forests may also have spelled doom for the animals unable to adapt to new environmental conditions.

Evidence of the Paleo-Indian population, apparently never very large, disappears from the archaeological record. Remnant groups of these big game hunters were probably absorbed by new Indian groups moving into the area and carrying a culture or way of life more suited to the new environmental conditions.

The earliest evidence for the Archaic Stage in Southern New York dates from about 4,600 BCE. There are numerous archaic camp sites on Long Island, though few of them seem to date much before 2,000 BCE.

These sites are fairly small, suggesting resident bands of fifty people or less. Shellfish are the primary food, with soft and hard clams, oysters and scallops. They were steamed in pits heated by burning coals or hot stones. Thousands of fragmentary deer bones indicate that this was the animal most commonly hunted. Bird bones and box turtle shells are also commonly found. One site has yielded a few fish bones and some notched stone sinkers for use with seine nets.

Finds of charred hickory nutshells and other seeds and pits suggest that wild vegetable foods may have formed an important part of the diet. No evidence of the Indian houses have been found at the Long Island sites. They probably lived in wigwams — small dome shaped huts made of framework of saplings and covered with bunches of grass, woven mats or bark. It should be noted that the conical skin tent or tepee was never used by the Indians of Long Island.

Archaic tools and implements were made of stone, bone and undoubtedly wood and plant fibers. Stone projectile points are the most commonly found artifacts. They were probably used on spears that were thrown with the aid of a spear-throwing stick. The dugout canoe was probably introduced during this stage. Animal hides were pierced and sewn with bone awls or needles.

This stage is radiocarbon dated at about 1000 BCE. The Orient burial sites suggest elaborate ritualism associated with the disposal of the dead. One might say that the Orient people lavished their wealth on death.

The Woodland Stage may be dated from roughly 1000 BCE to the time of European contact. Agriculture was introduced from the south or west. Wooded areas were cleared for small fields of corn and probably beans and squash. Agricultural activities are reflected in such artifacts as hoes, shallow stone mortars and pestles. Wild plant foods, including hickory nuts, were gathered in season.

Hunting was less important than in earlier times. The bow and arrow was probably introduced to Long Island during the Woodland Stage. Groups of Indians moving from the west or south brought the Windsor Culture to Connecticut and the coastal New York region about the time of or soon after the Orient Culture. These people spread out over Long Island.

New groups of people, with a new complex of ceramic traits - the East River Culture - appear in greater New York and western Long Island. The Massapequa tribe was on the south shore of Long Island in the 17th century. Generally speaking, the people of the East River culture are believed to have been the Algonquin-speakers. This ends the archaeological profile. We saw nothing in the report that discouraged us in our digs in the Long Island area. Even the findings of numerous fluted arrowheads on Staten Island was okay. We would expect an area with width and depth or kind of rectangular to make better hunting grounds than the long, narrow spit of Long Island.

I had to see Julia and have her sign a bunch of legal documents. They produced a girl to escort me to Julia's office. Everyone seemed to be dashing about in a dead run. There seemed to be inner spaces and outer spaces. These were no doubt that the inner spaces were for meetings with customers and for glamour while the outer spaces were for the working space machinery and seamstresses. There was a constant whirr of sewing machines. There were also designer notions, their ideas of new fashion designs.

"Shaun," she said, "She was rising up from her desk and work table that was strewn with photographs, artist drawings, fabric samples and all the tools of her trade.

"It is so wonderful to see you."

"OK, where are the papers you want me to sign?"

I produced these from my attaché case and laid them out in order on the work table. When she was finished, we talked small talk for a few minutes. Then I asked her to join me for dinner that night. This was a false hope since she opened her arms to the desk and table and said, "Look. Does this look like I can get away? Some other time and I am sorry."

I took my papers and left. It was a long shot in any event.

CHAPTER 55

Masada

After WWII, Paris was the center of the fashion industry surrounded by hundreds of 'wannabes' and New York was the center of fashion consumers with hundreds of wannabes.

These consumers ranged from basement store bottom-end buyers, to a department store crowd seeking mid-level smart clothes that moved millions and millions of dollars every year, to a designer crowd with clothes costing so much they had to give them away. Or, the designers begged to dress them on high paid models on runways. The streets of New York often had so much red carpet that the high-end patrons had Stiletto heels that rarely touched the macadam pavement. If that did not suit you, most houses were more than willing to set you apart for specialized custom outfits. Buyers roamed the world and when they bought, it numbered in the millions.

It was that kind of frantic world when Julia entered the Fashion Institute school and even more so when she worked for Dr. Ahmed.

One of the wannabe fashion centers was in a small school in Israel. For some reason, Israel had a large group of immigrants on Long Island and Manhattan. The government, or at least I conjecture that the Israeli government backed the expensive fashion houses in Jerusalem and Tel Aviv that aspired to become a center rivaling New York.

While Julia was taking classes in the fashion school in New York, she met an Israeli there. Both were students. Her name was Ruth Levine. They liked each other when they first met. They often were in the same work classes. They attended concerts and 'happenings' together and fitted perfectly. Ruth invited her to Israel three times and she accepted. She stayed with the Levine family. These and their fondness for the same things brought them close together.

During these times, Ruth struggled somewhat and was not really cut out as a top clothes designer. She finally became a buyer for a large fashion house in New York and Israel.

Ruth immersed me in the Israeli history and culture. I can never repay her for that. She taught me many things. I was bordering on being a biblical scholar. It was stories in the bible that attracted me. These were mostly stories in the Old Testament but those of the New Testament also attracted me. The stories about Masada intrigued me and I made a pledge to myself to go there at any opportunity. Masada occurred in the first century so qualified as an antiquity. It was during the Roman wars or the uprisings as the Romans described it.

This friendship between Ruth and Julia went on for years. Even when Julia took over the company, she would see Ruth from time to time but Julia had already moved on in her career. Her Jewish experiences with Ruth would stay with her forever but she had moved on.

Julia was on the long drive to Montauk and it was early on this Monday morning. She wanted to stop the technical talk about DNA. She interjected, "I talked to Jacob last night. He is talking very positively. He thinks they will be in a position to say something about our dig in Israel before long." I knew she was talking about the digs we were sponsoring with the Israeli Institute. Julia was providing funding for this.

"Things are moving too fast for me," I said. "We've just announced the dig on Long Island and we are already getting prepared to announce findings in the Masada digs."

Masada is a fortress that once was King Herod's castle. It has become the most popular tourist attraction in Israel. Julia and I had connections there because of our connection with what we will call the Israeli Institute. Julie, being Jewish, felt obliged to make a very significant contribution to the Israeli culture.

Julia's conscience had always bothered her because she was not a practicing Jew. Some would say she is a cultural Jew. She had made arrangements to fund a digging with the institute in Israel. About the only thing she knew when she made the obligation was from a documentary TV series starring Peter O'Toole called Masada, made about 1981.

She collaborated with the Israeli Institute to select a site for digging. Julia agreed to make significant charity contributions where she and the Israeli Institute would be partners in a dig near Masada. By this, she would provide funding for the dig. We were now over two years down that road so we were beginning to press for results. We were amazed at the progress that had been made, but naturally there was never enough.

Then we heard the news of miraculous findings in Herculaneum. The digs in present-day Italy were accidental — a farmer was looking for water found them. We all were as thrilled as if they were our findings. We even celebrated the farmer's good luck.

The story of Pliny the Elder and his nephew, Pliny the Younger, was celebrated wherever there was anyone interested in archaeology or the history of antiquities. It was a thrill for them all. Imagine finding a diary of Pliny the Elder during the massive eruption of 79. This was a miracle indeed. No one even suspected that there was a diary or a written word description recording the event. The fact that it was in a scribe's shorthand Latin helped to confirm its authenticity.

Although the finds by the farmer were unintentional, our find if we made one, would be intentional. The Israeli Institute had a list of potential sites and we were now digging on one that is on the list. The Israeli institute had a list and we chose from that. Julia was the final arbiter for the choice and this gave her a great charge. It was clear that the Israeli digs were her greatest priority.

Masada has become one of the Jewish people's greatest symbols as the place where the last Jewish stronghold against Roman invasion stood. Masada is located atop an isolated rock mesa about 1,200 feet high at the western end of the Judean Desert overlooking the Dead Sea.

After leaving Jerusalem for 50 miles or so, one sees the Dead Sea on the left and a sequence of high mountain ridges on the right. These are stacked up with caves but they are too high and steep to crawl up along the ridges. On the right, at just about the head of the Dead Sea on the left, is where the *Dead Sea Scrolls* came from or were found.

Proceeding on a few miles, one stops at a small building reception center where Masada is about 1200 feet upward, again almost too steep to climb. There is a cable car from the little building to the Masada mesa on top. There are also dual paths to drag yourself upward if one is so inclined, but it is a hard climb.

The region in the summer months, especially, is desert-edge steaming. There are many tourists that did not know what they were in for, but they committed to go there regardless. They are lying down on the steep mountainside and panting for breath. The Dead Sea is about 1200 feet below sea level and it is truly dead. It is not easy to get to. It is also filled with toxic chemicals and crystal forms that rise up from the sea, leaving the possibility that one of them might be Lot's wife.

I have been through that region many times. One incident in particular comes to mind. My friend and I came to a stoplight on the road just described and a cross road going down to the Dead Sea. There was an old Palestinian walking with his sheep. At just this moment, an Israeli police car with four uniformed policemen inside pulled up to the light and stopped. The Palestinian continued his slow walk. The sheep surrounded the police car. The policemen blew their horn over and over. Then they yelled out of their car's open windows.

The Palestinian stood at the intersection while his sheep surrounded him and his animals but the police could not move. Finally, the Palestinian walked up to the police car and gave the third finger salute. He held it on the windshield so they were bound to get the message. The yelling stopped. The car horns were quiet. The policemen had clearly got the message.

On the right, just off the road, there were the foundation stones for the Roman soldier barracks. They looked consistent with more than the 5,000 men purported to be encamped there for months while the siege took place. On the east side, the rock falls in a sheer drop of about 1200 feet. On the western edge, it stands about 260 feet above the surrounding terrain. The natural approaches to the cliff top are very difficult.

The only written source about Masada is Josephus Flavius's book, '*The Jewish War*.' He had been appointed governor of Galilee. Calling himself Josephus Flavius, he became a Roman citizen and a successful historian. According to Josephus, Herod the Great built the fortress of

Masada between 37 and 31 BCE. Herod had been made King of Judea by his Roman overlords and "furnished this fortress as a refuge for himself." It included a casemate wall around the plateau, storehouses, large cisterns filled with rainwater, barracks, palaces and an armory.

Some 75 years after Herod's death, at the beginning of the Revolt of the Jews against the Romans in 66 CE, a group of Jewish rebels overcame the Roman garrison of Masada. After the fall of Jerusalem and the destruction of the Temple in 70, they were joined by zealots and their families who had fled from Jerusalem. There, they held out for three years, raiding and harassing the Romans.

Then, in 73, Roman governor Flavius Silva marched against Masada with the Tenth Roman Legion, auxiliary units and thousands of Jewish prisoners-of-war. The Romans established camps at the base of Masada, laid siege to it and built a circumvallation wall. They then constructed a rampart of thousands of tons of stones and beaten earth against the western approaches of the fortress and, in the spring of 74, moved a battering ram up the ramp and breached the wall of the fortress.

Once the Zealots' leader, Elazar ben Yair, concluded battering rams and catapults would succeed, he decided the defenders should commit suicide. Josephus dramatically recounts the story told him by the two surviving women. The defenders — almost one thousand men, women and children — led by ben Yair, burnt down the fortress and killed each other. The Zealots cast lots to choose 10 men to kill the remainder. They then chose among themselves the one man who would kill the survivors. That last Jew then killed himself. Elazar's final speech clearly was a masterful oration:

> "Since we long ago resolved never to be servants to the Romans, nor to any other than to God himself, who alone is the true and just Lord of mankind, the time is now come that obliges us to make that resolution true in practice. … We were the very first that revolted, and we are the last to fight against them; and I cannot but esteem it as a favor that God has granted us, that it is still in our power to die bravely, and in a state of freedom."

The story of Masada survived in the writings of Josephus but not many Jews read his works and for about 2,000 years it was a more-or-less forgotten episode in Jewish history. Then, in the 1920's, Hebrew writer Isaac Lamdan popularized "*Masada*," a poetic history of the anguished Jewish fight against a world full of enemies. According to Professor David Roskies, Lamdan's poem, "later inspired the uprising in the Warsaw Ghetto".

The heroic story of Masada and its dramatic end attracted many explorers to the Judean desert in attempts to identify various remains of the summer home and fortress. The site was identified in 1842, but intensive excavations took place only in the mid-1960's with the help of hundreds of enthusiastic volunteers from Israel and from many foreign countries.

To many, Masada symbolizes the determination of the Jewish people to be free in their own land.

Ruth was acting as a guide here. She knew the stories well. She related these with great authority. Julie was still acting as a student but she was coming along fast. The Masada dig was producing minor artifacts from the beginning. There were shards from household pottery. There were shoes. There were construction materials and there were all kinds of shattered pottery and broken frescos.

The flat plateau of Masada measures upwards of 1,000 by 500 feet. The casemate wall (two parallel walls with partitions dividing the space between them into rooms) is about 2258 feet long and 8 feet wide. It was built along the edge of the plateau, above the steep cliffs, and it had many towers.

Three narrow, winding paths led from below to fortified gates. The water supply was guaranteed by a network of large, rock-hewn cisterns on the northwestern side of the hill. They filled during the winter with rainwater flowing in streams from the mountain on this side. Cisterns on the summit supplied the immediate needs of the residents of Masada and could be relied upon in times of siege.

To maintain interior coolness in the hot and dry climate of Masada, the many buildings of various sizes and functions had thick walls constructed of layers of hard dolomite stone, covered with plaster. The higher northern side of Masada was densely built up with structures serving as the administrative center of the fortress and included storehouses, a large bathhouse and comfortable living quarters for officials and their families.

On the northern edge of the steep cliff, with a splendid view, stood the elegant, intimate, private palace of the king. It was separated from the fortress by a wall, affording total privacy and security. This northern palace consists of three terraces, luxuriously built, with a narrow, rock-cut staircase connecting them.

On the upper terrace, several rooms served as living quarters; in front of them is a semi-circular balcony with two concentric rows of columns. The two lower terraces were intended for entertainment and relaxation. The middle terrace had two concentric walls with columns, covered by a roof; this created a portico around a central courtyard.

The lowest, square terrace has an open central courtyard, surrounded by porticos. Its columns were covered with fluted plaster and supported Corinthian capitals. The lower parts of the walls were covered in frescos of multicolored geometrical patterns or painted in imitation of cut marble. On this terrace was also a small private bathhouse.

Here, under a thick layer of debris, were found the remains of three skeletons, of a man, a woman and a child. The braided hair of the woman was preserved, and her sandals were found intact next to her.

Elaborately built, this structure probably served the guests and senior officials of Masada. It consisted of a large courtyard surrounded by porticos and several rooms, all with mosaic or tiled floors and some with frescoed walls. The largest of the rooms was the hot room (caldarium). Its suspended floor was supported by rows of low pillars, making it possible to blow hot air from the furnace outside, under the floor and through clay pipes along the walls, to heat the room to the desired temperature.

The First Jewish–Roman War (66–73 CE), sometimes called the Great Revolt was the first of three major rebellions by the Jews against the Roman Empire, fought in the Eastern Mediterranean. After the fall of Jerusalem in 70 CE, the Jewish-held fortress of Masada remained the only point of Jewish resistance. In 72 CE the Roman governor, Flavius Silva, resolved to smash this outpost. The assault against Masada had begun.

He marched against Masada at the head of the Roman legendary Tenth Legion, its auxiliary troops, and thousands of Jewish war prisoners, a total of ten to fifteen thousand people. The troops prepared for a long siege; they established eight camps at the base of the Masada rock and surrounded it with a high wall, leaving no escape for rebels.

Then, Romans started to build an assault ramp to the top; thousands of slaves, most of them Jewish, did that in nine months. After the ramp was completed, the Romans succeeded in moving the battering ram up and to direct it against the wall. They broke the stone wall, but the defenders managed to build a wall of earth and wood that was flexible and hard to break. Eventually Romans managed to destroy it by fire, and decided to enter the fortress the next day.

This ramp had a concave shape, rising from the taller mountains behind Masada and rising again against the Masada rock. The builders brought buckets of dirt to the ramp and emptied them for another round. This ramp probably was hundreds of feet high at its mid-point. In the movie, O'Toole sat in a huge chair on the nadir of the ramp. Drums beat out the rhythm like that of the oarsman on Roman ships. Leather whips accentuated the drumbeat; this was probably realistic at Masada and on the Roman ships too.

At night Eleazar gathered all the defenders and persuaded them to kill themselves rather than fall into the hands of Romans. The people set fire to their personal belongings, and then ten people chosen by a lot killed everyone else and then committed suicide. In the morning Romans entered a silent fortress and found mostly dead bodies. Two women and five children survived the mass suicide by hiding in a cave; they then came out to the Romans. Josephus describes all the dramatic details of the last hours of the Masada defenders as told by these survivors.

Evidence of a great conflagration were said to be found everywhere. The fire was probably set by the last of the zealots before they committed suicide. Josephus Flavius writes that everything was burnt except the stores — to let the Romans know that it was not hunger that led the defenders to suicide.

A Roman garrison was stationed in Masada for some time after the fall. During the Byzantine Period or that of the Eastern Roman Empire, the ruins of Masada served as a retreat for monks; they also built a small church there. It was inhabited during the Crusader period. Later, the place was abandoned and its identity lost.

The location of the historic Masada remained unknown until 1838 when illustrators of '*The Jewish War*' by Josephus stumbled onto it. Some say this happened in 1842. Archaeological expeditions were then made by Americans, Germans and French.

Masada and nearby Qumron were central locations for the Essene sect. Both lie on the Dead Sea, only a short distance apart, probably less than a half dozen miles. Masada was the last bastion of Jewish independence. The Romans army had very cruelly put down the rebellion in Jerusalem. They had hung a large number of rebels and crucified others.

Now they took care of the fighters of Masada. Many locations in Jerusalem were covered with crosses. Josephus says that the crosses were thick and stood all around Jerusalem as a testament of what happens to those who refuse to submit to Rome's authority.

Herod was about 71 years old at the time of Jesus's birth or he was born in 71 BCE. The great volcano at Pompeii occurred in 79. Josephus Flavius, the historian that reported Masada events was born in 37 CE. Pliny the Elder, was the historian that reported the great volcano events of Pompeii through his nephew, Pliny the Younger.

The Elder was commander of the Roman Navy at Pompeii. The elder was born in 23 BCE. He died while using the Navy to save people in 79, during the great volcano catastrophe. These dates are conflated for comparison of important events.

The might of the Roman Army was brought down on the Zealots who defied them. The Romans were there for years but there could be no doubt of the outcome of any confrontation. The Roman Army had brushed everyone aside in its assault on Jerusalem and its environments like ants. The 10th Legion was then stopped but it was only a matter of time. In 1838, it was re-discovered.

Julia's office was in Manhattan; however, the Israeli connection had a high priority with her. She kept pretty close communication with the Israeli Institute, with Ruth and with me at the dig site. She had made three visits to Israel and the Masada dig site by this time.

The area of our Masada digs was taken over by a consortium of diggers. They continued the work smoothly. There was no doubt that it was an important find since it provided a huge number of artifacts that could be placed together like a giant jigsaw puzzle. It did not have the excitement of an original find but there was often more than we could digest. The Masada dig was a major accomplishment by our team. We loved the adulation that came from our work and Julia especially reveled in this.

CHAPTER 56

Shelter Island Vikings and Masada

The Hopkins-Rhodes digs on Long Island finally started after all the arrangements were made. This Shelter Island dig was much closer to Manhattan then the first dig at Montauk. This made it more convenient for us all since it was so close to Manhattan. Further, many of the diggers lived in Queens, Long Island — the bedroom of New York.

We continued the Montauk dig since there were some artifacts teasing of something more. For a while, Montauk and Shelter Island were worked simultaneously. The Montauk dig continued to tease us but after a while, it was declared inoperative and closed down.

"Shaun," said Julia. "Masada is famous because tourists seek out the dramatic geographical site of the mountains of Judia, the Dead Sea Valley, the edge of the Negev desert around the site, the lowest sea on the planet, and the Roman siege destruction of the 1,000 defenders. It has so many superlatives that it is hard to make the choice of which one we must concentrate on."

"Even so," she said, "The tourists come for the wrong reasons. The Dead Sea Scrolls are different in that there is little attention paid to their surroundings. In fact, the local mountains play only a minor roll because they are so remote and difficult to get to. They also stand out because they have an end result and they increase our academic knowledge.

"The Masada findings are famous because they are easy to get to, there is hardly a limit to the number of tourists that can be accommodated and the geography is so dramatic that it is compelling. I hope this is not just a showplace in the desert.

"I assured her the best I could that this was not just a tourist trap but had academic value and contributed to our understanding of the past."

What was happening to the Vikings after this Masada period in the first century? Time had marched on as the Eastern Roman Empire continued its erratic rule through Byzantium. This was after the first century CE through the period of the Vikings in the 9th Century.

It is well known that the Vikings provided Varangian Guards to the Eastern Roman Empire from as early as 875. That put them contemporary with the early Vikings. In times of stress, the Gaurds sent mercenaries down through the Dneiper or Volga Rivers on the Black Sea in response to pleas from the Guards. Sometimes, they arrived from the Western Mediterranean Sea as well as from the Eastern Mediterranean, the Levant and Middle East. Their source was from Scandinavia by way of the Baltic Sea in the North down through the Dneiper River to the Black Sea and the Volga River down to the Caspian Sea. The Volga defined the demarcation between Europe and Siberia.

The Rus were Norsemen descended from Sweden living in what is now Ukraine and Belarus. They provided the earliest members of the Varangian Guard. They were in Byzantine service from as early as 874. The Guard was first formally constituted under Emperor Basil II in 988, following the Christianizing of Kievan Rus' by Vladimir I of Kiev.

After these early dates, there were frequent interchanges between the Vikings and and the Eastern Roman Empire. Soon, the empire was split where Constantinople formed the seat of power of the Eastern Empire. It became the beginning of the Byzentine Empire and that ruled for centuries.

On this date, Julia was with the dig site people and with me. We all sensed the excitement that was to come. Our dig site was now over two years old. The enthusiasm was becoming palpable. They had found what looked like a fragment of a piece of paper but there was no writing on it or marks of any kind. As fate would have it, Julia was again at the center of a finding.

Then, the dig was beginning to yield roughened dirt obstacles. The consistency of the strata dirt looked different somehow. Julie did not want to get out of the hole. She remembered the Long Island dig and how thrilled she was when they finally got results. This time was different. She composed herself and gave the appearance that it was all in stride. I kept talking to her and telling her exactly what was happening in the hole and elsewhere in the dig.

She would not forego that Long Island excitement again. She stayed in the hole. She finally found the corner of what looked like a note pad. It had writing on it.

We all examined the find but could make nothing of it. One might expect it to be on a scroll but that was not a shape to find out there. This Pompeii scribe for Pliny the Elder was equipped to write legibly on a reasonable paper form. For all the world, it looked like a diary, reminding us of the Pliny find at Herculaneum. We did not know but I would be willing to bet the scribes in those days are like our own in our courthouses. They make funny marks and slashes that are *shorthand* and allow rapid writing in this personal code. I am willing to bet the writing is in a personal shorthand Latin that will soon be decoded

I put it in the truck and drove off to Jerusalem while Julia made arrangements by cell-phone to show these to experts and put them in a safe vault. We all knew this was the denouement of all the hardships of digging in the dirt.

No one had doubt. We all believed the dig was hugely successful and the find was very important.

Now we had to take care of all kinds of duties. Not least of which, one of the men pulled out several bottles of champagne. The party and celebration had begun.

Julia was ecstatic. She had made her mark once more. She really enjoyed the recognition and celebrations around her.

For several years, when she was invited to a function in Israel, she would jump on an airplane and go although it was a long way from Jerusalem to her Manhattan office.

The find consisted of nails, tools, construction drawings, timetables, copies of official correspondence with Rome, the diary, if that is what it is, and numerous other items.

Mostly, she and I reveled in the booklet we found. Unfortunately, it is in a strange language that has not been translated yet.

CHAPTER 57

American Vikings

By this time, no one doubted the role Julia was playing. She had funded most of three successful digs. One could not argue that she was an amateur or didn't know what she was doing. She had even shared in the decision to move the Montauk or Long Island dig westward. There was no hard evidence that this should be done but everyone felt the urge.

There was just a feeling that pointed westward. We had no idea how far we should move. We finally decided to move the Montauk dig to Shelter Island, about 20 miles southwesterly from the Montauk dig. We wanted to find a place with plenty of water for landings and that was relatively secure from local Indians or a place where the Indians were friendly.

We also wanted quick access to the open ocean and not too far from the ocean and the Grand Banks fishing area. We also wanted access to fresh water, to abundance of shell fish, to large fish passing through the area and to a large number of mammals like whales, seals and other wild life.

Shelter Island on Long Island seemed to answer this.

We surveyed the area the best we could. This included satellite images, aircraft sensors and archaeological profiles of the area. It also included ground conductance or surface radar that we rolled along various paths in a search pattern. We also used algorithms that we were just developing and they were showing promise.

In other words, we were applying any technology that we could find. Our strategy was to keep digging at Montauk while we started up a new dig on Shelter Island. By our digging at Montauk, we knew the Vikings had been there. They left markers although they were very sparse. These certainly were not rife with life nor with the intent of permanent settlers.

We have described the sparse artifacts that led up to our first find. Importantly, the archaeological profile had paved the way on what we should do and how to do it. We followed that path as best we could. Very soon, we began to hit pay dirt. There were quick results. Our quick-look survey had been critical in making this new find. The day we decided that we had indeed made a new find, our news spread rapidly.

The analysts did a couple of 'high fives' but that was it.

Julia and I and a few analysts had been watching this with real anticipation. We had watched the data come in. The 'find' was at the east end of Long Island in New York. This was not the final conclusion. However, the 'quick analysis' confirmed that it looked very good. It looked like it was sure to be confirmed with continued analysis. It had to meet the standards, in any event. It had to appear conclusive. It had to provide evidence through various weather systems including heavy storms and floods. It had to satisfy the diggers. On and on, it went. It was a long and painful process. But, the analysts had faith that this 'quick look' would prevail.

"And why not," we asked. "It provides convenient landing for the longships. There was protection from the wind and storms. There were forest trees suitable for ship repair. There was a profusion of sea life. It looked like crops would grow. The Indians appeared relatively benign. Maybe we can live with them. In the days of a thousand years ago, this was just barren land with little attraction. Yet, there had been several encounters between the Indians and Greenlanders that resulted in fighting and killings. This did not bode well."

This Shelter Island find was all a big secret. After a while, the excitement drifted away as did the interest in the story. We were safe now, at least for a while.

We had to share some of our knowledge with our museum partners. That was alright. They too had been sworn to secrecy. No one outside a few analysts with Julia and I knew much about the secretive algorithms.

America had always had to live with neighboring Indians and their tribes. After Columbus, the Indians diminished because of warfare and disease. We had been working this Montauk dig for over two years. We had pulled up a number of artifacts that indicated that there had been Indian villages there off and on for centuries.

We finally have found the strata for the Viking years. From there, we had excavated evidence of occupation representing their stay there. The digs were to be held separately: the first dig at Montauk and the second at Shelter Island, both on Long Island. Our second dig was much more fruitful than the first. We therefore concentrated most of our resources there.

We had extracted several artifacts. These included many iron nails consistent with boat building and repair. We also found many wooden pieces. We found many stone arrowheads. The findings also yielded several items that we could not identify.

One in particular was a leather garment of some kind. We thought it may be stirrups but we could never verify the identity. There were also several items that appeared hand-made iron implements but we could not identify these either. These have all been sent to the lab for testing of identity and age but the final versions of some of them have not been made.

There were also several battle-axes. This was a very significant find; perhaps the most significant of all since the wooden handle could be aged very accurately through its DNA. Further, the Indians had no iron so this was also a very important find. The Vikings knew how to make bog iron that was needed for construction and maintenance of their boats and building structures. There was considerable disagreement as to whether the find was legitimate. One has to expect that sort of thing in this business.

"I told Julia and other officials that there is no doubt in my mind that this is a legitimate find and the artifacts are representative of that time period. I predicted it would soon be confirmed by the labs.

The press conference unfolded our finds in sequence. First, the guests and employees were invited to drinks and finger food. The finds of the dig at Montauk was then revealed from a dais. The resulting artifacts from that first dig caused an uproar. I presented them in sequence.

"First, the excavation at Montauk left no doubt that Vikings sometimes operated from there.

"Secondly, the find at Quebec was revealed. This was astounding. The Canadians loved it.

Several Canadians attended the conference.

"Third, the find at Masada fits Julia's style." Her friend, Ruth, hugged Julia.

"Lastly, the find at Shelter Island was the fourth and it gave a cornucopia of artifacts." The overall response was breathtaking. Julia was the queen of the ball. It had been her money and her foresight that drove us all.

This was a no-nonsense crowd. Their response was to cheer Julia and slap each other on the back. At the concluding remarks, they all stood and clapped hands. It was a better ending than any Broadway play

This has been a real adventure for me. We know conclusively that Vikings were in North America long before Columbus. They built on Newfoundland and on the east coast of Labrador. The Vikings were settled on Greenland about as long as we Europeans have been in America after Columbus.

There are probably thousands of diggers right now searching for evidence of the Vikings moving south to permanent locations. Julia and I and many others believe that permanent settlements were made by Vikings in America long before Columbus. We believe it so strongly that we have spent our own time and treasure to confirm it.

We do not believe the Vikings just lost their enthusiasm, their propensity for exploration and their drive for North American adventures. If they did pursue their dreams, they had permanent settlements a thousand years before us and 500 years before Columbus.

We do not want to refute history. We do want to expand our horizons to find a much broader wander in our journey.

The End

www.ingramcontent.com/pod-product-compliance
Lightning Source LLC
Chambersburg PA
CBHW070636310726
48982CB00001B/291

9781604149920